GREEN BUSH

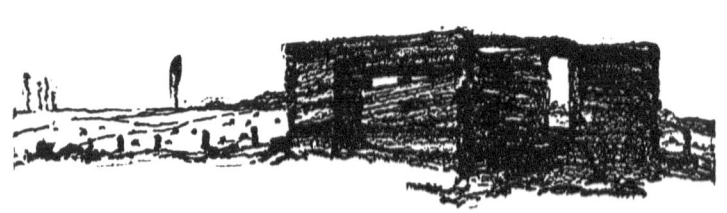

"Beyond was the grey bulk of an unfinished log house."

JOHN T. FREDERICK

GREEN BUSH

with nine drawings by
GEORGE L. STOUT

GREEN BUSH

CHAPTER I

THE sunlight of late forenoon filled the little clearing. Close to the trail huge blackened stumps rose from the even, full-seeded grass. Beyond them was the grey bulk of an unfinished log house. The clearing was walled by dense masses of young trees, behind which a ragged fringe of towering hardwoods made the sky-line.

Frank Thompson shifted his position in the light buggy, and frowned at the grey sand through which the wheels dragged heavily. Dust had settled on his brown oxfords and grey trousers. He glanced at the old house, and his face lit with a faint interest. Stopping the horse in the shade of a poplar, he climbed from the buggy, stretching his long legs stiffly, and brushed the dust from his thin shoulders.

He picked his way toward the house through matted blackberry vines and sweet fern, and peered through the blank window space. The smoke-grey walls had never been chinked with mortar, and within the doorway, in the roofless enclosure, the grass grew tall and straight between the hewn sills.

Frank was young enough to find something of romance in a deserted farm, familiar as the sight was: in his morning's drive from Green Bush he had passed three such abandoned places, where the trees which the settlers had cut down were growing up again, soon to cover the marks of their ploughs and the ruins of their

3

buildings. But this small clearing with its unfinished house seemed a little different.

Behind the house a clump of young birches grew lustily, and beside them Frank's foot struck a rusted ax-helve, half buried in the thin sod. He examined it thoughtfully, wondering what hands had dropped it here. Then he straightened and walked slowly back to the buggy.

The sand of the roadway gave suddenly to close-packed gravel, on which the wheels grated noisily, and Frank found himself at the top of a short, steep hill. The road led down between two small lakes that gleamed like metal in the cool sunlight. Beyond rose wooded slopes, dark with pine and hemlock among the birches and poplars, and beyond these rolled other hills, steep and rounded, mile after mile of brush and swamp and woodland unbroken by a field or a mark of human habitation, until a long, low range bulked purple-blue against the bright horizon.

Frank straightened in his seat and grasped the lines more firmly. The old horse shambled down the hill and stopped on the low causeway between the two lakes, nosing toward the water which stood only a few inches below the level of the road. Frank jumped from the buggy, pulled a dusty tin pail from beneath the seat, and dipped it full of the cold clear water. While the horse drank, the young man watched the small fish that swam lazily back and forth close to the road: chubby, vividly coloured blue-gills, striped grass pike, dappled rock bass. Farther out a white pond lily floated in a small cluster of pads.

As he climbed into the buggy again, Frank noted a hayrack in the marsh at the far side of one of the lakes, half loaded with the wild hay that grew in a yellowish-green band, thick with goldenrod and rosy-purple Joe Pye weed, down to the water's edge. A girl in a blue dress was building the load, handling the heavy forkfuls with practised ease and walking sure-footed on the yielding surface of the hay. As she turned the team to drive to another windrow, the pitcher came into sight—a thick-chested giant of a man whose bare head was covered with curly reddish hair. Frank could see his huge brown arms, and his brown, hairy chest where the blue shirt gaped open.

The old horse, timber trained, took Frank's buggy up the steep hill beyond the lakes at a rush, and in a moment he was out of sight of the marsh. Along the clay bank by the roadside, here, wild blackberries hung in heavy clusters, and Frank sprang from the buggy to gather hungrily a handful of the soft, fragrant fruit. Down another slope he drove, to cross on a rough bridge of cedar poles a swift stream, crystal-clear, a foot deep and two or three yards across. Leaving the buggy again, Frank knelt on a log that lay half-way in the noisy water, and, leaning down precariously, drank thirstily from the stream; then he washed the dust from his face and hands, and dried himself with a soiled pocket-handkerchief.

A gleam of red caught his eye. In the lush, yard-tall grass by the stream's edge grew a spike of cardinal flower, a slender tongue of flame in the warm yellow-green of the grasses. As he squatted by the water, Frank looked at it, his face lighting with pleasure. Then he returned to the buggy and drove on. The horse mounted another slope with reckless energy, and slowed to a sleepy amble once level ground was reached.

The trail turned suddenly to the left and joined a wider road which was graded a little, and fenced along one side with two barbed wires on heavy cedar posts. Directly in front of Frank, as he gained the larger road, was a small field of oats already in thick shocks, the heavy heads hanging down in festoons. Beyond the oats field was a patch of corn, and beside the road, set in a small orchard of close-headed trees, was a low grey house.

Frank drove toward this slowly, consulting first a folded map of the county, which he drew from beneath the buggy seat, and then a small pocket note-book.

A rickety tin mail box was nailed to a post at the roadside in front of the house, and the name lettered on it in neat, even characters, now almost defaced, confirmed the information which Frank had drawn from his notes. He climbed briskly from the buggy, tied the horse to the fence of pickets split from cedar, and walked up the grassy path between clumps of roses and seeded iris, and lace-like plants of "old man." Clusters of pinks edged the door-step, and at the end of the house, shaded by a low apple-tree, were the bright brown and blue faces of Scotch pansies.

A noisy shepherd dog greeted him doubtfully. Then a short woman with lively dark eyes, and dull black hair that edged her brown face, came to the door.

"Is this where Mr. McCune lives?" Frank asked her.

"It is. Won't you come in?" She held the screen door open for him.

"My name is Frank Thompson," the boy said. "My father publishes the *Oscona County Gazette*, and I am going through the country this summer to call on the people. I believe Mr. McCune used to take the paper, did he not, and let his subscription lapse two or three years ago?"

"Yes, he quit the paper. You might talk to him about it. He'll be in soon. Just have a chair."

The woman turned to the big black stove at one end of the room, and Frank sat down by a window. The sash was propped up with a small board, and the breeze blew a plain net curtain against his shoulder. "My, it's pleasant in here," Frank remarked. "It feels good to get inside, the sun is so bright to-day."

The woman laughed deprecatingly. "It gets hot enough in here sometimes," she answered, "especially in the afternoons." Frank watched her as she sifted flour into a large yellow bowl, and beat the mixture vigorously. The long room was clean. A rag carpet covered the rough board floor at the end at which Frank was sitting. Near him was a small oak table covered with brown oilcloth. A square of bright linoleum lay before the stove. The walls were lined with heavy paper of a dull, faded blue, tacked down neatly, and marked with nails and pegs on which hung hammers, lanterns, kettles, and, at one end of the room, two shot-guns and a heavy rifle. In the corner farthest from the stove were a small writing-desk and a little iron safe. Beside these stood a surveying instrument, hooded in a buckskin bag.

"You have a nice place here, Mrs. McCune," Frank ventured, looking out the window toward the stable, a low structure of logs and rough boards with a thatched shed against one end. Hay stuck from the open win-dow of the upper story, and beside the door was a round, half-built stack of the marsh grass.

"We like it here," the woman answered simply.

A short, plump old man appeared suddenly from the stable door and busied himself about the stack, raking down the sides with a pitchfork and gathering up the scattered bits of hay.

"Is that Mr. McCune?" Frank inquired.

"No, that's Uncle Marion—my father's brother, Marion Bouchard." She smiled at him. "My husband is in the marsh for hay. We don't usually cut the marsh, but Neal doesn't want to sell any stock this fall, the market is so bad; so we'll need lots of feed."

Frank nodded. "Oh, yes—I guess I saw him."

"Did you come by the lakes?"

"Yes—there was a girl loading——"

"That was them all right—my husband and my daughter."

At this moment the old man, setting his pitchfork by the stable door, appeared to notice Frank's horse and buggy for the first time. He stared at them a moment, then came briskly toward the house. His round, wrinkled face was brown as a nut, and edged by thick white hair. He paused outside the screen door beyond the stove, to spit a quid of tobacco carefully into a lilac-bush.

"How do ye do?" he greeted Frank in a cheery, high-pitched voice. His black eyes were as alert and eager as a child's.

"This's Frank Thompson—the editor's son from Green Bush," Mrs. McCune paused in her work to say. "He wants to see Neal about taking the paper."

The old man shook Frank's hand heartily. "Put your horse in the barn and have dinner with us," he said at once.

"Oh, I'd better not stop," Frank protested.

"Sure, sure, come on an' put your horse in."

"It's quite a ways to the next house," the woman agreed. "We'd be glad to have you stay."

"Sure, sure, we always like company."

"Well, thank you, I will stay then," Frank decided, not without enthusiasm.

The old man laughed brightly and led the way outside. He opened the gate of cedar poles for Frank to drive into the barnyard, and together they unhitched and led the horse into the cool, dry stable.

"Put him in the back stall," Uncle Marion directed. "Better pull the harness off'n him. Just hang it behind there." He was filling the manger with fragrant hay.

Before Frank had finished he heard the rumble of the wagon, and when he stepped from the low door into the brilliant sunlight the load was already beside the stack. McCune was standing in the middle of it, his legs apart, grasping a pitchfork. The girl had disappeared.

"This's young Mr. Thompson from Green Bush, Neal," Uncle Marion addressed the man on the load. "His father's the editor."

McCune greeted Frank gravely and silently with a nod and a steady look, then thrust his fork into the hay and swung a huge mass to the stack. Uncle Marion had scrambled nimbly up a short ladder and stood near the middle of the stack ready to receive it.

Frank watched the two men as they handled the hay: McCune steady, sure, lifting the heavy masses without apparent effort; and the old man scarcely seeming to work at all, but maintaining all the while the shape of the stack as it rose in a perfect cone, always a little highest at the middle, but never a forkful slipping from the edge.

In an incredibly short time the rack was emptied and driven away from the stack, the horses were unhitched

and fed, and the three men started for the house.
"That's a fine stack," Frank told Uncle Marion.

"I'll rake her down after dinner," he replied, glanc·
ing appraisingly at the even sides.

"You didn't seem to have much trouble pitching it
off," Frank remarked to McCune.

" 'Twas well loaded," the man agreed briefly. Frank
glanced at him curiously, struck by the restraint of his
speech and bearing in contrast to the open and buoyant
manner of the older man. His skull was large and massive under the exuberant reddish hair, curly and dulled
by the sun. From beneath bushy brows, fiercely in-
telligent eyes looked out with brooding intentness. A
stubble of rusty beard covered his heavy chin and edged
the large mouth with its thick, full lips. There was
strength and intellect in the man, and something gross
as well, Frank reflected, watching him as he bent his
strong body by the wash·bench in the back yard to
douse his head and arms with the ice-cold water from
the wooden pump.

Within the house he found the girl, helping her
mother prepare the meal.

"Mr. Thompson, this is my daughter Rose," Mrs.
McCune told him, pausing with a dish of beans in her
hand. The girl turned from her work of mashing potatoes and smiled at him shyly, her plain, strong face,
reddened from the heat of the stove, flushing still more.
She had the tawny hair, short and abundant, and fair
skin of her father, he noted; but her eyes, though blue,
were warm and vivacious like those of her mother and
Uncle Marion.

The table was set for six, and now Frank noticed for
the first time a chunky boy of ten or twelve who sat

in one corner, regarding him intently from under a shock of wavy black hair with black eyes of the utmost alertness.

"Come to the table, Neal," McCune commanded him, yet with a faint accent, Frank thought, of tenderness and pride.

The meal was served at once, and Frank ate, almost as freely as the men, of the thin stripped bacon, cream gravy, potatoes, string beans, white bread, sweet firm butter, and quivering carnelian jelly.

Uncle Marion maintained a constant conversation with Frank during the meal—about the weather, the crops, the political situation, and the prices of farm products.

"You just home for the summer?" he inquired. "Been away to college?"

"Yes, I've been down to Ann Arbor."

"Oh, yes. Big school there, I've heard."

"Yes, about ten thousand students enrolled last year."

The old man stared uncomprehendingly.

"Is *that* so? Going back next year?"

"Yes—I guess so. I was graduated last year, but I guess I'll take a year of graduate work."

"Takes a long time, doesn't it? What you studying —to be an editor like your father?"

"I guess so," Frank answered whimsically. "I'm not taking law or anything like that," he added.

The other members of the family listened to the conversation but did not speak, except to ask for food or to offer it to Frank and to one another.

When a huge bowl of fresh blueberries and a pitcher of cream were set upon the table, and dishes distributed, the boy slid from his place silently and left the room.

McCune laughed quietly, and spoke for the first time during the meal. "He had too many of 'em yesterday, when they were picking," he remarked.

"I'll take him a piece of cake," Rose volunteered. Her mother slid a big yellow cake from the oven, and the girl took a steaming slice on a plate, while Mrs. McCune filled a larger plate for the table. Frank realized that this cake had been added to the menu since his arrival.

Directly the girl had left the room, her mother addressed Frank. "Mr. Thompson, do you happen to know of any place in Green Bush where a girl might get a chance to stay and help a little for her board while she goes to high school? Rose finished eighth grade two years ago, and her father wants her to go to high school. But Rose wants to work for her board and room like Newton Henderson's daughter does. Seems so far like we can't find a place for her. We don't get out that way very often."

Frank found McCune's eyes upon him, gravely considering.

"I'll inquire about it," he promised readily. "Maybe my mother will know of someone." Both parents seemed relieved.

"Rose's real smart," Uncle Marion was beginning, but the girl re-entered, and the subject was dropped.

As soon as he had finished eating, McCune rose and went to the desk in the corner. As he opened it, Frank could see a few books, and ordered bundles of papers. Seating himself, McCune wrote a cheque, in a firm, easy hand, and gave it to Frank. "You can send me the paper for a year," he remarked with a degree of friendliness. "The boy and the womenfolks like to read it." He and Rose started at once for the barn, and Frank saw the girl leading out one of the horses and helping to hitch them to the wagon.

"Going on to Wilberville to-night?" Uncle Marion inquired.

"Yes, going to stay all night there and work back to-morrow; guess I'd better be moving on. I certainly enjoyed the dinner, Mrs. McCune." He had learned not to try to pay for such meals.

"I'm glad you did." She came out to the barnyard as he was ready to start. The wagon was rattling down the road toward the marsh, McCune seated and the girl driving, standing easily at the front of the rack. "You'll let us know if you find out anything?" the woman urged Frank.

"I surely will. I'll do my best."

"Thank you truly." She went back to the house without more words. Uncle Marion opened the gate, waving a friendly farewell, and the horse jogged slowly past him and out upon the highroad.

CHAPTER II

FRANK thought briefly of the McCunes, especially of the girl, as he drove slowly down the sandy road toward Wilberville. But the good dinner had made him sleepy, and he drowsed as he drove along, wondering vaguely how long it would take him to reach the town, how many subscriptions he would sell there, and whether he would find the hotel as pleasant and interesting a place as some of the other country hotels he had visited during the summer.

He fell to dreaming sleepily of the University and his friends there—particularly of Steen, the tall Hollander, now an instructor, who had been his roommate for two years and who was his chief confidant. He thought of courses in philosophy, in which he liked to dispute gravely with his professors concerning the validity of the ideas of Berkeley and Hume; of exacting hours in the biology laboratory, which Steen rallied him for enjoying—"pursuing the phantom of reality," Steen called it; of courses in romantic poetry and in Shakespeare, made dramatic by the personality of the teacher; and, more vividly, of fine evenings with Steen and perhaps one or two cronies, when books were pushed aside and problems of the universe were settled vociferously, with the aid of much tobacco and perhaps of a little beer or a pint of wine brought surreptitiously from Detroit.

As he drove, the character of the country changed. He entered an expanse of "plains"—level, sandy land set sparsely with jackpine and scrub oak which now edged the track and now opened broadly into lanes and vistas.

The trail wound irresponsibly across this expanse, branching and reuniting unaccountably. More than once Frank found himself puzzled as to the way to take, and had to trust to the instinct of the horse. There were no signboards or landmarks, and the near trees made the horizon, except for occasional glimpses of a chain of purple hills far away to the northward. The earth was cool and quiet under the immense and vivid sky, with its leisurely companies of sharply edged grey clouds. It was slow going, too; the wheels ploughed deeply in the fine grey sand, and the old horse pulled steadily, stopping occasionally in the shadow of an oak to rest briefly, and starting on of his own accord. Frank fell to watching the foreground, close to the slowly turning wheels. It was vivid with low scarlet bushes against the dulled green of bunch grass. In some places little jackpines grew in thick, even nurseries. Once he found a place where a few late-ripening blueberries clung to their low, leafy plants in scattered clusters of pure blue faintly silvered; and, stopping the old horse, he gathered a handful, eating the berries by twos and threes as he drove on.

Finally the trail twisted down a short slope into a swampy place where alders were growing, and the buggy-wheels bumped cedar ties left at the removal of an old railway. Back in the black depths of the swamp a young maple glowed with early autumn colour, red as flame.

The road emerged gradually from the swamp on the straight narrow grade of the old logging track, shaded by rough-barked birches and flanked by grazed land

studded with black stumps and occasional towering,
blackened trunks, broken, or carved by fire, into jagged
and grotesque outlines.

A half-mile farther on, he passed, close to the grade,
a large grey house, boarded up and deserted—a lumber-
man's lodging-house when Wilberville had been a centre
of the industry; and here the road swung away from
the grade, past a group of large, well-painted farm
buildings, to enter Wilberville itself : an irregular string
of small dwellings, with two stores and a schoolhouse,
facing a broad, tree-girt lake glittering in the late
afternoon sunshine.   In a hollow close to the lake was
the stack of a small sawmill, idle now and silent.   Most
of the houses were low and unpainted, but flowers
grew around them, bright against the cool grey of the
weathered walls.

Frank stopped his horse at the watering-trough in
front of one of the stores and entered the long narrow
room with its barrels of oil and sugar, shelves of calico,
cotton gloves and work-shirts, and small show-case of
candies and scrap tobacco.   From the proprietor, a
monosyllabic German, he secured the promise of his supper and a room for the night : for this store was also a
hotel.   He attended to his horse with the help of the
proprietor's son, a spindly boy of about Frank's own
age, as talkative and ingratiating as his father was silent, and enjoyed the hearty supper, served in heavy
dishes on a clean red table-cloth.   After the meal he felt
too drowsy and indolent to go out soliciting subscriptions, and so joined the group of settlers in the front
part of the store.   Three or four men sat about on kegs
and boxes, discussing excitedly the events at a dance at
Wilberville two or three nights before.

"I guess they was plenty to drink fer once, eh?"   A

"Towering, blackened trunks."

skinny, dark fellow in a red shirt leaned forward, smacking his full, bristly lips.

"Say, if I'd had a few drops more I might a' known how moonshine tastes." The speaker was the loudest of the group and evidently its favourite humorist, for a roar of laughter went up at this. He was a short round man in a grey shirt and baggy brown trousers, with a bald head and a droll, grimacing face.

"You hadn't ought to talk that way, Tubby," one of the men admonished him. "You might not get elected." Frank looked at the fat man with interest. So this was Saunders, whose announcement of his candidacy for the office of sheriff of the county the *Gazette* was printing weekly. And the talk was that he would be elected.

"Well," spoke up a tall, well-proportioned man in neat overalls with a hard, clean-shaven face, "all I got to say is, if they want to drink the stuff, they ought to keep it away from our dances. We'll get a worse name 'n we have now, if this goes on."

"That's exactly my feelin'," declared Saunders very solemnly, and again everyone laughed except the tall man who had just spoken.

"You know what I mean, Tub," he argued hotly. "It ain't jest old fish like you 'at takes it. It's the young kids—even the girls."

"God, yes," the thin man agreed loudly. "'D yuh see that Moler girl? She had some, all right."

"Guess she had something else before she got home, eh—heh, heh?" remarked Saunders, leading the guffaw at his own ribaldry. "What's this guy sellin'?" he added suddenly, to the storekeeper, jerking his thumb toward Frank. "Soft soap or cow soup?"

"He ain't sellin' nothin'," Hartman replied, when the

inevitable laugh had subsided. "He's the editor's son
from Green Bush, an' he's out lookin' over the candidates for county office, to see who the paper'll support."

"Holy Mister!" ejaculated Saunders. "Now I bet I've
went an' damaged my reputation. You know," he went
on gravely, addressing Frank, "I used to be an awful
bad man—a terrible bad man. Yes, sir, I wuz. You
might not believe it, but I wuz as bad a man as ever
walked on three legs. I loafed, an' played rummy, an'
went fishin' on Sunday, an' swore, an' told naughty
stories—yes, sir—an' I drank—drank whisky! But
that was before I reformed." His audience roared at
this, unable to restrain its appreciation longer; but
Saunders went on, sober as a judge. "Yes, sir, I got con-
verted, an' I'm a good man now. At the big camp-
meetin' it was, early in the summer." This was evidently an especially favoured local hit, for even the
storekeeper joined in the applause. But the neat man
in overalls shut his pocket-knife with a click and
stalked out the door.

Half an hour later Saunders got up from the keg on
which he had been sitting, opened the show-case behind
him, and took out a fistful of candy.

"Show's over till to-morrow night," he announced
briskly, distributing the candy to the group, a piece
to each. "I don't care whether your paper supports me
or not," he told Frank, "but if I ain't elected I won't
pay fer my announcement." He thrust the rest of the
candy into his mouth, and strutted out into the darkness.

By mid-forenoon of the next day Frank was on his
way to Green Bush, having completed his business in
Wilberville. He drove for a time through unfenced
grass land, set with stumps and the gigantic blackened

trunks of fire-killed trees. He stopped at two or three homes of settlers on his business for the paper: small frame houses set among patches of potatoes, silvery buckwheat, and corn. Toward noon he came to a fertile slope on which the ripe grain was shocked in thick even rows. At the base of a long hill, by a swift clear stream, were a shingled cabin and a long red barn, flanked by loaded apple-trees. Here he stopped for dinner, to eat fresh biscuit with honey from the hives so near the house that the hum of bees through the open window made low accompaniment to the creaking voice of a grey old man. He told of the days when the tall timber was standing: "Forty years ago, when I was a young man like you. Yes, I've lived on this place twenty-nine years—ever since I got caught by a falling limb." Then he showed a maimed and twisted forearm and a stiffened leg, and told how when chopping a big maple to clear a roadway through mixed pine and hardwood—"we never bothered with the hardwood in them days—just took the cream o' the white pine"—a dead limb had come down without warning, catching and mashing one side of his body. "Yes, me an' the old woman did all this clearin'. She did most o' the work at first. The children helped. But now they're all gone—to Flint and Detroit." The old woman, gaunt and powerful despite her thin white hair, smiled at Frank with eyes dimmed a little by the years, and urged on him more biscuit.

As he drove away from the grey house and up the steep rise beyond the stream, Frank looked back speculatively. He tried to understand what it was that made men and women cling to the land like this— twenty-nine years on this remote, rough farm, unvalued for all its fertility. "There's something in it that gets hold of a man," he concluded, gazing at the vivid grass beside the brook, the firm, bold rise of the great hill with its pattern of rich fields and the orchard clothing its base, and, beyond, the gigantic arch of blue fretted by the uneven sky-line of the hardwoods. Dimly he sensed what a man must feel who had lived for thirty years between that hill and stream, and who had given half his lifetime to the clearing and tilling of those fields and the care of that orchard. "He is rooted," Frank thought, "rooted like a tree, for all he moves about." And remembering the quiet, work-lined faces of the old man and woman, clean and gnarled like the bark of trees, the boy smiled to himself, pleased with his figure. "Strength of that soil, purity of that water," he said to himself. And then, thinking of Saunders and his group at the store, he smiled again, wryly. "What a little world in itself this country is," he reflected. And slapping the old horse with the reins, he fell to watching the second growth, of young birch, poplar, oak, and cherry, which lined the track here on either side—taller than a man on horseback, luxuriant in its fullness of leafage around the black stumps and prostrate logs and gaunt, towering, fire-scarred trunks of the earlier forest.

At last the narrow, ill-made road gave suddenly to a gravelled pike. The old horse, realizing the nearness of stable and supper, settled into a steady jog-trot. In a few minutes they topped a rise, and through the deep cut between clay banks crowned by bushy white pines, Frank caught a glimpse of Lake Huron—the distant glow of vivid blue that always quickened his heart a little. Down the slope they jogged, past little farms and a cemetery, and from another ridge he looked down at the village of Green Bush, between the hills and the Lake.

CHAPTER III

THE hill swept down in sunburnt buff cooled now by shadow, for the sun was low, to the masses of dull green that edged the streets, outlined the grey roofs of houses, and bordered unevenly the shining water of the great Lake. Through the middle of the village the highway Frank was following clove a clean grey line straight to the water's edge, bordered briefly by stores and dwellings among the trees, and dipping suddenly beneath the bright green water that became vivid blue farther out and dulled at last to purple-grey where it merged with the horizon.

Frank's eyes warmed to the sight. He drove slowly down the hill, past cherry orchards and outlying dwellings. Just where the single track of the railroad cut unexpectedly across the street between two huge maple-trees, he turned to the right, and proceeded slowly down an unpaved street so thickly shaded by the meeting branches of close-set maples that it seemed already half dark.

On the right a gentle slope, where grass grew thinly under the low-topped trees, led up to two square brick buildings, the courthouse and the schoolhouse, which drew from the old-time dignity of their design and the spaciousness of their setting a certain beauty.

Facing them on the other side of the street was a row of old houses, well spaced by shady lawns and fenced with pickets. Frank drove into an alley between two of these, and turned into the yard between a house

23

and barn, both painted a weatherbeaten brown, and having in their design common elements of tall, narrow windows and boldly executed wooden ornaments in dormers and gables.

As Frank began to unhitch the horse, his mother came from the vine-enclosed back porch down the board walk toward the barn. She was a tall, well-formed woman, and had dark curly hair combed carefully around a serious, sensitive face. She wore a light grey house dress and a ruffled white apron.

"Hello, Boy." She kissed Frank quickly and brushed the dust from his shoulders. "Did you have a good trip? We missed you at the social last night. Lots of people inquired for you."

"Oh, I guess they could spare me all right. Yes, I had a good trip," he added, leading the horse toward the barn. "Got eighteen subscriptions."

In the cool, quiet house Frank found that his mother had heated water for the bath she knew he would want after his dusty trip, and had laid out fresh clothing on his bed. "We'll have supper at six," she told him. "I'm going to Mrs. Steele's to-night. Your father's at the farm, so we won't wait for him."

"Is he cutting the alfalfa?"

"I don't know. I didn't ask him. I told him he shouldn't go to-day, when there was no one to leave at the office."

Frank went upstairs without replying.

They were just beginning their supper when Mr. Thompson entered the house. They heard him washing at the sink in the kitchen; then he entered the cool dining-room, where steps were hushed on the plain rugs, and ice tinkled in the tea-glasses.

"Hello, father," Frank greeted him. "Been cutting the alfalfa?"

"Yes." The older man sat down wearily. His tall, thin frame sagged a little, and his face looked worn and pale. "Couldn't get a team and mower, so I mowed it by hand," he explained. "Just a little patch—but I'm not a very good hand with the scythe."

"You should have waited till to-morrow, so I could have helped you," Frank remonstrated.

"Well, it was just ready, and the rain night before last has started the new growth in the crowns. We might get another crop yet this year."

"You are just as unreasonable about that alfalfa as everything else about the farm," Mrs. Thompson put in. "You could just as well have waited until to-morrow. Now you've completely tired yourself out. You won't be worth anything at the office to-night."

"I'm quite all right," he returned, straightening himself and unfolding his napkin. "Will you kindly pass the bread?" he added testily.

In a few minutes Mrs. Thompson had eaten, and retired to her room to dress for the evening's visit at Mrs. Steele's. The men finished more slowly, and then cleared the table together, in spite of Frank's appeal to his father to sit still and rest a minute.

The older man then took a grey alpaca coat from a closet, and a yellowed straw hat, and they set off together, walking briskly toward the main street of the village.

They turned in at the lighted front of a small frame building which a painted sign proclaimed to be "Steele's Drug Store." Frank opened the screened door between two small show-windows, one of which contained a display of patent medicines. The other was piled high with geological specimens—geodes, a petrified snake, fossils, and a piece of wood from the lake shore curiously carved by the waves to the likeness of a human hand and arm.

The store was already lighted by kerosene lamps hung from the ceiling. A short, thickset man with bushy white hair advanced slowly behind the counter, limping slightly. His brown eyes smiled at them from behind gold-rimmed glasses. Without further greeting he opened the cigar case, selected a box, and held it out to Mr. Thompson. He chose two cigars, sticking one into the front pocket of his alpaca coat and lighting the other at a small spirit lamp which burned on a bracket at the end of the counter.

"Been out to the farm to-day, Frank?" the druggist inquired of Mr. Thompson. The younger man noted with familiar pleasure the richness and deepness of his quiet voice, and the reserved affection that was apparent between the two men without the need of words.

"Yes, cut the alfalfa this afternoon. It's better than I thought it was."

"That's good. Hope for another crop?"

"Well, there's a chance for it." They puffed awhile in silence. "Guess my wife's going up to your place to-night."

"Yes, so Mrs. Steele said."

"Well, son, let's step around to the office. Good night, E. J."

"Good night, Frank," the druggist replied.

"Mr. Steele is a fine man," Mr. Thompson remarked to Frank for the hundredth time, as they strolled on down the darkening street. "You haven't found any better at the University, I guess, have you?"

"No, I haven't, father. He would have made a great scientist if he could have had the training. He has the mind all right. I've often wondered why he came here—and stayed."

"His brother was a doctor here, in the early days. He got E. J. to come here and make his pills. Then the brother died, and E. J. stayed on. My, how he has grown into the life of the town!"

At the post office a short, erect young man in a grey suit, with a ruddy, serious face, greeted them quietly. "Good evening, Mr. Thompson; good evening, Frank." He held the door open for them to enter.

"How are you, Harrison?" Mr. Thompson answered, friendliness and respect in his voice, stooping to unlock one of the two drawers below the small range of locked boxes.

A kindly bearded face with twinkling eyes looked out from the window at Frank.

"Evening. How's the back country? Say, Frank," addressing now the father, "see the news from Washington in to-day's paper?"

"No, I'm just getting my paper now. Been out to the farm."

"I declare I don't know what to expect next. This new congress's as unreasonable as a mule with a cocklebur under his tail."

"Frank doesn't quite get that," laughed his father. "He's never seen a cocklebur."

"Nor a mule either, hardly," Frank agreed. "There was McGilvray's mule, that used to walk into town on Sundays in the winter and eat the hay out of the sleighs standing at church."

"Yeh," chuckled the postmaster. "Mule would walk

on the sidewalk and people take to the street."

"Well, he got a good feed that way. Let's step over to the office, Frank. Good night, Dave." Mr. Thompson led the way across the street.

"Good night, Frank," called the old man reluctantly after them.

"Dave sure does hate the Democrats," remarked Mr. Thompson as he fitted the key in the door of the small brick building with "Oscona County Gazette" lettered on the window.

"And he sure does like to talk," Frank agreed.

His father lit the lamps above the job cases in the back room, and, hanging the alpaca coat behind a curtain, he put on a printer's apron. It was characteristic of Mr. Thompson that only now did he inquire as to the success of Frank's trip.

"How'd you come out this time, son?"

"About like last time. I got eighteen subscriptions—only got turned down about half the time. I got a sale bill at Wilberville—for the twenty-fifth."

"That so? You did well. Let me see the sale—guess I'll set it up to-night instead of finer stuff."

"I'll set up the new names for the mailing-list, before my notes are cold." Frank also donned an apron, and the two men set to work.

"Will Harrison be re-elected, do you think?" Frank inquired as they were settling down to work.

"I think so—though there's lots of opposition on account of his activities in the liquor troubles. I hope he will," he added. "He's the best attorney the county has ever had."

An hour later the older man climbed from his stool. "About done, Frank?" he asked.

"Just about. I'm working on this new ad for the bank."

"Just put the list and the cheques and money in the desk then. Guess I'd better get home and to bed. Will you stop around for mother?"

"Surely, I'll be glad to." Frank watched anxiously as his father hung up his stick and apron, washed his hands, and drew on his coat. Utter weariness was in every gesture.

"Will we put up the alfalfa to-morrow, father?" the boy inquired.

"No, it will need another day. It's mighty heavy. We can get the paper out to-morrow night and put it up Thursday morning."

At nine o'clock Frank turned out the lights, locked the office, and walked briskly down the street. He had no coat, and the stiff breeze from the Lake made him shiver. The post office was closed now, the drug store was closed, even the small confectionery and pool hall. Through all the little town the voice of the Lake resounded continuously, a rush and rustle of water and a grating roar of rolling stones.

At a small white house a few squares from his home he knocked sharply, for voices were gay within, and Mr. Steele opened to him at once. Mrs. Steele was behind him, her full figure gowned in brown silk and her beautiful, refined face, framed in white hair, quietly radiant.

"Come in, Frank. We were just speaking about you."

"I hope you weren't saying too many bad things about me," he challenged her kindly.

"No, we were just saying you will soon be starting back to the University."

His heart always warmed to Mrs. Steele's hospitality. Many a long winter evening he had browsed among Mr. Steele's books—geologies and travel, for the most part, with a few volumes of poetry—while the druggist and his father played checkers, and the women talked quietly over their fancy-work. Then Mrs. Steele would sit down to her old rosewood piano and play simple melodies with exquisite feeling. Often he had spent the night there: the Steeles had been childless except for a foster-daughter who had died, and they would beg his parents to "lend them a boy."

Thought of these things was in his heart as he took Mrs. Steele's hand and led her to the piano.

"Not to-night, Frank," she objected gently. He now noted that in addition to his mother two other women were present—the Methodist minister's wife, Mrs. Strout, a large woman with a shrewd, appraising look in her sharp eyes; and her daughter, a slender, dark-eyed girl with abundant black hair. "We were just urging June to play," Mrs. Steele went on. "We have finished our business, I think."

"I thought you people had completed that program of yours long ago," Frank laughed.

"This is the last meeting, I think," his mother answered. "Shall we have the music now, June?"

"No, I won't play!" the girl flashed. "Frank don't want me to."

Frank was silent. He detested June's playing. His mother rose to the occasion. "I guess we're all tired," she said. "This hot weather——"

Protracted farewells were said. At last Mrs. Strout and Mrs. Thompson started down the walk together, leaving Frank and June to follow.

"Was I mean to-night, Frank?" the girl whispered, slipping a hand through his arm and pressing it slightly. "I'm afraid I was awful."

"Oh, that was all right." Frank disliked the girl

more than ever. The warm soft hand on his arm irritated him.

"I do get so tired of old Mrs. Steele."

"I think Mrs. Steele is a mighty fine woman," Frank stated emphatically.

"Oh, now I *have* made you mad!" She clung to him, looked up with dark eyes filling with ready tears, small red lips parted.

"Oh, pshaw," Frank consoled her hollowly. She was too soft and too close. He looked ahead. "They're waiting for us," he lied desperately, and, grasping her arm, he hurried her down the walk.

CHAPTER IV

THE next day Frank and his father were at the little office early. "Getting out the paper" had been the crucial event of each week ever since Frank could remember, and he had helped in some way since he was a small boy. Now he was able to get out an edition of the small sheet by himself, and he and his father would have found their day's work together comparatively easy had it not been that the items of town news were still largely unset. It was late noon before the composition was completed, and by the time lockup and makeready had been achieved and they were actually ready to print, it was apparent that they would have to work well into the night to finish.

"I suppose I'm unreasonable, Frank," his father remarked. "I *would* like to get at that alfalfa early in the morning, while the dew is on. It is so leafy and nice, and the dew will help it to hold the leaves."

"It would be a shame not to get it up in the best shape possible, it's such a nice crop," Frank agreed.

The older man said no more, but Frank was glad, as they worked on together, that he had not urged the postponement of the task.

At supper Mrs. Thompson had a plan for an evening call, on the part of Frank and herself, at the home of the Strouts. "They invited us over," she explained.

"I'm sorry, mother," Frank answered cheerfully, "I'm going to work at the office to-night."

"Haven't you got the paper out yet?"

32

"No, not quite. If I get through early I'll come up awhile," he encouraged her.

"Let it go till morning then—there's no use killing yourselves. You can finish it by noon mail time, can't you?"

Frank hesitated. Mr. Thompson had busied himself with his supper, making no contribution to the conversation. Now he spoke almost defiantly. "Frank and I are going to make the alfalfa hay in the morning."

"Oh, the hay, the hay!" Mrs. Thompson exclaimed. "Make the hay just the minute you want to, even if you do have to work your son to death the little time he's home from college. That's always the way with the farm—it comes before the paper or your family or anything else. And what does it amount to?"

"I'm glad to help," Frank tried to interpose. But his father had risen from the table, his thin face flushed darkly. He replaced his chair quietly and put on his coat and hat.

"You go with your mother to-night, Frank," he said. "I'll get out the paper." He closed the door firmly behind him.

The boy knew that it was useless to protest. "He's getting more and more unreasonable about that farm," his mother remarked, still angry herself. "The paper is running down, and he knows it."

Frank felt his own temper rising. He tried hard to control it. "I don't care for dessert," he said unsteadily; and, rising, he made his way to his room.

He wanted to rebuke and reproach his mother for her harshness and lack of sympathy, for the unnecessary unhappiness for all of them of the scene he had just passed through. He wanted to tell her that he would not go to the Strout's, that he hated all of them.

"Damn them all," he muttered petulantly, staring through his window into the branches of an old apple-tree, loaded with green fruit.

He opened his trunk and drew out a secreted copy of Baudelaire—the "Poems in Prose"—and began to read, enjoying the boyish gesture of revolt, and at the same time ashamed. He knew that in a few minutes his mother would call him, and he would go. She would have her way. His rage did not cool.

When his mother called he came slowly down the stairs, and they walked in silence the two blocks to the parsonage. He sat glumly while Mrs. Strout and his mother discussed various plans for the church. Later he listened mechanically to June's playing, trying to think about a concert he had heard at Ann Arbor the year before. The girl was very pretty, as she sat at the piano, the shaded light glinting on her black hair and the dull red silk of her dress. In spite of himself, she attracted him. But, he felt, she was silly; her interest in him was too manifest. He was glad when his mother rose to go.

On the way home she reproached him a little for his attitude. "You were scarcely courteous," she told him. He did not reply, and she said no more.

He was up early in the morning, and ready to eat a silent breakfast and start for the farm with his father. The older man's face was drawn and haggard, but Frank forbore asking any questions as to the evening's work. Mr. Thompson had engaged a team and wagon for the haymaking from a retired farmer at the outskirts of town, and the team was hitched and waiting when they arrived. A cheery old man in faded denim gave the lines to Mr. Thompson. "They're real quiet," he recommended the plump, sleepy greys. The wagon rattled out of the grassy yard, past little houses set between huge clumps of lilac, and on to the grass-edged country road which wound away to the north where the great grey hills shouldered it close to the Lake.

The farm was at their left, covering the base and most of the side of one of these hills. There were no buildings, but next the road was a small orchard of young trees—cherry, plum, and apple. Beyond was the little field where the alfalfa lay in matted swaths, and beyond this a small patch of short-growing corn, thick-leaved, and coloured with silks and tassels. Above the corn the grass-covered slope ran up smoothly, marked with boulders and black stumps, to a sky cloudless and intensely blue.

As they drove into the hayfield and Frank began to pitch the heavy fragrant stuff direct from the swath, it seemed to him that his father already had grown younger. A fresh breeze was blowing sharply from the Lake, whipping the blood into their faces, and driving the waves booming against the point only a hundred rods away.

The hay was perfectly cured, a beautiful dull green, still toughened slightly by the dew. Mr. Thompson began to talk of the probable tonnage of the crop, comparing it with earlier crops and those of other years. He always talked when they worked at the farm, Frank reflected.

"Would alfalfa grow just as well back from the Lake, father?" he inquired. He remembered that his father had been the first to make alfalfa grow in this region.

"Better—they have better land for it back there. Oh, it might not do so well away inland—but anywhere in this county it would be all right."

"They ought to get it back there. They were making

marsh hay one place I stopped. That reminds me," he added suddenly. "I promised to ask mother if she knew of a place where a girl could work and go to school. I had forgotten all about it."

"That so? Who is the girl?"

"Mr. McCune's daughter—Rose, I think they called her."

"Oh, Neal McCune's daughter?"

"Yes. He subscribed to the paper. Why, do you know him?"

"Only slightly. He surveyed this place for me when I bought it. He's the only good surveyor in the county. He's a real engineer."

"Is that so?"

"Yes—University of Toronto man, I've heard. Came here I don't know why—some say to get away from liquor, some say from some other trouble. I imagine he just came in fishing or to see the country. Anyway, he married a girl in the settlement, and never went back."

"Maybe that's why he wants the girl to go to school. He seemed a strange, silent fellow."

"I seldom see him in town. Well, I guess we've got to make two jags of it. Let's go with this."

Frank climbed on the load and made a place to sit in the fragrant hay. They drove slowly down the road and through the village, along a street that paralleled the Lake, where branches brushed the hay, to the barn of a man who had several dairy cows, and hence wanted the alfalfa. As they unloaded, Frank could see from the barn window the green water rolling up the beach of hard grey sand and breaking in lacy masses of foam, and the lazy flight of big white gulls over the waves and back to the posts of a ruined pier.

The second load was to go to their own barn. When it was ready Mr. Thompson slid from the rack. "Let's step over into the corn," he said, "and see how it's doing. It will only take a minute."

They tied the team to the fence, and walked slowly between the rows of corn. The tassels were as high as their heads; and the beautiful silky tips of the ears, rose-coloured and tawny, were already turning brown. "A few days of good weather, and this corn is made," Mr. Thompson was saying.

"You've surely got it clean," Frank remarked. Not a weed was to be seen in the mellow yellow soil.

"It was pretty clean. But I hoed most of it anyway. We'll get horse feed here for the winter. If the settlers would only raise corn like this, they could feed cattle and make money." Frank thought of the labour his father had put into the making of this field—hard, menial labour—hours spent hauling manure from the village, spreading lime—and of the evenings when he had studied farm bulletins and farm magazines.

They came to the edge of the corn and stood looking out along the range of great hills that shouldered toward the Lake, narrowing the tree-clad shelf at their base.

Just beyond their land was a luxuriant tangle of second growth—birch and ash, wild cherry and basswood, mixed with willow and sumach—a dense, almost impenetrable mass. It was a real achievement, Frank reflected, to transform such wilderness into the ordered and useful beauty of these fields. He looked at his father with affectionate respect. The older man pointed beyond the second growth to a bare, unfenced hillside, where a few scrawny cattle were grazing.

"We ought to get a fence around the outside of the

farm," he remarked. "There are cattle grazing on all sides, loose on the commons, and when the grass is short they're half starved. I worry all the time for fear they'll get into the crops."

"That would be a good idea," Frank agreed.

"This land in front of us here is just the same as what the hay and corn are growing on," his father went on. "It needs only a little work and money to make it all productive. Well, son," he added, turning suddenly to Frank, "I don't know whether you'll ever have any use for this place or not. I expect you'll go on and be a professor like your mother wants you to. Maybe I could have done more for you some other way. But it's seemed as though I couldn't help doing this. My father moved off the farm when I was a little boy, but he always wanted to get back, and I've always wanted to farm. I'd have sold the paper and moved out here. But your mother wasn't cut out for a farmer's wife."

Frank was thinking of the old man with the crippled hand and leg, in the grey shingled house by the long red barn and the orchard and the stream, of Marion Bouchard, of all those who clung to small clearings and refractory fields while high wages lured them to the lights of the cities. He saw that there is a call of the soil, like the call of the sea, which is in the blood of men and holds them. He thought of lake sailors he had known, who could not give up their dangerous calling. His father was like one of these.

"I don't know, father," he said thoughtfully. "But I think you've done a mighty fine thing here."

The older man did not reply, but his averted eyes were wet as he led the way back to the wagon.

CHAPTER V

FRANK'S father was in good spirits at the supper table that night, and the meal progressed pleasantly. Mrs. Thompson had dressed herself in a fresh, cool voile, and her grey hair was crinkled prettily about her even, sensitive face. Her daintiness and freshness, and the shining linen doilies, the fragile china, and the carefully prepared food—meat loaf, chocolate, escalloped potatoes, amber jelly—were in strong contrast to the plain, work-soiled garments and plebeian hunger of her husband and son. Nevertheless, they talked together very happily. Presently Frank was surprised to hear his father remark: "We were speaking about your getting a schoolgirl to help you this year, Mina—like Mrs. Becker had. Frank knows of one you might like."

"Who is that, Frank?" his mother asked. "Someone you met on this last trip?"

"Yes—Mr. McCune's daughter, from out in the south settlement. Rose, I think her name is." He described the home briefly, and told of the questions of Mrs. McCune. "I'm sorry I didn't mention it right away when I got home," he concluded. "I didn't think of your wanting the girl yourself."

"Your mother hasn't been well for a long time, Frank," his father interposed, "and she *will* keep things up just so." He indicated the table with a sweep of his hand. "She needs help, but she hardly wants a girl all the time. I've been thinking about it ever since you told me about this girl this morning."

"What is the family, Frank?" Mrs. Thompson asked, addressing her husband now.

"McCune is a surveyor. I've been told he is an educated engineer—a University of Toronto man. I don't know certainly as to that. But he has the speech and accent of a man of some such experience—wouldn't you say so, son?"

"Yes, I would. I couldn't help wondering how he came into this country."

"Well, it was as I told you—he came into the country on a fishing or hunting trip, and stayed to marry a girl in the settlements. He farms a little, too; perhaps he saw the possibilities in the country."

Remembering that his mother had been one of the officers of a local temperance organization, Frank understood why his father forbore to mention the part liquor was rumoured to have played in McCune's history.

"You say the home is neat and clean, and they have some flowers?" his mother was asking him.

"Yes—it was unusually nice for the settlements. And the food was especially good and well cooked. Evidently the mother is a good housekeeper, and I think the girl knows how, too." Frank found himself and his father somehow in the position of advocates for the McCunes in general, and Rose in particular; and hence, knowing his mother, he omitted mention of her work in the field.

It was characteristic of Mrs. Thompson that she should act, promptly and carefully, once she had satisfied herself as to the facts in the case. She wrote a note to Mrs. Neal McCune, inviting her and her daughter to call, and directed Mr. Thompson to post it after supper, so that it would go out with the rural carrier in the morning.

"An old pier ran out into the Lake."

The next afternoon was cool and sunny. A drowsy quiet held the streets of the little town as Frank and his father walked toward the office after lunch—the complete and pervasive somnolence of summer afternoons in little towns. The streets were empty. No one swung the screen doors of the drug store or meat market. Barber-shop and pool room were closed. On the side porch of the hotel an old man was stretched out in an easy chair asleep, a quilt drawn over his knees. Everywhere was the sunlight, brilliant, cool, quietly exhilarating. As they turned a corner they came in sight of the Lake— an incredible field of colour—deep purple in the cloud shadows—clear green above the shoals—rich vivid blue where the sunlight struck deep water: at the horizon a band of hazy beryl, marked minutely by the faint smoke-trail of a steamer and a tiny spot of brightness where the low sun was reflected from her deck house: above, the sky—a sea of kindred blue, where sculptured clouds swam, weightless and motionless.

There was little to do at the office, and after a time Frank sauntered out, leaving his father drowsily read-ing exchanges; his big shears clacked at long intervals as he made a clipping. A light breeze had sprung up from the Lake, and scenting eagerly its keen, sweet tang of woods and water, Frank crossed the street and took the path to where an old pier ran out into the Lake, for a hundred yards or more, from the end of the quiet street. Its grey piles were lashed together by heavy chains above the bright water. On the widened por-tion at the outer end, the weathered red walls of a small freight-house glowed dully in the clear sunlight. He had slipped a book into each pocket of his coat before he left the house—a thin volume of Pater in one, and in the other a small, leather-backed portfolio of photographs of Rodin's sculpture. He walked slowly out the long pier, over the uneven, rotting planks, and found a place at the corner of the old freight-house, where the sun beat down warmly on his back and the breeze filled his nostrils. He tried to read, but Pater was too remote from what seemed to him at the moment a perfected beauty: blue sky and water, sunlight, and grey planks on which to lie. He relaxed utterly to the rhythm of waves thumping dully against the piling, of small clouds milk-white against the blue, of wind that brought crisp, tanging fragrances of wood-smoke and pure water. For an hour he drowsed, thinking idly of school—Steen—his beer and his pipe—of a girl in the biology laboratory—of another girl, very pretty and very awe-inspiring, who presided at a registration desk. He wondered if she would be there this fall.

An uneasiness stirred him, and he drew out the Rodin portfolio, staring long at the leaves. The wind had heightened, and moving masses of vivid green water stretched from the pier toward the point with its slender lighthouse a half-mile away. They went sweeping toward the shore, swifter and swifter, until suddenly all along their crests a cream of foam appeared, and they broke with crashing that shook the pier, sweeping the brown sand of the beach with swirling lather of white. Overhead the clouds were larger and lower, heavily shaded with grey and silver beneath their fluffy, milk-white domes, and they passed swiftly inland, great purple shadows fleeting beneath them over the turmoil of vivid blue and green.

In the pictures before him, miserable reproductions though they were, Frank found some satisfying relationship to this vivid, moving world of which he seemed a part: in the Burghers of Calais, the Thinker, the Adam and the Eve, the Balzac—something of stress met with strength, of tremendous vitality, elemental and dynamic, which moved him with profound satisfaction. In his mind stirred vigorously the desire to understand, to feel adequately this tremendous place of beauty and power, this drama of lake and land and sky. He felt keenly that really to understand, to compass however briefly the meaning of what he saw, would be a creative act of highest significance. He sprang to his feet, paced back and forth across the pier. At last, filled with the necessity of doing something, he started back toward the town.

As he regained the street, Frank saw his father walking slowly away from the office with a square, erect old man in a rusty brown coat, whom he recognized as Dr. Pratt. His father appeared to be listening quietly while the doctor expounded something vehemently, gesturing with a cigar. Frank smiled. "Father will have a good half-hour," he reflected, knowing the rare quality of the intellectual comradeship of these two men. He walked on up the street toward his home.

At the post in front a team was standing, hitched to a spring wagon, and Frank thought he recognized one of the horses as McCune's. In the living-room he found Mrs. McCune and Rose, talking with his mother. The country women sat stiffly on their chairs, and greeted him shyly when he entered. He noted the constraint of their attitudes in contrast to that of his mother, at ease in her grey silk. Mrs. McCune wore a tight black dress, and high black shoes carefully polished. Rose's dress was a rather painfully elaborate affair of pink, with ruffles and a sash, and she, too, wore shining high black shoes. She looked a little frightened and very countrified, and Frank thought with secret amusement of her easy mastery of the pitchfork and the team.

"We have just arranged for Miss McCune to stay here this winter, Frank," his mother was saying. "You see, my son will be away at college, so there will be just the two of us," she added to Mrs. McCune.

"We appreciate your speaking to your mother for us," Mrs. McCune managed to tell him.

"I was glad to do that." He paused a moment, impatient to get away, then passed on through the house and began to push the lawn-mower back and forth across the yard. The fat black horse next to the walk snorted as he approached.

A week later, on Saturday afternoon, Uncle Marion brought Rose to the Thompson home, and Frank helped him to carry her small black trunk from the spring wagon to the upstairs room which she was to occupy. The old man was loquacious as always, his high-pitched voice cheery and musical. But his jolly brown face grew serious when he came to bid good-bye to Rose. And as the girl followed him out to the wagon and stood talking with him, Frank realized suddenly what a break she was making in coming even from the settlements to Green Bush, and how much it must mean to all the members of her family.

At the meal that evening it was Mr. Thompson who engaged Rose in conversation about her neighbours in the settlement, and the crops. Frank saw that she liked him instantly, as young people always did, and that she was at her ease with him, while she still stood in awe of his mother and himself.

The next morning, awkward and self-conscious in her ruffled white dress, new hat, and tight black shoes, Rose went with the Thompson family to church. Frank noted with some disgust the curious looks which were directed at her, across the bare little church, particularly the level, appraising stare of June Strout, in the choir. He felt his usual twinge of disgust for the girl, attractive as she was in a yellow silk dress, with her dark eyes, rich black hair, and round, colourful face and piquant lips. He vouchsafed to her thunderous father only the external semblance of attention during the long and fervid prayer and the rambling, text besprinkled discourse which followed it. He shifted about on the hard, golden-oak pew, staring out a slit of window into maple boughs where the inner leaves were yellowing. At the end of the service he found June beside him in the crowded aisle as he neared the door.

"Who's your friend?" she challenged him in a whisper.

"She's a girl who's going to work for mother," he answered stiffly. "Her name is Rose McCune."

"Oh! I thought perhaps she was a college girl." June dropped her eyes flirtatiously and turned away.

Frank felt the gibe, and did not answer. He wondered if Rose, standing beside his mother a few feet away, had heard. She looked red and uncomfortable.

After the usual sumptuous Sunday dinner—served with the best linen, silver, and china, to Rose's silent amazement—Frank's father proposed a trip to the farm. Somewhat to Frank's surprise his mother consented, on condition that they should return early. Frank changed his clothes, curried the old horse, and cleaned up the ancient two-seated surrey which stood in the barn, seldom used, while Rose washed the dishes, his mother rested, and his father read a farm magazine. They drove slowly down the shaded street, past houses where people in their Sunday clothes sat on porches or walked about their gardens. Frank and his father rode in the front seat, and his mother and Rose behind. But at the farm it was Rose who walked with Mr. Thompson out into the alfalfa, while Frank sat with his mother in the surrey.

Below the vivid sky the tangled second growth beyond the fields was shot with yellow and crimson where birches and maples were already turning. The smooth contour of the hill nearer at hand was russet, and the tassels of the corn showed brown in even rows. The little field of alfalfa was a square of intense green, the young shoots already ankle-high. The man and the girl stood in the midst of it, he gesturing and pointing and she listening quietly, and Frank felt a sudden pang of alienness, almost of jealousy. He sensed a profound kinship between this girl and man, who stood so surely on the fruitful soil beneath the enormous sky— a kinship born of their knowledge of the earth and love of it. And he desired keenly to cross the fence which separated him from the field, and share their talk. But he remained sitting nervously in the surrey with his mother, who toyed with the lace collar of her modish silk dress, and was already impatient to return to town.

"I am confident we'll have a third crop," his father told them as he returned to the surrey. "Just see what a start it's making. I think I've persuaded Rose to get her people to try alfalfa out there."

In the days that followed, Frank saw a real friendship rapidly growing up between Rose and his father. Mr. Thompson took the girl to the shop and explained to her painstakingly the different machines and the process of getting out the paper. He announced that after Frank left he was going to depend on her to help him out. The two talked of farming often, and Frank saw that from her reading of farm magazines and her personal experience Rose knew far more about it than he did—enough to make his father listen to her with interest, and ask her for opinions. It was the older man to whom she occasionally appealed for help in her new and strange studies—algebra and Latin—rather than to Frank or his mother.

The relationship pleased Frank immensely, for he saw that his father enjoyed it, and that it kept the girl from home-sickness. If Mrs. Thompson did not wholly approve, she made no sign. Manifestly she was pleased with Rose as a helper, in any case, for the girl was clean, quiet, and competent, and eager to learn. The opportunity to help her with clothes, and to show her little refinements of cooking and serving, delighted Mrs. Thompson; and Frank remembered that once or twice he had heard his mother express a wish for a daughter.

One day in early September came a high wind from the north which died down at evening, leaving a cold calm through which the stars shone with wintry brilliance. "Hard frost to-night," Frank's father remarked as the boy started for his room. And as he lay in bed reading, he heard the older man moving about the house, and passing out into the back yard to test the air and look at the thermometer on the porch. "He's worrying about that alfalfa," Frank remarked to himself. In the forenoon Mr. Thompson disappeared from the office, and he was able to report at luncheon that he thought the alfalfa "wasn't hurt much." But the maples had felt the chill, and, in the week that followed, Frank could see them brighten visibly day by day, until the street before his house was roofed with red and gold. On the last afternoon before his departure for Ann Arbor he finished his packing about four o'clock, and find-

ing the house somehow oppressive with the demonstra-
tive tenderness in which his mother always prepared
for his going away, he set out for a walk. At the street
he met Rose, and on an impulse invited her to join him.
"I'll ask your mother," she answered, flushing with
pleasure.

He stood on the sidewalk, his eyes lighting as he
looked down the arch of colour. In a moment she was
back. "She says be home by five," she reported. Frank
frowned.

They crossed the school yard, where a group of boys
were punting a scarred football back and forth in an
opening between the brilliant trees, and took a winding
road that led back among the hills. In a little while
Frank turned aside, and showed the way up a steep incline to the edge of a grove of dark pines at the very
crest of the hill. They turned as their feet touched the
carpet of needles, and looked back.

Under an utterly cloudless sky the Lake was all one
tone of shining, sapphire blue. Against its edge, at the
foot of umber slopes, the little, tree-filled town lay glowing like a jewel of gold and crimson. Rose caught her
breath and stood silent, her soft lips parted, her wide
eyes, blue as the Lake, shining with delight. To Frank,
who had seen this sight before, her positive response to
its beauty was a surprise and a revelation. "Do you
like it, Rose?" he asked gently.

"Yes," she breathed. After a little while she added:
"We'd better go back now."

It was with a new appreciation that he listened to her
talk with his father at the supper table that evening,
and, later, noted the quiet effectiveness of her assistance to his mother in serving tea and cake to the callers
that evening—the Steeles and the inevitable Strouts,

invited because it was "the last evening before Frank goes away."

An uneasiness which he supposed to be a desire to get back to school had been growing on Frank for days, and he found even the Steeles a bit banal this evening, and the Strouts downright oppressive. He felt June's patronizing attitude toward Rose, and would have liked to say or do something to hurt the girl. He was glad when the callers had gone; and though it was evident that his father and mother wanted to talk with him, he retired at once, on the plea of a hard trip on the morrow. It was with a sense of positive relief that he settled himself at last in the seat of the south-bound train the next morning, after waving good-bye to his father and mother on the platform, and drew from his bag the new novel which Steen had sent him and which he had saved for just this time.

CHAPTER VI

THE novel proved dull, however—less dramatic and absorbing than the landscape which flowed past the windows of the little train. Frank found himself turning again and again to note the exuberant colour of a stretch of hardwoods, the dull greygold and russet crimson of a swamp, the yellowed green of fields and pastures, stretching far, far away to the blue of Lake and sky. Rusted goldenrod and azure asters bloomed in the right-of-way. Drift of downy seed of thistles blew from a weedy field. As he watched all this, Frank felt brief twinges of regret—a certain distaste for the crowds and cities he was approaching, and a desire to stay in this land of clean winds, where the earth was a constant, unveiled reality. He felt a warm kinship with the folk who greeted the train as it stopped at each tiny village—the farmers with faces and hands the colour of clay, who delivered cream cans and crates of poultry to jocular trainmen. Presently he laid the novel definitely aside and, slouching on the hard cushions, surrendered himself to a passive mood in which in swift succession the colours and forms of earth impressed themselves powerfully upon him, made him their instrument; and he responded in vivid joy and pain to the swift passing of beauty.

As the train neared Bay City, toward the hour of noon, and a succession of summer cottages—nearly all closed now—obtruded themselves between him and the Lake, Frank found his mood of exaltation giving way to

a more commonplace one. He observed that the train
was on time, and calculated with satisfaction the near
approach of a meal.

In the brief interval between his arrival at Bay City
and the departure of the Detroit train he lunched,
hurriedly but heartily, at a little restaurant across the
track. He was served by a pretty, dark-eyed French-
Canadian girl in a clean white uniform. And this brief
experience was sufficient to swing the balance definitely in his mood, and to set him, as he went on to Detroit, thinking with pleasure of his friends at the University and of the life he would soon be living there.

His year of graduate work should, he reflected, be
more memorable than those which had preceded it. He
recalled rather pityingly his first two years at the University, when he had been so very much alone, con-
strained to look on at the spectacle of University life
rather than to share in it. He had been very young,
for he had "skipped" certain grades in his grammar-
school career and had finished high school at sixteen.
And although he was already tall when he went to the
University, he was under weight, awkward, shy, and
acutely conscious of his social imperfections. He had
liked best to be let alone, preparing his assignments
with conscientious brilliance, and reading incessantly in
the University library, where all the treasures so tanta-
lizingly hinted at in his high-school literature books were
at last within his reach, and many others concerning
which the literature books had been strangely silent.
Certain cynicisms as to University "society" that he had
developed then had stayed with him: his contempt for
the "glad hand" of the Y. M. C. A., his dislike for
fraternity men and their affectations of superiority.
His cynicism in regard to courses and instructors had

come later, he reflected—since he had met Steen.

That had been the one real event of his college life: the evening at the University library when Steen had observed him reading the poems of Sidney Lanier and had led him outside for a "little talk." The talk had been prolonged far into the night, and resumed next day. Common tastes and background had soon brought him close to the lanky, studious Hollander from a tiny town on the west side of the peninsula. In a few weeks he knew Steen's three or four friends, and University life had taken on a new meaning for him, in which long walks over the hills around Ann Arbor, and talks around the back tables of restaurants or in smoke-filled rooms of students, replaced courses and lectures in the place of first importance. There was Devereaux, a dark, shy fellow, slender and silent, who now and then read his simple poems, of remarkable delicacy and precise beauty, in a flute-like voice with curious slurrings of French-Canadian accent; Dutton, plump, rosy, well-dressed, inclined to be pompous and often a bit inebriate, but capable of reciting Swinburne, Dowson, Wilde "by the armful," as Steen put it, and also, when well provided with liquor, given to long bursts of Latin and Greek which no one understood but which no one interrupted—relics of some ecclesiastical training in his past, Steen explained—just what, Frank never understood. Occasionally Haller joined the group—a small, vivid boy of German descent, with a square jaw, keen black eyes, and a tremendous voice in which he would hold forth for hours on politics, religion, philosophy, or literature.

Frank felt himself rather a negative and colourless member of this group, but he was accepted because Steen vouched for him. The Hollander, who seldom spoke and then usually in monosyllables, was clearly the centre of the group—the pivot on which it swung. He was the object of a self-forgetting fidelity on the part of Devereaux, of a bluff, whole-hearted admiration from Dutton, and of his sole respect from Haller, who would even pause in his periods when he felt that Steen had something to say. When Steen invited Frank to be his room-mate, at the end of Frank's junior year, the boy felt that the highest privilege the University could afford was being held out to him.

Frank's senior year, which they had spent together, had fully come up to his expectations. They had procured a large, rather bare room, a short distance from the campus, in a house in which they were the only students. Their life together had been largely a matter of live-and-let-live, as is necessary in such cases: each had his own work-table, his own bookcase, his own bed and clothes-press. But there were frequent hours of freedom from study, when they would smoke, talking at intervals or keeping silence as they happened to prefer. Sometimes one or all of the others would drop in— Devereaux with a new poem, Dutton with a couple of quarts of beer or a flask of whiskey, Haller with a new plan for a campus magazine, or a new theory of taxaion, or a theme for a novel; and the talk would be fast and furious till well past midnight.

The coming year Steen would be a half-time instructor in English, while continuing his graduate work. It was rumoured that he was "slated" for a high position on the faculty, for he was as highly thought of by his teachers as by the few students who knew him.

Lost in memories and plans, Frank made the swift trip from Bay City and Saginaw to Detroit without noticing the passage of time. At the Pere Marquette sta-

tion in Detroit he took a cab, for he had only a few minutes in which to catch a fast train for Ann Arbor. The
crowded streets were thronged and brilliant with lights,
but nearer the Michigan Central depot the cab roared
through dark, shaded avenues of small residences and
lodging-houses. His ticket purchased and trunk re-
checked, Frank walked about the spacious, towering
marble rotunda for a few minutes, hoping to meet an
acquaintance before he boarded the crowded train for
Ann Arbor. He shared a seat with a very fashionably
dressed young lady with a sorority pin and many bundles, wearing a corsage bouquet somewhat faded.

A long, jolting street-car ride, this time standing up,
and he reached his rooming-place at last. Steen
greeted him with a big hand outstretched, quietly exultant, his lank form draped in a grey bathrobe, and the
inevitable black pipe poised in his left hand.

The next day Frank set about the business of registration. It was a less complicated process than that he
remembered as a freshman, but still sufficiently tedious.
The campus was crowded with students in bright-
coloured suits and caps, filling the walks under the
huge elms, sitting in little knots on the grass in the narrow spaces between buildings to study programs and
registration cards, and diving headlong through tunnel-
like corridors in search of elusive deans and heads of
departments. He was glad that in the evening Devereaux, Haller, and Dutton appeared, the latter provided
with oranges, ginger ale, and a quart of gin. Steen
begged a piece of ice from the landlord, and there was
convivial talk until morning. It centred about a project for a campus magazine, which Haller was to edit
and Dutton to finance, and to which the others would
contribute: "a really live sheet, which will make the

powers sit up and roar most engagingly," as Haller put it.

A week later Frank had settled down to the business of attending classes and mastering assignments, varied by the occasional talk or tramp with Steen. As the fall advanced, the campus walks were littered with golden drift of elm leaves, and some of the older buildings took on a cold autumnal beauty. But to feel his pulses stirred and quickened by the loveliness of earth, as so often at Green Bush, Frank had to walk with Steen out over the steep and rounded hills beyond the town, which were painted by the oaks in bold splashes of crimson, scarlet, and vermilion across the dulled green of pasture and the brown of ploughed land.

His mother wrote regularly each week—long, pleasant letters of the town news, with many personal reminders as to his health and his work; and Frank replied as regularly with details of his courses and the events of the school year. He had only one letter from his father —a brief scrawl written "because your mother is laid up with one of her sick spells. I am worried about her.

"I have cut the alfalfa. Had a nice crop but had to stack it on the place as no room in the barn. Rose helped me. She is good company for us since you are away, and helps me some at the office, but I miss you and am kept pretty busy.

"YOUR FATHER."

His mother had written of how hard Mr. Thompson was working. "I guess he didn't realize how much you had done during the summer," she had said. Frank was worried for a time about both his parents, but was soon absorbed in the daily routine again.

He chose for his master's thesis a topic in American

literature which really attracted him, and began a series of readings which gained in interest as he advanced.

On one memorable afternoon the head of the English
department, a precise, grizzled little man who talked
with sharp inflections, called Frank into his office "to
talk over your plans with you," as he explained directly.
"I have watched your work with high interest, Thompson," he went on. "I hope you are having a good year."

Frank flushed with pleasure.

"What are you planning to do next year?" the professor asked.

Frank explained that he had no definite plans—that
he was interested in writing, and had considered teaching.

"I am glad to know that," the professor answered at
once. "I believe you could teach well. Come and see
me about it a little later in the year, won't you? Perhaps—well, we'll see later."

Steen was jubilant when Frank told him of this inter-
view. "Old Wright likes you, Frank," he declared.
"You're a lucky boy. There's a berth in line for you
here if you want it."

"I'm not sure that I want it," Frank answered slowly.

The campus magazine project had been given up because of the unexpected appointment of Haller as liter-
ary editor of the campus *Daily.* He had enlisted all
available helpers, including Frank and Steen, and was
filling the "mag" with stimulating and readable, if not
always well-considered, reviews and criticisms, sprinkled with verse and brief excerpts from current books
which appealed to Haller's taste or to his sense of the
ridiculous. To this development the University as a
whole was totally apathetic, though there were occasional snorts of protest from students and faculty mem-

bers whom Haller defined as "Kiwanians and right-thinkers."

For a time Frank neglected his studies to become general "fetch-and-carry boy for Haller," as Dutton genially expressed it—writing occasional reviews to fill space, and using his practical knowledge in "making up" the paper. Finally Steen protested, and Frank threw enough of his energy into his school work, before the coming of quarterly examinations in November, to enable him to pass them creditably. Nevertheless the examination week was one of rather gruelling effort, and when at last the final test was over, Steen took Frank home promptly after their restaurant supper—"to put in one quiet evening before you die, young man."

CHAPTER VII

IN the big bare room that November night there was a calm of lassitude and exhaustion. Steen had placed one of his favourite records on his small portable graphophone, and had shut the machine in the clothes-press. Very softly, as from far away, Wieniawski's *Melody* came to them: Steen lolling in his bathrobe in the big arm-chair, his feet on the littered table, pulling dreamily at his black pipe; Frank half undressed on his bed, staring at the ceiling in a sort of dazed inattention.

Into this quiet came the brief rasp of the door-bell from below, voices, and a call up the stairs: "Telegram for you, Mr. Thompson."

"I'll bring it for you, Frank," said Steen quickly, and, getting up from the chair, he hurried down the carpeted stairs.

Frank sat on the edge of the bed to tear open the yellow envelope, and read the line of purple capitals a second time before he understood: "Your father died 6:30 of pneumonia Could not save him Better come at once.
                                                "DR. PRATT."

Frank sat dumbly on the bed, staring at the slip. Steen reached out and took it. From the closet came the soft wail of the closing strains of the *Melody*.

"Well, Frank," said Steen after a moment, "I guess we can make the next car. I'll go to Detroit with you, anyway." He laid a hand hesitantly on Frank's shoulder, then drew it back abruptly. "Come on, old man, get your things together. I'll call a cab. We've just twenty minutes."

Frank rose uncertainly and began fingering things on his dresser. "I can't believe it," he muttered, unconscious that Steen had left the room to go to the telephone. He was back in a moment, and Frank went on, almost accusingly. "I didn't even know he was sick. Why didn't they write me? Dad——" he choked, his eyes filled, and he sobbed harshly.

"Come, Frank," Steen spoke firmly. "Here's your suit. Get into it right away while I pack for you. We've got to make that car if you're to get home in the morning."

Mechanically the boy drew on his trousers, laced his shoes, adjusted his collar and tie. Each movement seemed filled with an intolerable burning agony. It was an hour, he thought, before Steen was leading him down the stairs to the waiting taxi, carrying the loaded suitcase.

The express car ground its swift way through the night, leaping, jolting, screaming at crossings and sleeping towns, throwing the white pencil of its headlight across dim fields and pastures and mist-haunted woodlands. Frank rode silent, staring out the window or at the seat ahead, steadied and yet embarrassed by the presence of Steen. There was the transfer at Detroit— a hurried flight in a bounding cab over ill-paved, darkened streets where yellow lights glared dimly. They scrambled from the cab, and as Steen thrust into his pocket for the fare Frank gasped: "It's the wrong depot."

"Thought you said Grand Trunk," the driver announced truculently.

Steen thrust close his big angular head and swore

savagely. "The Pere Marquette is due in five minutes. If you don't get us there, I'll kill you." They dived back into the door and the cab roared away, through misty, foul-smelling alleys between warehouses, across a brilliant, hazardous boulevard, and stopped with a lurching rush at the curb where a big lighted clock in the tower showed "11:50," the hour of the train. Frank dashed wildly through the door and across the waiting-room, banging his suitcase against the knee of a sleeping labourer who awoke to jabber fiercely, and climbed aboard a chair car as lanterns were swinging and bells pealing. Once seated, he thought of Steen, left standing on the sidewalk by the sputtering cabman without a word of farewell.

"Good old Steen," he thought remorsefully. "He's been so good." And with this reflection came a sudden softening and loosening of the intolerable strain in his throat and heart, and, slumping into the seat, he hid his face behind his hand.

Presently he straightened up, and to get himself under control he walked up to the smoker and lit a cigarette. It was tasteless, and the strain of waiting began to close upon him again like a tightening vise. He thought of taking a berth, but knew he could not sleep. Finally he went back to the chair car, adjusted the seat, and, lying with his face toward the window, gave himself up to watching the swift flight of shadowy indistinguishable forms. Presently a late moon appeared and arched a low arc across the dull black sky. In its light the broad fields were grey and lifeless, and the denuded trees stark and unreal through the silvered folds of trailing smoke.

Frank saw the eastern sky pale at last, and a faint rosy flush crept into it before the sun, a dull orange ball, lifted suddenly across the flat marshy fields at the edge of Bay City.

An hour later he was speeding northward again, on the last lap of his homeward journey. In the brief wait between trains he had tried to eat oatmeal and cakes at the restaurant across the tracks; but the food disgusted him after a few mouthfuls, and he lit another cigarette and walked stiffly back to the train through the bright, chill morning.

He watched Lake Huron brighten swiftly as the sun climbed and the clouds thinned, until a path of blinding brilliance was flanked by intense and living blue. The cottages that fringed the Lake near the city were boarded up, the trees about them bare and lifeless, the marsh grasses browned by frost. Farther up, the bare little towns were stark under the sky which had filled with clouds again. In the midst of the bare brown fields, the clusters of low, unpainted stores and houses seemed unspeakably paltry and frail, set in an illimitable sterility of water and land. A grey mist began to drive in from the Lake, and blurred the window through which Frank had looked. His mind went ahead of the slow train to his home. Against his will he dozed a little, and dreamed that his father was alive and well, ruddier and stronger than he had ever seen him, and that he met him at the train with a hearty handshake. He was aroused by the brakeman's call, "Green *Bush!—Green Bush!*"

As he crept from the train, feeling somewhat faint and tottery with the weight of his suitcase, he came face to face with Rose, grey and frightened in the clinging mist. "I came to meet you," she said. "I thought you would be on this train." Frank could say nothing. She reached for his suitcase, and they walked down the platform and began to follow the track toward his home before he realized that she was carrying it, and took it back again. The action aroused him to speech. "How did it happen, Rose?" he asked, and added before she had time to speak: "It was good of you to meet me." He had a sudden sense of the bleakness of the place if she had not been there, of comfort in her presence.

"He went out to the farm last Wednesday afternoon," she answered. "Some cattle were at his alfalfa stack and I guess he got overheated driving them out. Then" —she hesitated—"he worked nearly all night at the office. He didn't change his clothes or—anything. The next day he had an awful cold, but he wouldn't see the doctor. Sunday morning he couldn't get up, and the doctor said he had pneumonia—awfully bad already. He didn't see how your father had kept going so long, and scolded him. I don't know why your mother didn't wire you then. She didn't realize, I guess. Then— Sunday night his heart just stopped—the doctor was there——"

She bit her lip and looked away. Frank strode uncertainly down the gravel, staring into the mist.

There followed in rapid succession the meeting with his mother, who clung to him brokenly, the preparations for the funeral, numerous condolences of neighbours and friends. He was conscious of his mother, removed, the object of solicitous inquiry and fervid exclamations of sympathy—her position grotesquely enhanced and glorified by her bereavement; of Rose, somewhere in the background, cleaning rooms and furniture, cooking for the relatives who arrived from Ohio, washing dishes, accepting tactfully proffers of cakes, pies, and advice from sundry neighbours; of himself, a baffled, numb, undirected organism responding mechanically to the stimulus of situation after situation, and feeling all the time only a consuming ache that had come first when he looked down on the sharply chiselled, statuesque grey face, with its strangely definite expression of the calm acceptance of defeat.

The funeral itself seemed obscene to him, with its spare clutter of hothouse flowers, the sentimental mouthings of Strout, and the sniffling of the women. He felt his first sudden warmth of genuine human sympathy when the old doctor held his hand in a big, hard fist and looked into his eyes without a word. He remembered suddenly the years that these men had known and loved each other, the doctor and the man in the coffin, and realized that the doctor was suffering yet the more keenly because his friend's life had been laid for a little time in his own hands, and had slipped through. He clasped the doctor's fingers tight.

He could not but admire his mother's self-control, in the midst of much display of emotion, even though he realized that it was her keen sense of the dramatic that upheld her. He was glad that she did not cling to him at the grave, but stood alone and unmoving. The sky was grey, but an offshore wind came shouting over the hill where they laid him, on the broad pine-dotted slope facing the Lake—a wind clean with the breath of inland forests and meadows, cold and boisterous. There was something primitive in the tiny group clustered there on the great hill-side among the low stones, about the grave dug deep in the yellow sand. The grave and all those about it seemed brief and small in the presence of earth and Lake and sky. Slowly Frank felt his grief dissolving into a peace not unlike that of his father's face, now hidden for ever—a peace born of a sense of the submergence of every life in the immensity of space and time.

Back at the house after the burial service, he found the rooms crowded with relatives and friends, and noisy with the suppressed but obvious relaxation and relief. His mother went to her room and locked herself in. An aunt and two neighbours announced their intention of staying all night "to help straighten up," and attacked with Rose the task of preparing a meal of fried meat and mashed potatoes, canned fruit and cake, for the twenty or so people who were in the house. Presently Frank slipped out the side door, circled the house and barn to the rear, and strode off up the track—a raincoat flapping about his heels and his head lowered, for the wind had changed suddenly and was blowing wetly from the Lake.

Along the grade the grass was brown against the gravel. A few leaves clung to the red-stemmed dogwood in the fences, and blackberry leaves were bronzed and rusted crimson. He turned where the road crossed the rails, and followed the white sandy track unheedingly until he came to the wire gate at the corner of his father's farm.

About the low, conical stacks of alfalfa he found the traces of cattle—deep tracks in the sand, bunches of hay torn from the stacks and trampled, sodden now on the ground. He saw where the rusty wires of the enclosure had been freshly stapled—the last work of his father's hands on the beloved land.

Keenly he visioned how it had all happened—the excited angry chase, in grey mist blowing from the Lake as it was now, after hungry, prankish cattle, back and forth, back and forth—where the deep hoof-marks showed they had run across the stubble of the corn from corner to corner of the field; the desperate effort, in the swiftly failing light, to make the broken fence proof against further inroads; the tramp back to town through the dark and rain; the few bites of supper, the sharp reply of fatigue and discouragement to reproaches—the slammed door, and the hours of toil by lamplight in the unheated, draughty office.

An acute sense of the human nearness and reality of his father came to Frank as he stood there alone in the driving dusk—a sense of his flesh and blood, of his clothing and gestures and voice, of his plans and enthusiasms and unconfessed dreams—of all that had been the man: and with this a curious perception of his destiny—of the impersonal aloofness of the earth, of this little space which he had loved and which had destroyed him. Gazing into the mist, his cheeks cold and his throat dry and wrung with pain, in his ears the ceaseless increasing cry of the Lake, Frank seemed to himself almost to grasp the ultimate mystery of human life: the strange duality of the individual strength expended in effort, with reward and defeat—and the aloof, indivertible forces which, to the generality of men, gave or withheld irretrievably, and destroyed at last. For a moment he seemed to see these things, and himself with all men bound to a brief, half-illumined struggle with powers invincible and obscure. Then all he thought grew dim, and he was conscious only of fatigue, of loneliness, and of unappeased grief, as he trudged slowly back to town.

CHAPTER VIII

THE next morning his mother appeared, pale but quiet and controlled, at the lavish breakfast which Rose and her helpers had prepared. Frank found himself eating hungrily, and felt a warm glow of feeling for his mother as she pressed the food on him, though herself eating little. After the meal she took his arm and they walked into the front room, where Rose had rearranged the furniture to its accustomed order and raised the shades to the top of the windows to admit the morning sunlight. "We must talk about the paper, son," she began. "It isn't like some businesses, you know—it *has* to go on. I have thought it all over, and I am afraid you will have to stay at home awhile and keep it going, until we see what can be done."

"I'll be glad to, mother," Frank broke in. "Of course that's the thing to do. I'm glad I *can.*"

"We should both be thankful for that, I guess," she answered, looking at him consideringly. "It will save us from the necessity of a forced sale at heavy loss—if we could find a ready buyer at all. Perhaps you can study nights and keep up your work or part of it."

"Oh, that is easy to arrange," he assured her. "You see, we've just had quarterly exams, and I'm confident all the men will give me 'unfinished' and let me make up this second quarter some other time."

"I don't want you to regard this as a break in your school work, Frank," she urged. "I want you to go right ahead just as soon as we can possibly arrange it. ⁻ would rather you would do some studying right along."

"Well, probably I can," he conceded. "We'll see how it works out."

"The paper was due yesterday," she went on, "and of course there was nothing ready for it. You will have all you can do to get it out next week. But Rose can help you with the folding and addressing—your father used her sometimes." She put her arm about his shoulders. "Dear boy, this is *so* hard for you. I know how you are going to feel, going into the office and using his things. I am *so* sorry you have to do it, and that you have to stay out of school. It about breaks my heart. But promise me you won't let it interfere with your life work, Frank. You *must* go on."

"Oh, don't worry, mother. I'll get along all right." He held her close, kissed her again and again, and a little later hurried from the house.

He found the office stale and musty; and as he looked about at the unfinished work—the forms on the table, the apron hanging at the end of a case—he choked, and it seemed to him that he could not bear to touch these things. But he busied himself in building a rousing wood fire in the big heater, crossed the street to the post office to get the boxful of mail, with an additional bundle of accumulated papers which the girl gave him, and found things growing easier as he sat at his father's desk to glance over the exchanges and decipher the pencilled screeds of country correspondents.

By the end of the week he was fairly in the harness, and the following Tuesday he went to press at an early hour with a paper of the usual size, announcing briefly on the first page the reason for the omission of the preceding week's issue, and stating that F. J. Thompson, Jr., would conduct the paper temporarily in his father's place. On an inner page, at his mother's insistence, he printed the signed "obituary" by Strout, the banal floridity of which he mitigated considerably in the process of composition. The next day Rose helped him with folding and wrapping, and the paper was mailed on time. He returned to the office with a certain quiet elation, and set to work sorting the contents of two or three large "hellboxes." Later that day he wrote to Steen a full account of all that had happened, supplementing a hurried note which he had sent the day after his father's funeral. He thought affectionately of Steen as he wrote, realizing how much letters from him would mean in the weeks and months that lay ahead. He wondered when he would see his friend again.

In the week immediately following her husband's death Mrs. Thompson was taken ill. For several days she was confined to her bed, and Rose stayed out of school to care for her. When finally she gained the doctor's permission to get about, she was weak and easily exhausted, and seemed to Frank much older than she had before. He felt sometimes that she was harsh and exacting toward Rose, but the girl worked uncomplainingly, and found time to help a little at the office.

Frank was fortunate in the fact that immediately after he took over the paper the holiday season came on, with its extra advertising and special news of entertainments and Christmas services. For a month he was kept desperately busy; and he found a real exhilaration in matching himself against the demands of the office— working night after night at the case, and spending much of the day in gathering news and advertising. In this period he had little time in which to think of his father, or of the new issues in his own life.

But with the holidays past, and the work of the office fallen suddenly from the highest to the lowest point of the year, things were vastly different. The deep snow of the northern Michigan winter was banked along the sidewalks. Farmers made infrequent visits to the town in cutters and sleighs. There was little business—little advertising and little news. Frank could usually keep busy for the forenoon. But there were long afternoons in the office alone, with nothing to do but read or think or work half-heartedly over the correspondence courses which he had at last taken up at his mother's repeated request. The evenings were even more tedious, and Frank gradually formed the habit of spending them with Mr. Steele or Dr. Pratt. He found real comrade-ship with these old men. Mr. Steele would be alone in the drug store, sitting on the broad shelf behind the counter and reading from a worn volume of Dana or Darwin. He liked to have Frank tell of his work in biology at the University; and their common enthusi-asm for science in its broader and more philosophic as-pects drew the boy and the old man together.

He was likely to find Dr. Pratt in the back office of his rooms in the lower story of his little hospital, seated in an old rocking-chair with his feet on the fender of the rusted cannon stove and a faded dressing-gown around his shoulders, eating apples from a dish by his elbow and reading some romance of distant lands— Janvier or Rider Haggard, or Lew Wallace's "The Fair God," or a volume from his well-used set of Burton's "Arabian Nights." He liked to read aloud to Frank from these last, in a deep resonant voice that sounded and measured the prose. One zero night, as he was

reading, the telephone jangled; and Frank heard the
old doctor's brusque, impatient inquiries change to a
tone of reassurance as he promised to start at once on
an eight-mile drive into the country. He drew on extra
woollen socks and shouldered his tall, thin form into a
fur coat. Frank walked with him to the livery stable.

In Frank's home there was little change during these
weeks. His mother wore black whenever she left the
house, but at home there was no hint of mourning, and
no reference to Mr. Thompson's death. She watched over
Frank's health and diet very carefully—so carefully,
in fact, that he was made uncomfortable by her atten-
tions. She took a considerable interest in the business
of the office, and an even keener interest in his reading
for his thesis and his correspondence work. The routine work of the house—the cooking and cleaning and
dishwashing—she left very largely to Rose, in spite of
the fact that during the holiday season Frank needed
the girl much of the time at the office. Frank had moments of thinking remorsefully that Rose was working
too hard, and that something should be done about it.
But for the most part he noticed the girl very little.
He saw her rarely except at meal times, and she did her
work efficiently and cheerfully.

He knew from her infrequent comments that Rose
was enjoying her school work, and doing well with it.
In February she had a part in a play which the high
school gave, and of course Frank and his mother went.

They climbed the scarred, uneven stairs in the rickety
old school building to the "high school room" on the
second floor, a high-ceiled, box-like place with a huge,
rust-reddened cannon stove in one corner. Here a
stage had been improvised on the platform beneath the
bust of Cæsar and the portraits of Lincoln, Garfield,

and McKinley. The principal's desk was pushed aside, footlights were contrived by placing two lanterns in a dry-goods box, and a curtain was stretched across the front of the platform on a wire. A screened passageway was provided to the door of the tiny room which was used as a library, and this had to serve as a dressing-room for the whole cast.

June Strout had the lead in the simple little play, and dominated the first act. Frank had the uncomfortable feeling that the girl was playing directly to him. She was really lovely in a light dress of pale yellow, her naturally vivid colouring heightened by make-up. And she played her part feelingly, if a bit consciously. Frank was interested, and yet irritated by the strong physical attraction the girl held for him.

Between the acts Frank devoted himself to observation of the audience. He had insisted on sitting near the back of the room, and most of those near him were country people: grey men and women with hands and faces brown and strong like oak; abashed, self-conscious girls and their "fellows"; young fathers and mothers with two, three, even four little children. He counted eighteen children in arms, in the audience of perhaps a hundred people. The parents sat patiently in the old-fashioned, uncomfortable seats, their tired, weathered faces alight with eagerness. They were ready, like all the rest, to break into delighted applause at every opportunity. Frank felt inexpressibly drawn to these people, and somehow ashamed that they were not given something more worthy of their enthusiasm than the hackneyed little play. It seemed to him that for the first time he got a real glimpse of the folk of the soil— a sense of the vast reservoirs of life and strength from which the factories and the armies of earth are replenished; and he was profoundly sobered and impressed.

At the beginning of the second act came the important scene for the part which had been assigned to Rose—that of an attractive and aristocratic but ridiculous old lady. As the girl appeared on the stage and began to speak her lines, Frank was amazed by the transformation in her. He had known that his mother had given her an old dress for a costume and had helped her to fix her hair; but he was unprepared for her positive dignity and beauty. The dress was of rose-coloured brocade with full skirt and sleeves. Her abundant hair had been piled high on her head and powdered to glinting grey. She spoke easily and moved naturally, and as the scene progressed Frank became aware that she was really acting. She was gracious and self-assured, and yet incredibly funny. Frank knew that her triumph was the expression of reserves of capacity in the girl which he had sensed half-consciously, for the coaching had been mediocre. He pressed forward eagerly at the close of the performance to congratulate her. Finding June Strout in the aisle, he shook her hand mechanically, with a word of compliment. She held his fingers a moment, then looked away suddenly. When he reached Rose she was surrounded by her family, and he tempered somewhat the enthusiastic comment he had intended as he caught McCune's steady eye fixed on him a bit suspiciously. Rose was radiant, even more beautiful than on the stage, her blue eyes vivid and joyous as she listened breathlessly to Frank's words; and as he looked at her he was reminded suddenly of the afternoon in the autumn, when they had looked down on Green Bush.

CHAPTER IX

AS the long winter slowly passed, the close confinement of the office began to tell on Frank and he was nervous and irritable as he stood behind the type-cases day after day, or laboured desperately with the cumbersome, erratic old cylinder press. Rose helped him when she could, but his mother needed her much of the time, and the girl could not in any case relieve him of responsibility or of the more exacting work. He watched eagerly for the first signs of spring, and caught himself sometimes thinking regretfully of the campus at Ann Arbor, which he knew, from letters from Steen, was already greening. But the spring was late that year, even for the Huron shore. In late March the last ice went out with a whipping offshore wind, to be lost in the vivid blue of the rough, newly released water; but still the ground froze every night and the efforts of the villagers at gardening were all defeated.

Finally came an April afternoon shortly after Easter, when there was a mellow warmth in the sky, when the crows of roosters rang out bugle-like across the village, and the steady breeze that blew up from the south along the shore held the smell of grass and budding orchards. As he emptied a tin wash-basin at the back door of the office, Frank could see across vacant lots to where an old man and his wife were directing a very deaf man with a huge team—evidently hired to plough their garden. They shouted at him futilely, waving their arms and pointing. And the deaf man would nod reassuringly, wheel the huge horses, and start a furrow in another direction with the round little woman scrambling energetically beside him, gesticulating furiously to save the threatened permanent bed of asparagus or peonies.

It was a Saturday, and, locking the back door and hanging his printer's apron on a nail, Frank passed into the office where Rose was just finishing her balancing of the week's books.

"This is the best week you've had since I've worked in the office, Frank," she told him enthusiastically. "See!" She leaned back in the office chair and smiled up at him, pointing with her pen to the figures at the foot of the column.

"That 'Spring dollar day' ad we worked up helped out," he commented. "It has been a good week."

"You shouldn't say 'we,'" she corrected him.

"Yes, I should," he insisted. "The suggestions you made of what to get them to advertise were the best part of it. I couldn't have sold the ad without."

"I'm glad if I can help," she answered.

Their eyes met and held a moment. Then he reached for her coat and held it ready. "Let's walk down by the Lake," he suggested. "It's real spring to-day. I've finished up in the shop."

"I know it is," she agreed. "I knew spring had come when I first got up this morning. Feel o' the air, I guess. Uncle Marion will be ploughing to-day. The ground warms up faster, even that close inland, than it does here on the shore."

"I know—father used to say that," Frank replied, as they turned from the street that led on to the old pier and followed a path down to the beach. "Say, I'd like to walk out to the farm, I believe. Would you care to walk out there?"

"I'd love to!"

The clean brown sand of the beach was smooth and hard for the width of a rod back from the water. Beyond lay logs and drifts of rubbish, the débris of many storms; and behind these a steep bank, that rose to the level of the town, grass-clad and tangled with shrubs and vines, already held touches of green.

They stepped out rapidly over the smooth sand, Rose a little ahead with her firm, easy stride, her hair tangled about her ears by the wind, her eyes on the range of hills to the northward that swept toward the Lake and met it in grey curves and foldings at the horizon. Frank watched the lacy curl of low breakers that reached up the shelving sand toward their feet, and the ceaseless circling of shining gulls over the slanting black piles and ruined fish-traps out in the bright blue water.

They had little to say as they walked briskly along, past a little dock where a stout dory was moored and newly oiled nets were sunning, across a road that ran down to the very edge of the Lake, and close to the foot of a high bank which was topped by the grey board fence of the county fairgrounds. Frank found himself strangely eager for a sight of the farm. He had not been there since that November night when he had walked alone after his father's funeral. He had known that his mother had sold the stacks of alfalfa to a farmer, but otherwise he had given little thought to the land during the winter months.

They turned away from the shore, picked a course through wind-twisted bushes and low trees that grew in matted grass, and came out suddenly at the edge of the road that ran by his father's farm. Frank caught his breath sharply as he looked up at the great round of the hills above the little fields, clean and firm against the bright sky where floated low clouds of a fragile snowy lightness.

They crept between the wires of the fence and walked slowly across the alfalfa stubble, past the enclosure where leaning posts and sagging wires showed that the foraging cattle had returned. Frank looked away from these to the cornfield, lined with even rows of low grey stubs against the clean yellow soil.

"What would you plant where the corn was, this year, Rose?" he asked.

"You might try potatoes," she suggested. "Or you might sow oats and get it seeded. How did your father seed his alfalfa, Frank?" She looked critically and appreciatively at the grey crowns of the stubble, in the centre of which small green shoots like closed fingers were showing. "Looks like it's coming through the winter fine."

"I don't know," he confessed. "You see, it was when I was away at school and—I wasn't so much interested in the farm as I am now, I guess."

Rose dug her fingers into the soil at the edge of the cornfield judicially. "It's ready to plough any time," she announced. "It'll work up fine this year. We must be getting home," she added, glancing up as the sun flashed through a cloud, just above the shoulder of the hill. "I'll have to be getting supper." They walked back towards the road, passing the little orchard which Mr. Thompson had started. "I believe you would do well to get some small fruit in here, Frank," she commented, "raspberries or strawberries. You have good soil for them, and you could get pickers in the village, I

should think. I've often looked at the market reports
and wished we could raise some, but we are too far
back from the railroad—and we couldn't get help in
berry season. Raspberries are always a good price."

"I believe that's a good idea," Frank agreed, absently.
He was surrendering himself to his pleasure in the sight
of the sturdy young trees, the olive-green of the apple
twigs and the rich red of the cherries; to the vision of
loaded boughs, of acres of alfalfa and tasselled corn; to
the lift of the hill and the exultant spaces of the sky.

"Did you enjoy it away at school, Frank?" Rose
asked him, as they regained the road.

He looked at her quickly, wondering how much of his
thought she guessed. "Why, yes, pretty well," he answered.

"I've often thought I'd like to visit those places—Ann
Arbor and Detroit—maybe go to school, or work down
there. But I guess probably I'd want to come back up
here. I don't know, but I like it here."

"I guess you would, Rose. I don't think you'd like
the cities—not for long. You know," he went on after
a little silence, "I used to feel sorry for my father, away
off up here, when I first went away to school. I feel
sorry for him still, but in a different way—just that he
didn't fully succeed in what he tried to do, not that he
didn't undertake other things."

"Does anyone succeed fully in what he wants to do?"
Rose asked thoughtfully.

"Well, I don't know that he does. My father did
something, anyway. He made something useful and
beautiful from what was waste and desolate, out there."
His glance rested on the clean little fields and the smooth
round of hill. "And he built himself into the life of the
village—I'd like to be loved as Dr. Pratt and Mr. Steele

loved him. He wasn't a successful man, maybe—but he wasn't a failure."

"What is it that makes one successful, do you think, Frank? Is it being happy?"

"No, not that. Father wasn't happy. Neither was Lincoln, or Poe, or Hamilton. It's achievement, I suppose—doing what one is capable of doing—using one's powers."

"But wasn't he happy in his work? Weren't all those men? Didn't they have some compensation?"

"Why, yes, I suppose they did." Frank thought suddenly of his last conversation with his father at the farm, there at the edge of the cornfield in the August twilight. His eyes misted and grew luminous. "Father told me he was repaid," he told Rose, "the last time we worked there at the farm together—in the evening, standing at the edge of the corn."

She met his eyes understandingly. "I am glad he told you," she said. "But I would have felt sure he felt that way, even if he hadn't said so. He loved the land so much. And I guess there's something in it besides the crops."

"Do you know," Frank ventured, "I believe all living's that way. It takes whatever we will give and then destroys us. But if we have given our best freely, I suspect we are glad that we have lived." Frank paused, suddenly aware that he was becoming grandiloquent, and wondering at the fact that he was talking as he had never talked to anyone except Steen. He chuckled. "Do you know, Rose," he added, "you remind me of Steen!"

Her quick sense of fun made her laugh outright. "What—that lantern-jawed Dutchman in the picture on your dresser? Why, Frank, do I look like him?"

She turned a merry, mischievous face toward him, giggling, and he laughed with her. The contrast between her fair plumpness and the leanness of the saturnine Hollander was sufficiently comic.

"You don't appreciate the compliment I am paying you," he reproached her with mock sadness. "Steen is the one real friend I have ever had in the world. And I have just realized that I have been talking to you as I have never talked with anyone but him."

"I do appreciate that, Frank," she told him. "And—I guess I have never talked with anyone as I have with you."

They walked slowly through the breadth of evening, while the sun filled with golden light all the world of space above the hills that edged the little town.

As they reached the outskirts of the village, they passed a ruinous shanty where a dim light shone from a murky window. Two men were standing on the low, broken porch in the semi-darkness. They were silent as Frank and Rose passed; then one of them burst into cackling laughter. Looking back, Frank could see that the men were shambling toward town behind them.

"Those are the Butler boys," he told Rose in a low tone. "They're degenerates," he added tersely.

"Boys? They look like old men to me. I don't like them." She shivered. "They remind me of rats—a big one and a little one."

Frank smiled grimly at the accuracy of her characterization. They *were* like rats—both small, stooping men, though Bert was thick and muscular, while Benny was slighter and had something repulsively womanish about his appearance. His dark, dirty face had sometimes interested Frank. It seemed hunted and furtive, and in the eyes burned always a look acutely tragic.

"There are all kinds of people in Green Bush, aren't there?" Rose commented.

"Oh—there is everything in human nature here—everything from the Butler boys to Mrs. Steele. It's a world in little. That's the fascination of it to me—everything is so close and clear—one can see it all. Talk about a *Comédie Humaine!*"

"What's that?" Rose queried. And he tried to tell her something about Balzac.

"Maybe I'll try to write something like that some time," he added, in an impulse of confidence. "I guess everyone dreams of writing—every newspaper man, anyway. There's a fellow who has done it in poetry—Masters is his name—for a town out in Illinois. 'The Spoon River Anthology.' I'll show it to you if you like."

"I would, very much."

Later that evening, when Frank stepped into the pool hall to buy a package of cigarettes and chat for a few minutes with the proprietor, he noticed Bert Butler playing pool in the back of the room with some of his cronies—Tub Saunders, now the sheriff, and two or three others. As Frank was about to leave, Bert spoke to the group, in a confidential tone but loudly enough for Frank to hear: "Wonder if young Thompson's been walkin' out in the country any more with 'at girl 'at stays at his place."

Frank hesitated a moment. Physical violence was repulsive to him, and he would have liked to walk away, pretending not to notice. But there seemed only one thing to do.

He strode straight back and, thrusting himself close to Bert Butler's evil face, spoke sharply, holding his voice steady by an effort. "I heard what you said about me, and it's a dirty lie. If you ever mention that girl again I'll beat you within an inch of your life." He thrust a sudden fist to Bert's jaw and knocked him sprawling on the pool table, sending the balls clattering to the floor.

Frightened, Bert crouched away from him. "I didn' mean nothin'," he whined. "Keep him off'n me," he appealed to the sheriff.

The men stood perfectly silent, waiting. Frank paused for a minute without speaking, and lit a cigarette—conscious of the dramatic effectiveness of the gesture, and regretful that his fingers trembled and the match would not burn well. Finally he turned on his heel and walked away, trying to stroll unconcernedly.

At the office he found himself hot and cold by turns, as he thought of the incident. He decided that he must be careful not to be seen alone with Rose again for some time, for he knew how readily such a rumour would spread in the village. If it came to his mother's ears, no matter how little she believed it, he feared she would send Rose away.

CHAPTER X

THE next morning Frank declined to accompany his mother to Sunday School and church. While she was gone he rummaged through the boxes in which his father's papers had been stored and found farm bulletins on alfalfa-raising and the culture of small fruit.

"Do you know, mother," he greeted her from the easy chair by the bay window as she and Rose came in from the April sunshine, "I believe we ought to set a few rows of red raspberries out at the place this spring."

His mother glanced at him sharply in surprise for a moment, but passed into her room without replying. Rose hung her coat and hat in the hall and hurried into the kitchen to prepare the special Sunday dinner. In a moment Frank's mother returned, and, drawing a chair close beside him, she spoke to him in a low tone, leaning forward and running her slender fingers up and down the jet beads that hung down the ruffled front of her brown silk dress. "Frank Thompson, I am ashamed of you. Here you are, Sunday noon, unshaved and in your old clothes, reading farm bulletins!"

Frank laughed good-naturedly. "Never mind, mother." He patted her shoulder reassuringly. "I'll hustle into clean duds and be a real Christian the rest of the day." He laid the bulletins carefully on the bookcase, sauntered into the kitchen to get warm water for shaving, and bantered with Rose for a minute.

"Say the golden text, Rose," he commanded.

"Feed the hungry," she answered laughing, her face pink with the heat as she turned from the big range to face him. "Are you hungry?"

"Sure am—I've farmed all morning. Gee, that's a pretty dress, Rose," he added admiringly, glancing at the yellow folds of plain voile.

"I'm glad you like it. I just finished it last night and pressed it early this morning while you were still asleep."

"Did you make that yourself?" He turned back in astonishment.

"I surely did. Your mother helped me choose the pattern and the goods."

"You'd better open a shop." He sauntered off down the hall and whistled aimlessly as he shaved and dressed.

After the meal he offered to help Rose with the dishes, but his mother interposed. "I want to talk to you about the farm, Frank—now, while it's on my mind."

"All right, mother, fire away," he assented cheerfully.

Rose looked up, startled, from her work of clearing the table, and his mother led Frank into her room. It had been her habit since her illness to lie down after the noon meal for an hour each day, and after measuring a spoonful of medicine from a bottle on her dresser and swallowing it, with a wry face, she lay down on the bed and motioned Frank to a chair beside her.

"I want you to understand me, Frank," she began firmly. "I don't want you worrying about that farm. You have too much to do at the office as it is."

"But I need the farm work, mother, for relaxation and out-of-doors. I'll enjoy a little of it mixed along."

"That's what your father used to say. But it was always a burden, not a relaxation—and no return for it."

"But father just had got the farm to the point of making a return. I'm confident this next season——"

"He always said that too, but it never worked out. It was more money all the time for that wretched little place—spraying outfit, fertilizer, I don't know what all—and never anything for it." Frank wanted to say that his father had taken something from the land that she had known nothing about, but he was silent. "I'm not going to have you tying yourself to the land, or anything else here, Frank. You're too big a man for Green Bush, and the sooner you realize it, the better."

"But as long as we have the place, mother—we can't let it lie idle. And I'm confident that raspberries——"

"Yes—there you are—you would plant raspberries for someone else to harvest, and sink more money still. Don't you remember that you promised me to go on to school?"

"Well—there's no telling when—I'm in no hurry about that."

"Well, I am." She sat up on the bed and faced Frank, her mobile, sensitive features set and positive. "I might as well tell you, Frank. I've had the farm listed for sale for some time, and I've had several offers. I've held off because they weren't high enough. But now I think I'll sell."

Frank rose and turned to the window. He felt as though he had been struck a sudden, vicious blow.

"I think you might have consulted me before you offered the place for sale, mother," he said quietly. "Of course I know father left everything to you, but I—like the place, and father loved it. I was out there yesterday. I'd rather not sell it right away—not for a while, anyway."

His mother lay down again, and adjusted her pillows.

"There's no use arguing about it, Frank," she answered.
"I've had enough of that place in the last ten years. I
think I'll try to take a nap now. Will you lower the
shade?"

He drew down the shade and left the room sadly.
Passing across the dining-room and through the hall, he
left the house, walking slowly down the maple-arched
street. As he turned at the corner toward Dr. Pratt's
office and the drug store, it came to him sharply that he
did not want to leave Green Bush. He belonged to it—
this cluster of frail houses between the Lake and the
hills. He felt desolate in the thought of the loss of the
farm. He hesitated at Dr. Pratt's office steps—thought
of appealing to him to intercede for the farm on the
plea of his own health—but he knew his mother too well.
The little street was deserted, and he walked quietly in
the cool sunlight down the sidewalk and along the gravelled path that led to the old pier. He crept under the
board marked "DANGER—KEEP OFF" and picked his way
for a hundred yards along the worn causeway of grey
planks, rotting and broken here and there and showing
the green water underneath. Out on the pier itself he
circled the sagging, weathered warehouse and, passing
the sloping gangways where freight had been trundled
up and down to the decks of waiting steamers, he seated
himself on the round top of a mooring-post that projected some two feet above the floor of the pier, only an
arm's length from one of the outermost corners.

The Lake was alive and buoyant under the cool sun.
Small waves thumped incessantly at the piling, and all
about to the horizon was intense and quivering blue.
The space and colour rested him, and Frank sat motionless for a long time, humping his shoulders to the cool
breeze, and wondering what the future held for him.

Finally he turned back toward shore and trudged wearily to the office, but he could not bear to look up at the hills that stretched away to the north.

He had been at his desk but a moment when Rose rapped at the office door and entered. "Oh, you *are* here, are you? Your mother sent me to look for you. The Baileys have come to take us for a ride in their new car, and your mother wants you to come home."

"I don't want to ride with the Baileys, Rose," he answered. "I want to work here at the office."

"But—hadn't you better come, Frank? Your mother will be embarrassed if you don't. She said you would."

"She shouldn't be so sure about what I will do. Oh, well, that's a little enough thing. I wouldn't really work anyway. But sit down a minute, Rose, and then I'll go."

She sat in the chair facing him and looked at him questioningly.

"Mother wants to sell the farm, Rose, and I don't want her to," he said soberly. "She has offered it for sale already—has some offers."

"I guessed that was it," she answered. "She doesn't want you to be a farmer, Frank."

"She doesn't want me to be anything here, I guess. She's set on my going back to school and entering a profession—somewhere else, in some big place."

"Well, isn't she right, Frank? Do you think you could really be happy here—for very long? Wouldn't you get tired of it, and want a bigger chance to do things?"

"I don't know, Rose. It's all a question—what one can do, or when, or where. But I believe it's more *what* one is than where he is that counts. Anyhow, I like the farm—I wanted to see what we could do with the raspberries. And I believe that corn ground would be ready for alfalfa."

Rose smiled queerly, he thought. "Well, you'll have more time for the paper," she suggested. "You have lots of plans for that."

"Yes," he agreed, rising and looking out into the shop consideringly. "There's lots that needs to be done. You're a good pal, Rose," he added, holding the door open for her and turning to lock it. "It's helped to talk to you." He thrust the key into his pocket and turned away, and they walked slowly up the street.

CHAPTER XI

THE sale of the farm, the next week, diverted Frank's natural spring energy of planning and organizing wholly into the management of the paper. He made arrangements for the publication of regular "departments" of news from two neighbouring towns. In this way he hoped to secure advertising, as well as additional subscribers. He broadened the scope of his school department to include news from the rural districts, and wrote to each country teacher in the county, inviting her to send in regular news of her school. For his work in the neighbouring towns and his subscription campaign he bought, with his mother's reluctant consent, an old Ford car without a starter, which he could run over all kinds of roads and in the worst of weather.

The demands of the increasing business were greater than he could meet, with the very little help from Rose which his mother was now able to spare. Accordingly he engaged the regular assistance of Dale Quemby, the son of the local blacksmith, a lanky, silent boy who had been stranded in the eighth grade at school, but who had a natural love for tools and was quick at understanding anything mechanical. Frank set about teaching the boy the case, letting him distribute ads and sale bills, and had him kick the footpower press on small jobs. But the big press drew the youngster irresistibly, and within a month or two he had cleaned and oiled every part of it so zealously that it worked better than Frank had ever made it. Soon Dale was printing the paper regularly every Wednesday night, with the help of another boy, while Frank worked in the office.

The steadily mounting weekly income was a source of vast satisfaction to Frank, and he and Dale studied catalogues of presses and equipment, measured the building and estimated the cost of an addition, and dreamed of the time when they would operate "one of the neatest little plants in north-eastern Michigan," as Dale enthusiastically expressed it.

Frank's mother was very busy these days. She was a leader in local club and lodge activities, and had undertaken the management of a series of church affairs to raise money for redecorating the parsonage. "Your mother does too much," Dr. Pratt told Frank one time, when he stopped at the hospital with word that she had a headache and wanted medicine. "She won't remember what I tell her. I can't manage her any better than I could your father." He caught himself sharply, and turned away.

When he looked back into Frank's face the boy knew that the huskiness in the doctor's voice was for his father, though the concern he expressed was for his mother. "Your mother is not at all well, Frank, not at all. I am doing all I can for her, but there seems to be something I can't get hold of. She ought to go down to Ann Arbor for a thorough examination. I've told her so repeatedly, but she won't listen. And she *will* overwork. I guess you'll have to take her when you go back there, Frank—maybe she'll be willing then." He smiled at the boy.

"I don't know how soon that will be, doctor," he answered. "I'm busy, and I'm sure enjoying the work."

"But you plan to go back to school, don't you?" the

doctor insisted. "Your mother says you do."

"Oh, some time, perhaps. But I want to get the paper where it belongs first. I've got some other plans for it."

"Well, you're doing fine, Frank. We're proud to have you here." The doctor thumped him affectionately on the back and, turning his burly form to his desk, wrote out the prescription for Frank's mother.

Mrs. Thompson often asked Frank about the school work which he had made an attempt to carry on in odd hours at her insistence, and was pleased when he received letters from Steen. Once or twice she referred to his courses for next year, and once she asked him whether he was sure he could be reinstated at the beginning of the second quarter. She also took an increased interest in his work at the office, and followed his weekly financial statements closely. She had gone over the books with him two or three times, scrutinizing the inventory which he had made at the first of the year and insisting on his stating just how much he thought the paper was worth, and how much it was making and would make. He was gratified by his mother's interest, and told her fully of his plans for expansion, to which she listened quietly but offered no comment.

On Tuesday afternoon of the first week in June, Frank sat listlessly in the office chair, staring out the window. Beside the old dwelling across the street, now used as a store, a huge lilac-bush was misted purple with buds, the first flowerets of the clusters just opening; and beside it the even, blunt cone of a buckeye-tree was pearled with its first blossoms. Beyond, a dense mat of grass swept down to the blue of the Lake.

On the desk before him was the wet press proof of one side of the eight-page paper, and back in the shop the big press was rumbling with clock-like regularity as Dale printed the edition : fifty copies more than had ever been printed before, Frank reflected proudly. Part of these were necessitated by the recent increase in circulation, and part were for sample copies to be sent to a list of former residents of Green Bush, now scattered over the country, which he had secured from Dr. Pratt and Mr. Steele. The issue carried the announcement of the high school commencement exercises which would occur that week, as well as other news which he thought calculated to arouse the interest of former townsmen.

The office door opened abruptly, and a short, thick man with keen black eyes and swarthy skin bustled in, carrying a suitcase.

"I'm Finchburg," he announced, setting down the suitcase and looking sharply about the office.

"Queer way for a salesman to act," Frank reflected. Aloud he said pleasantly: "What can I do for you, Mr. Finchburg?"

"You're young Thompson, ain't you? I been inquiring about town. I'm the man been corresponding with you people about buying the paper, an' I've come up to look her over—from Pigeon, you know."

"Oh, yes!" Frank looked down quickly and cleared his throat, his heart thumping. So this was what his mother's interest in the financial statements signified. She was planning to sell the paper out from under him, as he phrased it to himself. Almost uncontrollable fury swept him. He wanted to fly at Finchburg and pound out his beady eyes. With trembling hands he selected a pencil from the tray on his desk and began to sharpen its tapering point.

"Well, you can see what there is here in the office," he managed to mutter.

Finchburg was already trying the keys of the type-writer, pawing at the huge volumes of back files of the paper which Frank's father had bound, and making notes on a mussy pocket pad as he ran his eyes over the shelves of stock—wedding announcements, ready-cut sale-bills, and small cards to be used for announcements by political candidates, or as tickets at chicken dinners.

"Well, the shop's the main part," he grunted. "I'll look at the books later." He elbowed his way through the door, and Frank followed trembling. He found that he could not muster self-control for displaying casually the meagre equipment which the shop contained. He realized as he paused at the door how fully he and the shop had grown together—how he loved the racket of the old press, the smell of ink and benzine, the shabby contours of the cases and tables.

"Dale," he called hoarsely.

The boy slowed the big press to a stop, climbed down from the feeder's bench, and approached curiously.

"This man wants to look over the shop. You show him around—you know what's here as well as I do. I got to step out awhile."

He caught the sharp, inquiring flash of Finchburg's eyes as he turned on his heel, and grasping his cap as he passed through the office, left the building.

Outside the door the voice of the Lake called him, and he turned mechanically across the street and down the gravel path to the old pier. He strode out the cause-way in the sunlight, bracing his shoulders against the brisk wind that was sending long rollers of bright water to crash in swirling, snowy foam along the yellow ribbon of the beach.

He passed the warehouse and seated himself on the mooring-post, looking out dolefully across the width of water. He submerged himself in the colour and sound, and an hour passed while he sat motionless, his mind whirling about the events of the past few days—the plans and eager calculations so suddenly destroyed. His hot anger toward his mother slowly cooled. He realized that subconsciously he had been expecting this, that he had sensed his mother's opposition to his devoting himself to the paper and the town; and he knew that she had proceeded secretly through fear of his opposition, and, too, that she was justified from her own point of view by the belief that she was doing what would be best for him. His deep and genuine love for his mother made his dominant feeling one of pain—the hopeless pain at misunderstandings and crossed purposes which had gripped him so many times while his father was alive, and that now settled with a smothering ache about his heart.

When he again became aware of his surroundings he saw that the wind from the Lake had died down and an unsteady offshore breeze had sprung up in its place, chopping the water into incessant trembling billows that threw changing facets to the light. Above in the sky a swifter air current from the west was bearing great grey clouds—grotesque, sprawling shapes that filled the sky with incredible swiftness even as he watched, cutting off the light and turning the blue of the water around him to an uneasy steely grey. Farther out it was cold, dull blue, and as the clouds reached the horizon the line between sky and water was almost lost, but held a faint narrow band of brightness. To the west a window of pale light widened in the sky above the hills, and long fingers of shadow reached out from the shore and broadened slowly.

Far down to the south a regularly spaced line of fish-traps ran out into the Lake—dim rectangles of grey stubs above the water. About them gulls began to rise and circle, whining and crying with eerie, half-human voices. From beyond the traps came a small, swift motor boat, the steady *put-put-put* of its engine now dulled by the offshore breeze and then coming clear again. Frank watched with irritation as it headed straight for the end of the pier. "Probably some idiot wants to warn me off of here," he complained to himself.

As the boat neared he could read the name "Lucile" on its bow, and saw that the two men in grotesque outing costumes were strangers. Opposite him they stopped the engine and one of them stood up precariously to hail him:

"Whajja call this town?"

"Green Bush!" Frank shouted.

"Bean Bush?" the stranger yelled, whether ironic or hard of hearing Frank could not decide. He nodded, and the man lurched to his seat, apparently satisfied. With a sputter the engine started and the little boat pushed unsteadily on.

Frank turned his back and looked toward the town. The window of pale light was ruddy now, and as he watched, the crimson, misted ball of the huge sun crossed it slowly, passing behind the fretted column of a Lombardy poplar. The sun sank swiftly, the red light seeped and dulled, and the sky was left to grey clouds, august above the hills. Under the waning light the little town lay in utter peace, its clusters of low houses marked by the first lights of evening, its new-leaved trees soft and mysterious with coming dark.

He knew that underneath this beauty crept ignorance and bigotry, petty jealousy, and spite and greed. But

"The little town lay in utter peace."

he felt that somehow the closeness of Lake and sky and wilderness set these things all in their right proportions—made them as little as they are in the lives of men. He saw keenly for a moment how the brevity and impotence of man's hold upon the earth, elsewhere cunningly disguised by the brave devices of palace and skyscraper, of avenue and apartment house, was here made inescapably apparent in the frail tenure of this little group of boarded dwellings between the hills and the shore. And it seemed to him easier to live nobly here, as it were in the ceaseless presence of life and death themselves, than in any place where men were always blinded by the products of their hands. He knew that he loved the Lake and the wilderness, and that he belonged to them.

His moment of insight passed. He walked slowly back along the pier, feeling now only a sick weakness and desolation, an unbearable hunger for sympathy and companionship.

CHAPTER XII

HE did not go home for supper. Indeed, he did not eat at all, but waiting until he was sure Dale had finished his presswork and gone away, he went to the office and locked himself in. He sat at his desk in the darkness, feeling a sickness of betrayal and defeat. The books and papers on the desk were eloquent of his plans and hopes. Here was a proof of a "last-minute" account of progress on a new school building, here a preliminary invitation to "Come to Green Bush to celebrate the Fourth." Homely, insignificant things, he knew, smiling at them wanly; but expressive of his thousand minute relationships to what he had come to call "his town" and "his work." The first violent flare of resentment toward his mother had died down. He knew well enough that she was acting for what she thought to be his good, and for his sake. But his anger had been replaced by a cold pain at the way she had taken to accomplish her purpose, centring in an acute physical dislike for Finchburg.

Presently he arose. He unlocked the door and lit the lamps back in the shop. It was foggy outside, and night had come early. But he remained sitting in the darkness by his desk, looking out blindly at the street of the little town. Soon Rose would be coming to help with the folding and addressing, as she always did on press night—for the last time, he remembered with a suddenly keener sense of misery; her school year was completed, and she would be going back to her home the next day. He found himself waiting for her eagerly. He saw the light disappear in the post office across the street; then the straight form of the old postmaster passed briskly down the walk and disappeared in the mist.

There was a firm step at the door, and Rose entered the office. She hung up her coat in the customary place, then paused beside him, her face dim in the half-light of the room. Her hair, dampened, gleamed with dull tones of gold.

"You didn't want to come home for supper, Frank?" she questioned. There was sympathy in her voice, and with a great wave of reassurance Frank knew that she understood what he was feeling.

"Was—this man—there?" he answered.

"Yes."

"I thought he would be."

"Mr. Henkel was there too," Rose added after a pause. "Your mother kept inquiring for you, but they didn't wait." She was silent a moment. Then she spoke quietly. "Frank—maybe I ought not to ask—but—did you know this man was coming?"

"No." The word was bitter.

When she answered, her voice was even lower than usual, and held its rare, rich note of anger. "I don't think it's right!"

Frank was surprised at her feeling. "Why, Rose——" he began.

"I don't care—it's wrong to encourage you to make the most of the business and then sell it without consulting you. Whether you want to sell or not— Well——" She turned toward the shop.

"Wait a minute, Rose. Did they talk as though the sale were—going through?"

"I thought so. They are coming down here in a little while to go over the books."

"They are! Well, I don't want to be here." Frank jerked to his feet violently, and spread out his books on the desk. "Henkel can find everything. We'll leave the folding and addressing till morning, for once. Come on, Rose, let's get out of here."

He was conscious that he did not quite conceal the break in his voice. Taking her arm, he hurried her from the building. As they neared the corner he heard voices, and, turning abruptly across the street, they walked down the dark path toward the Lake. At the old pier they turned and, looking back, saw the light flare up in the office, and figures cross and recross it. Stumbling, Frank led the way to the hard sand of the beach and hurried off along the shore, momentarily forgetful of his companion.

Rose restrained him. "Look!" she said. Frank paused, and, staring into the greyness over the Lake, he made out dimly the lights of a steamer, much closer in than was usual, and seemingly motionless. They stood together, silent, and watched. The lights made an irregular pattern like a dulled constellation, suspended strangely in the indistinguishable greyness of water and air. Gradually Frank became aware of the steady beat of the waves close beside him. "Rose!" he half sobbed. "I guess I'll go to Detroit and try to get a job on the boats. It would be good to be out there—on the blue water—all summer long—away from all this."

She was silent, and her silence refuted him. "You understand, Rose," he pleaded. "I don't really want to get away. I want to be here. But—I can hardly stand it, Rose."

"I'm sorry, Frank." Her voice was a caress, her warm hand lay lightly on his arm, and she looked up into his face. "I know how you feel about it, and—I'm glad you like Green Bush and want to stay here. I should think you'd *want* to get away."

"Do you, Rose?"

"Oh, I don't know. You see, I've never been away, like you have. But I've learned so much this year— had such a good year—I'd just like to go on like we have been."

Frank was silent a little while. The waves were steady, unceasing, at their feet. The ghostly lights of the boat grew dimmer in the endless greyness over the Lake. A cool, sweet fragrance came down from a little orchard of apple-trees at the top of the bank behind them.

Frank felt steadied and strengthened. The girl beside him seemed strangely dear and familiar, and with a sudden keen joy of assurance he knew that he loved her.

"Dear Rose," he said, "I don't know what I would have done to-night if it weren't for you. I would be all alone." She looked at him soberly, her face serious as she met his eyes.

"I am glad, Frank," she said.

"I want you to know that I love you, Rose," he told her quietly. "I don't know what this sale is going to mean or what I'm going to do. But I want you to know that—Rose——"

"Oh, Frank, you shouldn't——" Her hand against his breast trembled as though to push him away, but he saw a great happiness battling with doubt and surprise in her eyes. "You shouldn't say that."

"It is true, Rose—I may have to go away. I don't

know what I'll do—but I'll come back to you, Rose.
Do you think you'll be glad to see me?"

"Oh, Frank," she faltered.

"Dear, dear Rose——" He held her gently in his
arms, and kissed her hair. She pushed him from her,
trembling. "I want to go now, Frank. Please. I—
I'm glad, Frank." She touched his hand, then turned
and ran lightly up the dim beach toward the pier. He
followed slowly, smiling foolishly at the waves that almost touched his feet, and for an hour he strolled
dreamily through the deserted streets of the village.

There was a light in the house when he reached home,
and his mother was reading. She faced him defen-
sively, laying down her book, and he greeted her almost
genially. Seeing his mood, she reproached him.

"Son, I don't think you've been quite friendly toward
Mr. Finchburg. I wish you wouldn't act so."

"Well, mother, I don't think you've been quite fair to
me in bringing Mr. Finchburg here without warning
me. But we won't go into that."

"Why, son, you know, if you will only think, I've always meant to sell the paper. I hadn't expected to get
a buyer so soon—you know it's for your——"

"Yes, yes, mother, it's for my good. We won't discuss that." He sat down beside her and patted her
hand, and her eyes suddenly misted. She looked away.
"Did you make the sale all right? What are you getting?"

"Yes, I guess so. Oh, Frank, I wish you really felt
what you said. I do want to do the best for you——"

"Well, when is he coming on? I might get a job in
Detroit for the summer—or drop in at summer school.
I guess there'll be nothing here."

"Why——" she hesitated. "Mr. Finchburg couldn't

leave where he is right away—he hasn't really sold out there. And you had said you could take up your school work at the beginning of the second quarter where it was left off. So I thought perhaps possession about November first would be all right. That was what he wanted."

"Oh!" Frank's anger came flooding back, hot and choking. "So I'm to stay here and work for five months more, am I, building up the paper—for *him!* You sell it out from under me and expect me to go right on running it until that dirty little shrimp is ready to come and take it over! Not on your life. If I'm through, I'm through, I tell you. I resign to-night. The issue is printed—he can mail it out. I won't lift my hand——"

"Frank, don't you forget who you're speaking to? Why, Frank, you talk as though I had no *right* to sell the paper."

"You have right enough, I guess," he answered miserably. "But you can't ask me to go on working for him—you can't, and I won't do it either."

"You're perfectly unreasonable. I can't understand what's got into you. Go on to bed without another word, and possibly you'll feel differently in the morning." She stood tall and unyielding, yet pitiful, beside the lamp. Frank had a moment's impulse of sympathy, but his sense of outrage overwhelmed it. He turned abruptly on his heel and left the room.

In the morning he greeted his mother as usual, but did not speak further until, when Rose had gone up to pack her things and they were alone together, she asked him:

"Have you reconsidered what you said to me last night, Frank?"

"Yes, I have," he answered firmly.

"I am glad you have."

He laughed harshly. "I lay awake most of the night thinking about it," he told her. "I went over the whole matter in my mind. I can see your reasons for taking the business into your own hands the way you have—the plans you are working for. But I may have plans of my own some day and they're not necessarily going to be the same as yours. I think we might as well give up trying to work together. I've decided this, mother. I'll run the paper until November first, if you wish. But I'll do so for my own profit. I'll pay the running expenses, and turn things over just as they stand to-day. All I take in above that will be mine. I'll live at the hotel—or pay board if you prefer to have me here. But I'll not give another day of my time to the plant under any other arrangement."

His mother was silent. "Frank," she said at last, "you are grieving me. Your attitude is so unreasonable. Can't you trust me to decide anything for you?"

"You have decided enough for me already," he answered bitterly. "First the farm, and now the paper. Oh, well," he added, less harshly, "there's no use arguing about it all. Will you accept my offer, or shall I go ahead packing to leave for Detroit?"

She rose proudly, her mouth set in hard lines. "We will go down and have Mr. Henkel make out a contract," she said. She went to her room to dress.

A little later, Rose came hurriedly down the stairs to get something of hers from the kitchen. As she returned, Frank followed her into the hall. "Rose!" he called softly.

She paused at the foot of the stairs.

"Must you go this afternoon?" he pleaded.

"Uncle Marion is coming in for me. I'm sorry, Frank." She looked earnestly into his face, her eyes filled with sympathy and understanding.

"I'll come to see you as soon as I can," he told her, "next week, I hope." He tried to take her in his arms, but she gently held him away.

"Not here," she whispered. "Good-bye!" She went slowly up the stairs.

He looked after her sorrowfully, then returned to the living-room and sat staring out the window until his mother came from her room, dressed with her usual exquisite care in her black dress. Frank's heart was sick at the pain in her eyes, but he could not forget his own pain. They walked silently down the street together, under the bright new leaves.

CHAPTER XIII

THE strain of the day that followed was almost intolerable. From the bank Frank went to the office of the *Gazette* and mailed out the number, working savagely in silence, with the amazed and curious Dale repulsed and sullen. He took lunch down town and spent the afternoon alone at the shop, distributing type and clearing up generally. When evening came his anger had dulled, and he was very tired. He walked slowly home through the quiet streets. The house seemed deserted; Rose had gone and there were no signs of preparation for supper. He found his mother in her room with a hot water bottle at her head.

"I don't want anything—not anything but to be let alone," she told him. How often, he remembered with a sudden clutching of pain, she had used those words to his father. He touched her shoulder awkwardly, contritely. She thrust a trembling hand from beneath the coverlet and clasped his; her face, reddened by crying and the heat of the hot water bottle, turned toward him, and she looked up searchingly into his eyes. He returned her gaze miserably.

"Go away now, Frank," she said; "I'll be all right in the morning."

He prepared a cold lunch for himself, ate without pleasure, and went to his room. It was chilly and his feet were cold. He drew a note-book from the drawer of his table, and began to write a letter to Rose—haltingly at first, then more rapidly. He told her of the misery of the day, of his sense of loneliness (hinting and skirting the gulf that now he felt between himself and his mother). Eloquent phrases came to him as he wrote of Rose's meaning to him, of his love for her.

When he had finished, and read the pages over, he smiled wryly and, folding the letter, carelessly thrust it back into the table drawer. But he sat for a long time quietly in the chilly room, staring into the darkness outside the window. The noise of the Lake was outside, and the patter of wind in new-leaved trees. As he listened pain drew and furrowed his face into lines of age. Then he smiled, and his eyes were warm.

The next morning his mother in her dressing-gown came slowly into the kitchen as he was preparing breakfast. Her face was grey and haggard, and she clutched the edge of the table with a pale hand. "I guess you'll have to call Dr. Pratt, Frank," she told him sadly. "I feel pretty well used up this morning."

"Oh, I'm sorry, mother!" He helped her back to her room, made her comfortable with straightened quilts and two pillows, and telephoned for the doctor. He prepared toast and coffee, but his mother would not eat, though she sipped a little of the coffee.

Dr. Pratt came, bringing the crisp morning air into the quiet house with him. He frowned at Mrs. Thompson. "Up to your old tricks, are you?" he demanded. He talked with her jovially for a while, until she had gained a little animation. Then he left medicines, and told her to stay in bed for a week.

"I'll get Lizzie Barling to come around and help out with things," the doctor told Frank at the door. "You can keep your mother pretty quiet, can't you—stay here a good deal? She isn't well, Frank. I can't seem to get at the cause of these spells, and it worries me.

When she's all over this, I guess we'd better send her down to Ann Arbor for a thorough examination."

"I'll keep her as quiet as I can," Frank mumbled. He felt that he knew the immediate cause of the present illness; and, in spite of his persistent feeling that his mother had been unfair to him, he had a sense of guilt.

He had intended to announce casually, that morning at breakfast, that he would make the usual business trip to the inland towns that week—his real motive being his desire to see Rose. But his mother's illness, and her subsequent weakness, compelled him to postpone the trip for two and then for three weeks. His disappointment was keener than he had anticipated, and he found it hard to work at the office. He spent much time at home in reading—a set of Hardy which he had bought the fall before in Detroit, and some new plays by Galsworthy which Steen had sent him; the reading kept him from thinking about Rose, and he justified it by the need of his remaining at home with his mother, though she required little attention. In the evenings he did more reading, and wrote letters to Rose.

He did not tell his mother of his intention to visit Rose. He told himself that he was not sure he could really spare the time to go. Actually, he knew intuitively that his mother would disapprove, and he feared her opposition. He promised himself that he would tell her about the whole matter after his return.

He left Green Bush at last on a Thursday morning at the end of June, in a brilliant windy sunlight which made him stop the old Ford at the top of the hill behind Green Bush to look back with delight at the blue of the Lake. He had cleaned and polished the old car a little, rather shamefacedly, and had dressed himself with more care than was usual on such trips.

He found Rose and her mother and Neal all hoeing potatoes in the big patch near the house. The girl welcomed him with frank pleasure; and as he stood beside her on the brown soil, there between the rows of thrifty plants, and she turned her strong sweet face toward him, smiling gravely as she spoke, he had a swift, overwhelming certainty of his love for her. He was content to follow her silently, as she worked.

Mrs. McCune greeted him warmly, and immediately invited him to stay for dinner. When she went to the house a little later to begin the preparation of the meal, he took her hoe and worked beside Rose. He had often done such work at home, but he was not so adept as Rose. "Uncle Marion taught me," she explained. "He's wonderfully handy with all kinds of tools." The boy stayed well away from them; but Frank was aware of occasional swift, appraising glances.

At noon Uncle Marion was as whole-heartedly hospitable and loquacious as Frank remembered him; but McCune seemed dour and offish. This was only natural, Frank reasoned, and tried his best to be genial.

He had planned half-heartedly to go on to Wilberville in the afternoon; but before he forced himself to an announcement of his intention, Rose and Uncle Marion had struck on a plan to make an expedition for wild strawberries, with Frank and Neal as their helpers. Neal was wildly enthusiastic, and ran to get the pails; and Frank did not protest.

The boy led the way and he followed closely—across a small field of young corn, just ankle-high and freshly cultivated; around a patch of barley, rich stone-green in the brilliant sunlight; and so to a tract of unfenced hardwood land, which had been burned over two or three years before.

"You oughta seen the fire run in here when it burned," Neal boasted. He had become friendly now, and had talked constantly as the two walked side by side, followed by Rose and Uncle Marion. "It was roaring hot in here. It would 'a' taken the whole hardwoods, but the wind died down at sundown, an' the men worked all night over in there, and stopped it." About him Frank could see the blackened stubs and fallen logs, the wood weathered now, and spongy on its surface. Grass and small brush had sprung up around the stumps and logs, and with these were the wild-strawberry plants—rich, luxuriant clusters of vivid leaves, sheltering the abundant delicate sprays of little coral and flame-coloured berries, of ineffable aroma and flavour.

The hours of brilliant sunlight passed swiftly, out here on the hill-top where the sweet, strong wind filled one's face and throat. Frank paused now and then to look off across the country—to the irregular, ragged mass of hardwoods to the north, the sweep of hills and valleys back toward Green Bush, and the long stretch of unpeopled country to the west that rose at last to a chain of purple hills.

They gathered the berries in clusters, laying these carefully in the shining milk-pails which they had brought for picking. But Frank's pail was not half full when Uncle Marion called: "You'd better run across toward the lakes and look for the cows now, Neal. Rose, you and Mr. Thompson may's well go on in now, so you can help your ma a bit with supper. I'll pick awhile yet." Frank noted that the old man had al-

"The long stretch of unpeopled country to the west."

ready filled a large pail, and Rose had done nearly as well. He surrendered his pail to Uncle Marion in exchange for the full one, and walked slowly with Rose back toward the little grey house, with the sulphur-yellow mass of a rose-bush in full bloom beside it and the little orchard of low-headed apple-trees bright in their fresh leaves beyond.

"I mustn't stay for supper," he told Rose.

"Oh, please do!" She looked at him wistfully, and Frank agreed. He decided to ask her to go riding with him in the Ford after supper. And when she presented herself at the table in her best dress—the one she had made herself and he had admired—he divined that she anticipated such an invitation. McCune looked glumly at her, but made no comment.

The sun was still above the horizon when they drove away, taking the road into the plains that led toward Wilberville. They drove slowly along the narrow, winding trail. The air was cool and still. Jackpines threw long wedges of shadow across the park-like open spaces of the plains. Scrub oaks were chilled rose and tawny opal in their young leaves. Suddenly the sun was gone, and almost at once stars appeared in the vast, diffused brilliance above their heads.

Frank turned the car into a side road, off the beaten trail, and stopped only when the track ended at the brink of a steep descent to the cedar-filled level of a stream. The voice of the water came up to them softly in the hush. In the great basin over the stream, night-hawks circled swiftly, with their peculiar sharp cry—"*Speek! Speek!*"—and dived again and again dizzily, to right themselves with a curious thrumming boom.

Slowly darkness filled the basin. Frank drew the girl toward him gently, and their lips met again and

again. "Are you sure you love me, Frank?" she asked
him once.

"I am sure, dear," he answered, "more sure than of
anything else in the world."

At last they drove slowly back in the cold white
light of the late moon. The car ground and chugged
through the sand, ploughing a way through the silver
silence that closed again behind it.

The house was dark and silent in the moonlight, a
block of grey shadow. The chilled perfume of garden
roses hung in the motionless air about it. Rose kissed
him quickly once again, and the door closed softly behind her.

Frank's eyes were dim as he stumbled back to the
car. He followed the road to Wilberville like one in
a dream, a roaring stillness about him. In the little
town he found the hotel-store locked, and no one answered his repeated rappings and cautious calls. Finally he curled himself up on the back seat of the Ford,
drew an old blanket about his knees, and dozed uncom-
fortably the two or three hours until morning.

CHAPTER XIV

WHEN he returned to Green Bush, Frank did not tell his mother of his visit to Rose, as he had intended to do. In some subtle way the incidents at the McCune home had deepened his awareness of the breach between his mother and himself and he shrank from confiding to her his interest in Rose, lest it lead to another open break. He was not resigned to the sale of the paper, or convinced that his mother's way of effecting it had been either wise or just; nor could he be, in spite of his efforts to justify her action to himself.

He formed the habit of spending each Thursday—at least the afternoon and evening—at Rose's home. Except for these visits, and the thoughts of Rose and letters to and from her which connected them, his summer was unhappy.

In his mother's house he preserved an air of casual cheerfulness. Indeed, he tried to bring himself close to his mother, to gain a real sympathy with her point of view. But when he would leave the house and walk down the street of Green Bush to the office, the pain of leaving would come back; and he found that he could not forget the way in which what he had called his work had been taken from him.

He never tried to explain his attitude to his mother. He felt that it was hopeless—the more when he realized how incapable he himself was of meeting her half-way in her infrequent attempts at reconciliation.

117

Outwardly their relation was as before. In the house
they ate their meals in silence except for casual comments on matters of no importance. Frank took many
of his luncheons and dinners at the hotel, partly to save
them both the strain of these hours together, and partly
to relieve his mother of work. Her health continued
very uncertain and unsatisfactory all summer, and she
was willing to accept such help with the cleaning and
washing as Frank could secure in the village. He knew
that worry and unhappiness over their relation aggra-
vated her trouble, but he could not overcome these. He
accompanied her each week to church and Sunday
school, sitting through the sermon of the detested Strout
in smiling disgust. They would take Sunday dinner at
the hotel, and call on the Steeles in the afternoon.

Only to Mr. Steele and the doctor had he expressed
his real feeling in regard to the sale of the paper. He
was disappointed at first that the druggist did not offer
a word of encouragement or sympathy. Later he realized that Mr. Steele's fine courtesy, and lifelong friendly
respect for his mother, forbade any comment which could
be construed as criticism of her. The doctor was less
restrained. "Well, Frank," he decided, after Frank
had told him the whole story, "I see how you feel. And
it looks to me as if, even if your mother were right, she
shouldn't have—oh, well," he broke off suddenly. "I
have no right to judge. I'd like powerful well to have
you here, boy, powerful well. You know that. It's
too bad you've got to go when you don't want to. That's
all I can say."

To all others in the village Frank maintained a pose
of complete satisfaction with the sale of the paper and
with his mother's plans. And this, in the face of the

friendly inquiries of some of those he liked and trusted, was very, very hard.

In roundabout ways, by hint and questioning from Dr. Pratt and others with whom she had discussed the matter, he was reminded of his mother's hope that he would suggest that she sell or close the house, and go with him to Ann Arbor. About this matter he debated with himself long and earnestly. He felt only the mildest interest in returning to school at all, but there was a certain glow of anticipation when he thought of the fine freedom and comradeship of his life with Steen. On the other hand, he could see no reason for maintaining an intimate relation with his mother which both found painful. Time might close the breach between them, he considered. He might come to see the wisdom of her course—he admitted that; or he might cease to feel in her sale of the farm and the paper emblems of her defiance of his own and his father's ideals. He fancied in himself a sort of fierce, unforgiving loyalty to his father in his attitude.

Against all this perplexing and irritating network of false relations and uncertain plans he took refuge in the work of the paper. Here was something concrete, pliable, which he could and did modify to suit his will. He threw himself even more vigorously than before the sale into the task of getting out a better and more profitable paper. He did this partly for purely selfish reasons, of course. The mounting weekly balance was his, now, and it ran into a satisfying total to his credit even more rapidly than he had dared to hope. But he took equal satisfaction in the favourable comments which the paper occasionally elicited from various sources, and in the sense of demonstrating that he could continue to do well what he had set out to do.

He realized that he was skimming the territory closely in anticipation of the coming of Finchburg, but he had no compunction on that score. Indeed he took a certain fierce delight in wringing from reluctant customers the last bit of prospective job work, and stocked the banks, stores, and offices of the whole county with printed supplies of all kinds for a year to come. If this was not quite fair to Finchburg, he reflected that that gentleman had himself suggested the date of possession, and was doubtless doing the same thing in his own territory— if he was energetic enough. And, anyway, he disliked the man.

As punctuation to his weeks of planning and effort in the little office, or in the home where he seemed incredibly alien and alone, came the brief intervals of his visits with Rose. These hours in the fields or the woods, with the excellent meals in the little grey house and the pleasant, natural conversation with the people there, were inexpressibly recreative and enjoyable. He was tacitly accepted by all the members of Rose's family, even by McCune himself, who became, though still gruff, not unfriendly. The only hint of unpleasantness came when once at the table Frank remarked casually: "I hear there's some talk of liquor trouble out in this part of the county." McCune glowered and grew silent as a clam. Uncle Marion began to talk briskly about the crops. When they were alone together after the meal, Rose asked him hesitantly not to talk about the liquor troubles any more. "I'm afraid papa knows the men who are in it," she explained. She seemed so troubled that he did not question her. On his third visit Mrs. McCune suggested that he stay all night with them, and go on in the morning. He was given a tiny room just off the big living-room, which, he gathered, belonged to Uncle Marion. The clean little bed and washstand were of walnut, and the floor and walls were painted in blue, grey, and yellow. Through the small square windows blew the scent of the old-fashioned roses that grew against the house, and the rich fragrance of sweet corn in the garden a few feet away.

In the evening he walked with Rose a little way in the warm dust of the road. The sky was thick with stars, and she asked him the names of the planets and the constellations which she saw. She was cool and sweet in her plain blue gingham dress, her tawny hair brushed back from the smooth, firm contours of her face, and she seemed to belong beside him, there in the utter peace of the moonless summer night, with the dim land stretching away for miles on every hand in wooded folds of shadow. He felt a swift release from all the tautened worries and strains and subterfuges of the week, in her presence and in that of the unsleeping earth.

CHAPTER XV

ON a Sunday in late July, Frank sat with his mother at the table in the low-ceiled dining-room of the Green Bush hotel. "I want you to plan to omit your regular trip to Wilberville this week, Frank," she said suddenly, as the girl who had served them withdrew.

He looked up surprised, apprehensive.

"We have planned a surprise picnic for the Strouts," she went on. "He is to have a vacation in August, and Mrs. Strout told me confidentially that he is going to preach at a college town in the southern part of the state; he hopes to get the conference to move him there, so that June can live at home while she goes on to school. So we want to have this picnic now, while the weather is nice."

"Well, I don't know," Frank temporized. "I have some pretty important deals——"

"I guess they can wait," his mother answered, with the old, dominant ring in her voice. "You have been working too hard at the paper anyway. And I want you to be here. You haven't been near the Strouts all summer; and you don't even *look* at June. It's very small and silly of you to act that way toward the nicest girl in town, I think."

Frank did not reply. He wondered uneasily if his mother had heard of his visits at the McCune home. It was altogether probable that she had; and he felt that she would not only be hurt by the feeling that he had deceived her, but would be strongly prejudiced against Rose. He decided to capitulate. "All right, mother," he agreed. "I'll stay at home this week—till Friday, anyway. And we can use the car for the picnic. How are you planning to arrange it?"

"We will invite the Strouts to go out to the Point with us for a picnic. When we get there all the rest will come, and we will have a basket supper on the beach."

"That ought to work out well." Actually Frank already regretted his decision. With a sharp inward pang, he contrasted the prospective several hours in intimate association with the Strouts with the evening he might have had with Rose. But there was no backing out now.

That evening he wrote to Rose a lengthy letter explaining why he could not come on Thursday as usual; he did not know, he told her, whether he could come on Friday or not. He sent the letter out with the rural carrier next morning.

The day of the picnic was bright and warm. Frank went stolidly through the ordeal of cleaning the car and helping to pack the elaborate basket supper. Then his mother got into the back seat of the Ford with the baskets, and they drove to the Strout home. When the preacher and his wife had taken their places in the tonneau, with Mrs. Thompson and the baskets, there was no room to spare. The preacher held a large pan, covered with a linen cloth that flashed in the sunlight, on his lap. June sat with Frank, a smaller basket on her knees. She seemed strangely subdued, Frank thought. She greeted him and his mother in simple, friendly fashion, and had little more to say. He noted with approval her plain white dress, and watched from the corner of his eye, as he drove, her piquant, colourful face. The winding shore road to the Point was pitted and rough, and with a boyish, vindictive thought of the preacher, bouncing with his pan, Frank drove very fast. He passed the farm that had been his father's in a cloud of dust.

At the beach some of the picnickers had already arrived, and Frank was glad that there was work to do in building a table, carrying water, and collecting wood for a fire. The Strouts were elaborately surprised, as more and more of the congregation appeared. Finally the increasing noise of conversation and the confusion around the tables came to a climax as people found their places. The half-dozen younger people were seated together, apart from the vociferous children, and Frank did not try to avoid a place beside June. There was a moment of hush while Reverend Strout invoked the divine blessing with exceptional brevity. Then everyone fell to.

June ate little, and in a few minutes she was up helping some of the older women pass cups of milk to the children, and tea to the adults. She worked quietly and capably. Frank watched her, trying to analyse the change he began to sense in the girl: the slight ripening and strengthening of her slender figure, and the quiet neatness of her abundant black hair.

As soon as the meal was over, the two couples with whom Frank and June had been eating sauntered off down the beach in the pale mingled light of moonrise and sunset. June looked at Frank shyly.

"Want to take a walk?" he suggested.

She nodded, and they started off.

As he felt beneath his feet the hard sand of the beach, Frank thought, with a sudden quick sense of shame, of Rose. He was silent as they walked slowly over the patterned sand, stepping occasionally over little gullies cut by the water, or sticks of driftwood. June stumbled, and he took her arm.

"My shoes are full of sand," she said suddenly. "Let's sit down here." She pointed to a huge log, laid up by a storm a rod from the water's edge. Frank's mouth twisted in a wry smile. But he followed her. The girl sat on the edge of the log and pulled off her low slippers, brushing the sand from her slender, silk-clad feet. Then she crouched on the sand and laid back her head against the log. "How lovely the moon is!" she said. A bright opal glow arched over the yellow disk, just above the water. Little waves flashed blackly. The dim light rested on her long, slender throat, filled her face, glinted on her hair. After a moment's hesitation, Frank sat beside her on the sand.

They were silent. The waves lapped softly. A whippoorwill called far back in the brush behind them. June laid a warm hand on his arm, and turned toward him slowly a face rich in the pale light, and tremulous. She was lovelier than he had ever dreamed. He thrust an arm around her and drew her to him. Slowly her body turned to his; his arms trembled.

Suddenly she struck him weakly in the face, and twisted away. "Oh, you don't love me! You don't really want me!" she sobbed. "It's Rose McCune you want—that country girl. You've been seeing her every week—you can fool your mother, but I know. And now—oh!" She stumbled to her feet, ran a little way, dropped to her knees in the moonlight, and sank forward prone on the sand, hiding her face. Frank followed and knelt by her, touching her shoulder clumsily. "There, there, June," he tried to soothe her.

She shook off his hand. "I hate you! Go away!"

he heard her choke. She rose suddenly to her knees again. "Oh, what am I?" she pleaded. "I don't want to act this way—I want to be decent, and have you respect me and like me—I've tried so hard—and how you must despise me——" She rose uncertainly to her feet. Her face was very close to his, wet with tears.

"I do respect you, June," he urged. He grasped her arms and supported her.

She leaned against him, within his arms, and looked up into his face. He was amazed and shaken by her beauty, and by the strength of the desire which filled him. His hand caressed her shoulders, and he held her close.

Gently she turned away from him, her face averted, and he did not restrain her. "I guess we'd better go back now," she challenged him softly.

The beach was strange and chill about him. The moon rode whitely above the gleaming metal of the water. He drew a deep breath. "Perhaps we'd better," he said.

They walked silently, apart. As they rounded a bend in the Point, they could see the dark figures by the circle of firelight, a hundred yards away. Frank paused, and would have drawn the girl to him and kissed her lips. But she hid her face and pulled away.

Back in his room at last, Frank felt shaken, sick and muddied. He hated himself, hated and pitied June. The thought of Rose was an inescapable torture of shame and desire. Finally, mastering all his other emotions, came a deep, unreasoned resentment toward his mother, which persisted—a defence against his shame. He scarcely spoke to her for two or three days.

Before the next Thursday came, he grew intolerably

eager to see Rose. He could hardly endure the routine of getting out the paper. At last he drove swiftly from the town, over roads treacherous and sloppy from a recent rain. She came out to meet him as he stopped at the gate, and his pain and shame were all swept away and forgotten in the joy of seeing her.

That evening, as they sat together in the Ford on a side road in the plains, a mile or two from the McCune home, Rose told him that she had received a letter from his mother, asking her to stay and work at the Thompson home as she had done before.

"Frank," she asked, "didn't your mother want to go to Ann Arbor with you?"

"Yes," he answered, meeting her eyes. "I guess she did. But I couldn't see it that way. I can't bring myself really to forgive her—about the paper and the farm—and I know she resents my attitude just as much. And I don't believe in maintaining relationships like that when your heart isn't in them."

"I know how you feel, Frank. Of course, it's fine for me—gives me a chance to go on to school. But I'm sorry it has to be that way between you. She's your mother, Frank."

"Yes," he agreed miserably. "But—I can't help it, that's all. We don't see things alike. There would be only unhappiness for us both in going away together."

"Have you told her anything about—us?" she asked softly.

"No, not yet. I—I should have, I expect."

"She'll have to know some time, Frank."

"Yes. I thought maybe—if she got to know you better this winter, maybe—oh, I don't know, Rose—it seems as though everything's wrong between my mother and me. I don't know *what* to do. I've managed things poorly. And—I'm not worthy of you, Rose—I want to tell you——"

She hushed him with a finger on his lips, kissed his trembling face, drew his head against her firm shoulder. "Don't talk any more, dear," she soothed him. "Don't worry now. You're tired, and you've been worrying too much. Oh, I'm so glad to have you, dear." He was quiet in her arms.

CHAPTER XVI

IN the days and weeks that followed, Frank found increasingly dear to him his weekly visits with Rose, and the thought of her between these. He could hardly bear to contemplate the prospect of leaving her when he should return to Ann Arbor, and the necessity of his going took on a new bitterness to him.

He drew some comfort from the thought of the two months when they would be in Green Bush together at his mother's home, after Rose would return to school and before his work on the paper would be completed. Then, he promised himself, he would tell his mother of his love for Rose—they would announce their engagement; and, if she opposed it, he told himself fiercely, he would marry Rose at once, and take her to Ann Arbor with him—or to Detroit, where he could get a job.

Finally the day was set for Rose's arrival in Green Bush, on Wednesday of the week preceding the opening of the high school. Frank entered upon his usual duties of the week in a state of very pleasant anticipation. On Tuesday morning he went to the station at the time for the regular north-bound train, to glean if he could a few final "personal items" for the paper which would go to press that evening. He took down in his notebook the names and destinations of two or three villagers who were leaving, and went back to a seat in his Ford to watch the train come in. To his utter astonishment he saw Finchburg alight from the day coach, in a new straw hat and neatly pressed suit, looking about him with his

peculiar bright smile.   Frank started the engine and
drove away before he could be recognized.   His first
thought was a wild one of hope; perhaps Finchburg had
decided to try to get out of his bargain.   But no, he
would do that by letter.   And his spruce appearance
and possessive air as he had looked about the platform
could mean but one thing: he had come on to take possession now—September first—instead of November first
as had been agreed.

Instantly Frank jumped to the conclusion that his
mother had deceived him again, and hot anger filled him.
He drove madly down the street toward the office.   At
first he thought of trying to hold his mother to her contract with him.   She deserved the humiliation, he felt;
and his mind ran swiftly over the jobs he had been promised for the ensuing weeks—particularly, the dozen or
more sale bills and accompanying advertisements for
which he had contracted.

That course seemed the wrong one, however.   He was
not sure that his contract would hold.   Such a course
of action would lower him in the eyes of Mr. Steele and
Mr. Henkel.   And, anyway, he wanted now most of all
to get away.   He felt that he did not want to see his
mother again.   There was a biting thought of Rose, and
the two months with her at his home which he had
anticipated.   Then he was in the office, hastily counting
out the money in the till and withdrawing a few personal possessions from the desk.   He laid the account
books of the paper conspicuously on the desk, and with
them his memoranda of the jobs which were coming in.
Hurriedly he crossed the street to the bank, where he
deposited the money from the till to his personal account, verified his checking balance, and withdrew fifty
dollars in currency and a hundred in the form of a draft.

Then he climbed into the Ford and drove to his home. As he expected, Finchburg was there. His mother rose to greet him, and before he could speak she began: "Frank, Mr. Finchburg is here, and he wants to talk with you——"

"Yes," Finchburg broke in, "I got off a little sooner than I had expected down below, so I come on up and thought maybe I could start right in here now."

"I guess you don't want to talk with *me*," Frank answered wrathfully. "I guess you've settled it all beforehand, just as you did before. Well, I can stand it. Here's the keys, Mr. Finchburg. I resign right now." He laid the keys on the table and stormed up the stairs. In half an hour he was back, carrying a suitcase. He paused at the living-room door. "I'll tell Lindell to call for my trunk," he told his mother. "I'm leaving for Ann Arbor to-night."

"Why, *Frank*," his mother pleaded. "Don't act so! I didn't know Mr. Finchburg was coming. Why can't you be reasonable?"

"Well, you're agreeing to his proposition, aren't you?" he answered roughly. "You're letting him come in and steal the best two months' business of them all, right out of my hands. You've agreed to it, haven't you?" he insisted.

"Why," she urged, "I don't see that there's any other way—he's here ready."

"Well, then, I'm through," Frank cried.

"But vait," Finchburg interposed, "ain't you going to help me git started—tell me nothing about the shop?"

"I'll tell you to go to hell, you dirty little shrimp," Frank shouted, beside himself now. "I won't lift a finger to help you!" He slammed the door, threw the suitcase into the Ford, and tore off down the street.

At the depot he left his suitcase in charge of the agent, and sent a hastily written day letter to Steen at Ann Arbor:

"Am coming on at once Please try to get me job as compositor or makeup man on Daily Can work full time until November first if needed Details when I see you.

"FRANK."

Climbing into the car again, he drove swiftly out into the country and soon was speeding over the winding, sandy road toward the McCune home. He would see Rose again, explain the situation to her, and get back to town in time for the evening train.

He found her working in a hayfield beside the road, and, leaving the car, he crawled through the fence and crossed the meadow toward her. She was working with a pitchfork, piling the richly fragrant alsike clover into neat round shocks from the windrows which Uncle Marion left as he slowly circled the mown field with a small rake drawn by a fat white horse. "Father is away from home," she explained, "so I am doing this. But I like it. The hay is so sweet."

They stood a little way apart in the hot sunshine while he told her what had happened. "Are you sure your mother knew Mr. Finchburg was coming?" she questioned gravely, when he had finished.

"I'm confident she did; it's just like it was before," he answered hotly. But he remembered that his mother had denied this knowledge.

"Well, I'm sorry, Frank. I'm awfully sorry." She turned away, and Frank thought there were tears in her eyes. "It's time for me to go to the house now," she added after a moment. "I must help mamma with din-

ner. Come on and I'll ride with you." He was sure
of the tears now, and would have taken her arm, but
saw that Uncle Marion had turned his horse and was
regarding them curiously.

The family was strangely silent and preoccupied during the meal, he thought. Even Uncle Marion seemed
glum. After the dishes were washed Rose returned to
the hayfield, and taking McCune's long-handled pitchfork and a big straw hat of Rose's mother's, Frank went
with her to help with the shocking. Rose said little,
but it seemed to Frank that there was a new tenderness
in·her attitude toward him. It was an upland meadow,
and they paused now and then to look off across the rolling, wooded hills to the blue ranges in the west. As
they worked a cooling breeze sprang up, bringing to
their nostrils the clean fragrances of this world of woods
and water. Slowly Frank felt his anger seeping from
him, and a great peace and relief taking its place.

By mid-afternoon the field was finished. Near the
centre of the cleared area a single black stump had been
left, and from it a small birch-tree was growing, cast-
ing a feathery shade on the fragrant stubble. "Let's sit
here and talk awhile," Rose suggested. "You don't
have to start back to town for a while yet." She smiled
at him sadly, and Frank felt a tightness in his throat.
They drank in turn from the small brown jug of spring
water which Uncle Marion had brought to the field,
wrapped in a wet sack, and then sat on the ground together, looking across a stretch of the field to the highway and the brush land beyond.

"There's something I want to ask you to do for me,
Frank," Rose began directly when they were seated.
"Won't you please go back and have things right with
your mother before you leave? Weren't you maybe too

hasty this morning? Maybe she *didn't* know he was coming. And you won't feel right to leave things this way. Won't you, please?"

Frank was silent.

"And, maybe, if you feel you can, help this man just a little to get started?" she went on. "I'm not asking you to stay long, Frank. I know you can't—there's nothing for you here. But please have things right at home before you go. Won't you?"

"There's everything for me here, Rose," he answered warmly, turning toward her and taking her hand. "But I'll have to come back for that, I guess."

She blushed as she met his eyes. "But you haven't said," she insisted, "about your mother."

"Yes, Rose," he agreed humbly. "I guess I was in the wrong—to talk the way I did. Maybe she didn't know he was coming. It's his fault, anyway. Yes, I'll apologize to mother—before I go, and I'll help him get out the paper—if he acts half-way decent—I ought to be getting back, I suppose. She won't know where I am."

"You won't leave to-night, then?"

"No, there's no necessity of that. I want to see you again, Rose."

"I'll be coming in to-morrow afternoon, to stay," she reminded him shyly.

"Well, I'll see you to-morrow night, then. I'll stay over a day or two—I'd better be going now." But he stayed on while the sun lowered slowly, and they talked of inconsequential things. A Ford car whirled by; a team trudged through the dust pulling a loaded wagon, from the spring seat of which a girl waved to Rose.

Then from the side road came jogging slowly an old bay horse drawing a buckboard. In it was seated Tub

Saunders, the sheriff, apparently asleep under his broad straw hat. Between his knees was a large bundle wrapped in a horse blanket.

Rose giggled. "The horse is blind," she whispered. "See how he lifts his feet."

As they watched the slow passage of this outfit, a very large red cow suddenly appeared from the brush on the other side of the road and capered heavily into the track a few rods ahead of the buggy, staggering a little and tossing her horned head so that the bell on a chain about her neck jangled furiously.

"What in the world is the matter with her?" Frank asked. "She acts so funny."

"I don't know," Rose answered. "Look at her!" The cow stumbled clumsily, righted herself, and plunged uncertainly down the road toward the approaching buggy, shaking her head and bellowing.

"I believe she's drunk," Rose decided suddenly. "I saw a cow that way once before. She's found a still and been eating mash."

Two more cows appeared from the brush and lumbered into the road. The old horse stopped suddenly, listening apprehensively, and Tub Saunders, awaking with a lurch, brought the lines down sharply on his back. The old fellow sprang forward, and at the same moment the cow, prancing awkwardly toward the buggy, thrust her horns into the front wheel.

There was a crash of splintering spokes, a bellow of pain and rage from the cow, and a yelp of fear from the sheriff, who lost his balance as the buggy jerked ahead, and fell out sprawling across the rear wheel. In a moment the old horse was galloping desperately down the road, dragging a three-wheeled ruin of the buckboard, which disintegrated swiftly as he went. The bundle bounded out and revealed itself as an obese, black jug which broke with a gurgling crash upon a stone. The sheriff, 'rising to his knees, found himself face to face with the lowered head of the large red cow, one horn broken and bleeding. She lunged at him, and Frank and Rose sprang up, grasping their pitchforks, and started to run across the field. But the sheriff had scrambled to his feet and with desperate speed he scuttled across the road and clambered into the branches of a small scrub oak, hotly pursued by the bellowing cow. Her companions pranced unsteadily in the rear, and the three surrounded the tree, pawing and mooing. The sheriff clung frantically like a large porcupine, looking down at them, speechless with terror.

Before Rose and Frank could reach him a Ford appeared suddenly from the way the horse had gone, bristling with fishpoles. Four young fellows from Green Bush, in mackinaws and hip boots, climbed from it. Evidently they were bound for a night's fishing. They drove off the prancing cows with yells and stones, and the sheriff climbed down and scrambled into the car. But the young men were in no hurry to leave. They surrounded the ruins of the jug, sniffing at the fragments and guffawing loudly. They collected mementoes of the buckboard, pressing them on each other and on the sheriff with noisy delight. As the full ludicrousness of the situation became apparent to them they danced about the car, embraced each other, and shouted with laughter. Finally they solemnly collected the fragments of the jug, wrapped them in the blanket, and placed the bundle in the sheriff's arms like a baby; and, still whooping, they climbed into the car and drove away toward Green Bush.

Rose and Frank clung to each other, weak with laughter. They had to rehearse the scene to Rose's mother and Uncle Marion, with eloquent pantomime. It was not until he had bidden Rose good-bye, at almost supper-time, and started on the hurried drive to Green Bush, that Frank reflected on how little pleasure Mrs. McCune and her brother had appeared to take in the incident.

CHAPTER XVII

FRANK stopped the Ford before his mother's house as quietly as he could. It was hard for him to go up the walk and enter the door. But he crossed the living-room directly to where his mother was sitting by the window, looking up at him silently, and said: "Mother, I'm sorry I spoke as I did this morning. I've come back to tell you so, and to offer to help Mr. Finchburg get started, if he still wants me."

"I thought you would think better of it," his mother answered, repressed feeling cold in her voice. Frank flinched. "Why *will* you be so unreasonable? I declare, you are worse than your father ever was."

Frank stiffened. "Suppose we do not discuss it any further," he suggested quietly. "Is Mr. Finchburg at the office?"

"I don't know. He may be at the hotel getting his supper."

"I'll look for him there." There was a real pain of humiliation and disappointment in Frank's heart as he walked away from the house, leaving the car standing there. At the hotel he did not find Finchburg, in the smoky lobby or the low dingy dining-room; but his healthy appetite asserted itself, and he ordered supper and ate the meal of steak with onions, fried potatoes, coffee, and pie, before he went on to the office.

As he ate he listened to the hilarious talk of a group of townsmen. "The sheriff and the cows" was the sole

topic of their conversation, and the story of the afternoon's adventure, variously elaborated and adorned, was
repeated to each new member of the group. From the
comments Frank gathered that Harrison, the county attorney, was "up in arms," and that something would be
done on the morrow.

Leaving the hotel, he sauntered into the drugstore for
a smoke. He was reluctant, he realized, to face Finchburg and offer his services. When they were temporarily alone in the store, Mr. Steele spoke quietly to
Frank.

"Do you know whether McCune is mixed up in this
liquor trouble, Frank?"

"I don't know," Frank answered uneasily. "I hardly
think so."

"I hear his name mentioned repeatedly," the druggist
went on. "It seems to be the general belief that the
still is on his place, or near there. I am sorry on account of his daughter—the girl who has been helping
your mother. She seems such a promising girl. It
would be a shame for her reputation to be spoiled by
anything of this sort."

Frank started. He wondered if the old druggist had
suspected his feeling toward Rose; but his manner was
wholly innocent. In any case, this confirmation of his
own anxieties made him doubly uneasy, and he soon
excused himself and started for the shop. He had not
realized before how definite would be the effect upon
Rose's position in the little town of any accusation
against her father—even in the minds of such tolerant
people as Mr. Steele. He wished he could do something
to intervene. But he could think of nothing.

At the shop he found Finchburg labouring over the
mailing-list, and Dale sulkily working at the big press.

"I want to apologize for my conduct this morning, Mr. Finchburg," he said simply. "I'll help you get out the paper if you want me to."

"Huh? All right," replied Finchburg noncommittally. "I don't get on to this mailing-list very good."

Finchburg proved a slow learner, for all his seeming alertness. It was past midnight before the issue was finally ready for the mails; and Frank had agreed to make the regular weekly trip to the inland towns, for news and advertisements, so that Finchburg could put in his time in the office.

Early the next morning, as he drove up to the Ford garage for oil and gasoline, Frank saw the county attorney's car just pulling away. On the front seat were Harrison and Bennie Butler; on the rear seat Bert and the sheriff.

"They're goin' out still-huntin'," the garageman remarked with a guffaw. "Harrison said somethin's got to be done, so Tubby he swore in the Butler boys for deppities, an' they're goin' out to hunt. Reckon they ought to fin' somethin' all right—them Butler boys kin smell liquor 's far 's anybody."

Frank was worried. He paid for his oil and gasoline and drove as rapidly as he could toward the McCune place. He came within sight of the attorney's car several times, but did not overtake it; and about a mile from McCunes' he saw where the fresh tracks turned into the soft sand of a side road.

He hurried on, and called Rose out to the car from the garden where she was picking green beans. She came forward smiling, pulling a blue sunbonnet from her tawny hair. "Did you fix things up with your mother?" she greeted him.

"Yes, I guess so. But, say, Rose, Harrison's on the

war-path about the liquor business. He and Saunders and two deputies have come out this morning to look for a still. They turned into the side road back there about a mile."

Rose paled and turned away. After a moment she faced him, her eyes very grave. "Thank you, Frank," she said. "I don't know whether you've guessed it or not—but papa is into this business—I don't know how much. He isn't really away from home—he's back there in the swamp. I must warn him, right away." She started toward the house.

"Rose," Frank called sharply. He sprang from the car and followed her. "You *mustn't* go back there now. These deputies are the Butler boys. I won't let you. You tell me where, and I'll go."

"No—papa wouldn't like it—I'm not afraid."

"I'll not let you go," he insisted. "Tell me where, or I'll start out anyway."

"Go around the edge of the cornfield," she answered quickly, "this way. By the second post from the corner on the other side you'll find a path. Follow it as fast as you can. But do be careful! Oh, Frank—you'd better not go."

He had started already, circling the cornfield at a run. He found the path readily and trotted along it through the tall brush. After five minutes it bent sharply down into a ravine, then divided. He paused. Rose had not prepared him for this. One branch led back into the ravine, apparently toward the house. The other, almost parallel to the direction he had been following, was lightly but freshly blazed. He chose the latter, and was off on a jog-trot again through the arching birches and poplars. Presently he slowed his gait, realizing that the path was climbing a considerable ascent.

The climb became steeper, and he began to think that he had chosen the wrong branch. But it occurred to him that possibly this was a direct cutoff over a ridge and down into the swamp.

He continued the climb for perhaps a hundred yards, when suddenly the growth thinned, and pushing his way through clusters of willows and sumach to the foot of a short black snag, he found himself at the crest of a narrow ridge which fell away steeply, bare except for the low sumachs.

He caught his breath at the scene below him. Spread out maplike to his right was an irregular little lake, of perhaps twenty or thirty acres in extent, bordered by grassy marshes and bits of wooded swamp. To the right, at the head of the lake, was a great expanse of swamp-land—hundreds of acres of densely growing spruce and alder and balsam, set thick with the grey masts of dead tamaracks and cedars. No sound came from the swamp, no birds circled above it. It lay dark and silent under the sunlight and blue sky. A road ran along the farther edge of the lake, branching as it entered the swamp. And as he studied it Frank saw that he was too late for any warning to McCune. The attorney's car was half-hidden in a grove of poplars near the lower end of the lake, and the four men were already on the road at the end of the swamp. The path which Frank had followed appeared to end where he stood, and even if he could have descended the slope without being observed by the attorney and his men, he would not know where to enter the swamp to find McCune. It seemed futile to go back to the forks in the path and try again. His own passage through the swamp would be only too likely to guide the searchers to the still, now that they were on the ground.

He watched, fascinated, as they divided, evidently conversing in whispers, for no sound reached his ears. He pressed himself into a fire-eaten cavity at the base of a stump and remained there, confident that he was well hidden. The attorney took a road which ran directly back into the heart of the swamp. Saunders followed one which skirted the border at the far side, while Bert Butler took a similar road which ran along the base of the ridge on which Frank was standing. Bennie Butler was apparently left as a sentry and means of communication at the forks, for he remained there, darting nervously back and forth, first into one trail and then into another.

The attorney and Saunders soon passed beyond Frank's sight, swallowed in the vast and obscure silence of the swamp. Frank fixed his attention on Bert Butler. The man advanced steadily and carefully for perhaps two hundred yards, his thick figure moving slowly along the uncertain green line of the log-road between the thick, dark walls of trees. Then Frank saw him stop, peer intently ahead, and drop to his knees. Pushing aside the bushes and searching the trail, Frank finally made out what Butler had seen. Some fifty feet ahead of him a small stream ran out of a ravine at the foot of the hill; the road crossed this stream by a bridge of cedar. And on the end of the bridge, almost hidden in the weeds, little Neal McCune sat fishing.

He held a small pole firmly above the water, and was so intent on watching his bait that he did not notice Butler's approach.

Frank sprang up, intending to shout, to warn the boy, but he was too late. Butler had advanced with the silent swiftness of a snake. As Frank gained his feet he saw the boy jump up suddenly, and at the same moment Butler sprang for him and grabbed his arm. Frank saw the child back away, in terror and defiance, saw the ugly face crowded toward his, and knew that Butler was trying to frighten him into revealing the location of the still.

Frank saw Butler lift a fist menacingly. Then the child writhed away from him, and screamed suddenly with pain. Frank saw that the man was twisting his arm. "I'll bust yer arm," he heard distinctly.

The child screamed again, "Don't—don't——"

Frank sprang down the slope, but checked himself on the instant. The bushes parted suddenly on the edge of the swamp a few yards from Butler and the boy, and the huge figure of McCune sprang into the track. Instantly he rushed straight for Butler. The deputy dropped the boy's arm, and the child sank inert into the bushes. Butler backed away, snarling and fumbling at his belt. As McCune reached him, there was a single sharp shot, and at the same moment McCune swung a blow to his jaw that sent him sprawling face down in the weeds at the side of the trail.

Frank heard the sound of the blow even where he stood. Without a moment's pause McCune swung the boy over his right shoulder like a sack of flour, ran swiftly back the way he had come, and with a sudden spring gained the swamp and was gone.

Frank crouched in the sumach, watching. The deputy lay perfectly motionless in the weeds, one hand still clutching the revolver which glinted in the sun. There was no sign or sound from all the vast expanse of swamp, except that a crow flew up suddenly from the green depths and circled silently above the place where the man lay. With a swift chill of fear, Frank turned and ran back along the path.

He found Rose waiting at the edge of the cornfield, and quickly told her the story. She grasped his arm and hurried him toward the house. "You must go on, now, Frank," she told him. "You mustn't be found here. No one must know you've been here."

"No, Rose," he urged, "I must stay and see what happens. I wouldn't tell what I saw, Rose—you know that."

"I know—but you mustn't stay. Please, Frank. Don't you see, there is *nothing* anyone can do now but wait. We must go ahead with things just as if there were nothing happening. I'm getting ready to go to Green Bush—Uncle Marion will take me in this afternoon. *Please,* Frank, go right away before anyone comes!" Finally he climbed into the Ford, and drove away, leaving her, white and silent, by the gate.

CHAPTER XVIII

FRANK went through his business at the inland towns mechanically—collecting a few bills, placing advertisements, jotting down bits of news. He drove furiously between stops, and half the time forgot to tell his customers that Finchburg would visit them in his place the next week. His mind was with Rose, busy with thoughts of the possibilities involved in the situation at her home. Suppose McCune were wounded —perhaps seriously. Suppose his blow had killed Bert Butler?

The late darkness had come already when he had finished his work in the most remote of the three towns he visited. And as he neared the hotel where he had planned to spend the night he realized that he had not eaten since morning. He secured a room, washed his face and hands in a china bowl with cold water which the landlord brought in a pitcher, and ate an excellent meal alone in the lamp-lit dining-room, with its bright rag carpet on the floor and house plants in the windows. He paid for his room and meal, bade the landlord goodnight. Then he climbed the stairs to his room and went to bed, but lay awake for a time, worrying about Rose and her father. Finally he slept fitfully for an hour or so. He came broad awake to find the light of the old moon shining brightly in his west window. He had a vivid sense of imminent danger, or of need of him, and without delay he dressed himself, took his shoes in his hand, and went softly down the stairs and out to the

porch. His Ford was standing in the moonlight, one
wheel in the shallow ditch, headed downhill. He released the lever brake, pushed the car into the track, and
coasted silently down the main street of the village, past
the sleeping houses, the stores all bare in the moonlight,
and the grey steeple of the Methodist church. At the
foot of the hill he let in the clutch, and the engine started
with a roar. He took a road leading out of the town
directly into a stretch of sandy plains, for on an impulse
he had determined to drive by the McCune place, though
it was many miles out of his way. For over an hour he
drove through the winding road, between the clumps of
jackpines and scrub oaks that now closed together to
brush the sides of the car and now opened away into
parklike vistas through which the grey track wound.
There were no houses, no vehicles; and the track was
crossed and recrossed by diverging paths that seemed
equally promising. More than once Frank had to stop
in the moonlight and study carefully to decide which
way to go. For the most part he drove by instinct,
releasing himself to the spell of space and silence, the
immense blue distances of earth, the steadiness of stars.

Finally the trail wound slowly down between great
rolls of tree-clad sand, and Frank knew that he was approaching the settlement in which the McCunes lived.
He crossed a little stream, driving over a log bridge and
through a rutted, pitted swamp which tossed and
wrenched the light car fearfully. On the sand-hill beyond the swamp the engine heated unconscionably, and
he barely reached the top. Climbing out to investigate,
he found the radiator almost empty; the water trickled
steadily from a new leak at one side. He drove slowly
on the mile and a half to the McCune place, the engine
racketing wretchedly. The road before the place was

empty and peaceful as on the night he and Rose had last walked here. A deserted look about the house impressed him, and, crossing the yard, he found all the shades drawn, the windows closed, the door locked.

Wondering, he passed through the lot to the stable. The stalls were empty—the horses and cattle all gone.

He found an old bucket by the well, and, opening the petcock underneath the engine, he poured water through the radiator until the engine had fully cooled. Then he filled up the tank again, and drove away, taking the old bucket with him. As he looked back, the place bulked black against the setting moon.

He was compelled to drive slowly, stopping at streams to refill the radiator, and before he was half-way to Green Bush the sky ahead was brightening with the early dawn. Some two miles from the town, as he was driving faster into the rosy brilliance ahead, he was compelled to slow down suddenly in front of a farmhouse for a herd of cattle in the track. A man who had been milking one of the sleepy cows straightened up and hailed him apologetically, and Frank stopped the car. It was Elmer Bailey, a young farmer.

"I couldn't find the beggars las' night," he explained. "So I got out early to hunt 'em, an' here they was. So I thought I'd just milk here an' save driving 'em in the yard. You're out early," he added. "Been out getting news on the murder case?"

"Murder case?" Frank questioned sharply.

"Yes—didn't you hear about it?"

"No—I came from High Grove and had engine trouble—been on the way all night. Why, who's killed?"

"Bert Butler—Neal McCune stabbed him in the back with a knife. Leastways they've got McCune in jail, and things look like he was the man all right. He was

shot in the arm, an' there was one shot fired out o' Bert's
revolver. It happened out there in the swamp, right by
McCune's place."

"McCune's not the knife-using kind," Frank declared
impulsively.

"I don't know him," the farmer answered. And he
stood staring as Frank shot the car forward toward
Green Bush, swerving about the cows in the road.

As he drove, Frank's mind worked furiously on the
new problem. He reviewed vividly the events of the
day before. Manifestly, McCune had not stabbed Bert
Butler. He had seen every action of the man—and anyway, he was not the knife-using kind. He must talk to
Harrison at the earliest possible moment, try to do something. But first he must see Rose.

The town was still sleeping when he clattered into
Green Bush. He had forgotten the condition of his car,
and a column of steam rose from the radiator in the
chill morning air as he drew up before his mother's
house. Half wild with anxiety and fatigue, he hurried
up the steps. The door was locked, and he rang the
bell, then thumped loudly, hoping that Rose might come
to let him in. He was hungry for a sight of her. Instead, when the key was turned, his mother faced him,
haggard and inquiring.

"I want to see Rose," he greeted her breathlessly.
"Will you call her please, mother?"

"Rose is not here," she answered calmly. "What is
the matter with you?"

"Not here? Didn't she come in with her Uncle Marion yesterday?"

"Yes, she came. And she has gone away again."

"Gone away—where—why?" His tired mind grasped
blankly at the possibilities. Then his anger flared up

suddenly. "Did you dare to send Rose away?" he demanded.

"I don't care to be talked to in that way by anyone, least of all by my son," his mother answered firmly. "But I did not send her away. She went of her own accord."

"What did you say to her?"

"I told her that I thought she had better look for another place to stay—that I didn't care to have the daughter of a bootlegger and murderer in my home. I told her she could stay overnight—I wouldn't turn her out. But she left at once."

Frank gasped; the hot words that rushed to his lips were inadequate for the cold fury that mounted in him so powerfully that he trembled; he grasped the door casing for support. As he faced his mother he realized that now indeed they had reached a final break. His voice was curiously even, but dry and hollow, when he spoke. "Her father is not a murderer—I know that, and I'm going to prove it. And you are going to have Rose in your family, for I am going to marry her. But you won't have her in your house. I'll see to that. I'll never enter your house again. You've robbed me of the farm—the paper—but you can't rob me of her—oh, oh——"

He turned away from the white, shocked face, angry and unyielding, above the sharp shoulders squared under the faded bathrobe, dashed his hands across his eyes, and staggered out to the car.

"Where is she?" he leaned back to call hysterically. "Don't you know?" He started the car without waiting for a reply from the open door.

He drove to the hotel and hurried around to the kitchen. The proprietress was shuffling about on the rough floor, a grey, dingy figure in a grimy dress and tattered slippers, starting a fire. The blue acrid smoke of pine splinters seeped from about the lids of the huge, greasy range.

"Is Rose McCune here?" Frank inquired.

"Yes, she come here las' night jus' before supper." The woman stared at him.

"Will you call her, please, Mrs. Lacey, and tell her I want to see her right away? It's important."

"Why, yes, I guess so." She shuffled away across the empty dining-room and lobby, and Frank followed, to take a seat by the window and turn over an old newspaper nervously, folding and refolding it. He was surprised to see Rose following Mrs. Lacey back down the stairs, dressed in the plain blue suit which she had bought for school.

"I was already up, you see," she explained quietly. "But how did you get back from High Grove so soon? I'm glad to see you, Frank," she added, impetuously, coming close to him. "I was just writing a letter to you."

"Oh, Rose, I'm so sorry!" He was standing beside her, and as the old woman disappeared into the kitchen he drew the girl into his arms and kissed her lips. "Oh, Rose, Rose," he muttered brokenly.

"Frank, dear," she answered, holding him tightly for a moment. Then she pushed him away. "You have heard about father, then?"

"Yes—just this morning—a man I passed on the way in told me. Of course it isn't true. Have you seen him, dear?"

"Yes, I talked to him through—through the door."

She shuddered, and Frank had a fearful vision of McCune's huge, active, sun-loving body penned in the damp, narrow space of a cell at the county jail.

"Never mind, Rose," he assured her. "He'll soon be out, dear. Did he tell you anything—about it?"

"He told me Mr. Harrison was having Bennie Butler kept there at the jail, though he isn't locked up!"

"Is that so? I wonder—— I must see Harrison right away," he declared.

"Oh, Frank, I'm so wonderfully glad you're here!" She clasped his arm. "But how did you happen to start when you did, to get here so early?"

"I couldn't sleep—so I thought I'd like to drive back in the night," he answered easily. "But—I came by your place," he added, "and there seemed to be no one there. Are your folks here too?"

"No—they've gone away. They took the train from Black River last night. Father made them go. You see, he came back with Neal right after you left yesterday. And he made them get ready *quick* and go. He had a neighbour bring me in, and arranged with him to take care of the stock. He didn't want them to be mixed up in whatever was going to happen, he said. And then the men came and arrested him on this murder charge, and he didn't say a word, except told mother to 'go ahead with her plans.' You see, Neal fainted when Butler let go of him, and didn't see what happened. So he wouldn't be a witness. That was why papa had to carry him, like you saw. So they left last night— they'll be in Canada by night. And when I went to see papa at the jail last night after—I left your mother's— he made me promise to go to Detroit to-day. He gave me money. Mr. Saunders was real good to me—he let me talk with papa alone. Papa said I must go this morning, and get a nice place to stay and then get a job. He gave me all the money he had. He said not to write to him or let people know where I was. He said he didn't want me to be mixed up in it at all. I told him I couldn't bear to go and leave him. But he made me promise."

"Rose," said Frank earnestly. "I want you to stay till evening—I want you to marry me, Rose. Your father will be cleared soon, I believe—maybe we can take him with us. But anyway, I want you to marry me—to-day. I love you, Rose. I want you as my wife."

She looked at him steadily, proudly and gladly. "I can't, Frank," she told him. "It wouldn't be right. Not while this trouble is on—and anyway you don't know me well enough—not now——"

"Oh, I do, Rose. You know I love you. Tell me you will, Rose."

"No, it wouldn't be right. Your mother——"

"Don't mention her to me," said Frank harshly. "She's not my mother any more—not after the way she's treated you—and me."

"Don't say that, Frank. She thought she was doing right by me. She wanted me to stay, but I was—too proud, after what she had said about papa. It was partly my fault. No, Frank, I can't marry you—not now. But I love you." She had never seemed so beautiful to him as now, as she stood before him in the cool level light that filled the shabby room.

A waitress shuffled into the dining-room behind them, and began to clatter silver on the tables as a signal that breakfast was ready.

"Poor boy, you're so tired," said Rose impulsively. "I wish I could make breakfast for you." She blushed. "Come, let's get something." They entered the dining-

room together, and were soon joined by other early pa-
trons—rural mail-carriers, and a sleepy, very cross
travelling man who must take the morning train, and
who pronounced the weak coffee, sour cakes, and crisp
eggs as execrable as they were.

After the meal Rose paid her bill and brought down
her suitcase while Frank filled the radiator of his Ford
from the pump in the hotel yard, and they drove noisily
to the depot. It was a hard moment for Frank.
"Don't go, dear," he begged. "Wait until I can come
with you."

"I promised papa," she answered. "And anyway I
mustn't let people think you are too much interested
in me. It isn't fair to you—now that I'm in disgrace,
especially." She laughed, a little bitterly, he thought.
She would not stay in the Ford until the train came, but
when she had bought her ticket she remained on the
platform and they stood together talking.

"You will be anxious to hear how things come out
here. How can I find you when I get to Detroit—to-
morrow, if things go well, or as soon as I can?"

"What time would you get there?"

"At about eight o'clock in the morning."

"Well, I'll be at the general-delivery window at the
post office at nine—every day until you come. Or you
can write me there."

The train pulled in promptly, and Frank saw her on
board. As he walked back down the platform, past the
conductor signalling "all aboard," he saw Bennie Butler
appear suddenly around the front of the train and duck
between the baggage trucks, running toward the door
of the smoking-car. Impulsively he sprang forward
and seized the little man firmly by the arm. He

writhed and gesticulated fiercely, and Frank thought he was going to bite with his yellow, rat-like teeth. The train pulled away, and as her window passed him Frank caught a glimpse of Rose's face, surprised and questioning. He grasped his victim more firmly, marched him to the Ford, and drove off toward the county jail.

CHAPTER XIX

SAUNDERS met them at the door of the jail, his ruddy face a little anxious, Frank thought. "Why, hello, Bennie," he remarked, "didn't know you'd stepped out." He pushed the man inside and, closing the door, turned back to Frank.

"Glad you brought him in, Frank," he said heartily. "Say, don't tell Harrison he was out, will you?" he added ingratiatingly. "I don't know why he wants me to keep him here—ain't got no warrant for him. But I can't hardly refuse—the county attorney, you know."

"Well, you'd better watch him," Frank advised savagely. "I caught him getting on the Detroit train."

"So?" The sheriff gaped in surprise; turning, Frank left him staring, and crossed the gravel driveway to the courthouse.

Harrison was already in his neat office in the far corner of the old brown brick building, working at his desk. He rose with his perennial courtesy to greet Frank as he entered. "Good morning, Frank," he said. "What can I do for you?"

"I want to talk to you a few minutes, Mr. Harrison, about the McCune case. I have a little information about it."

"Sit down," said the prosecutor promptly. He pointed to a chair and, opening a box of cigars on his desk, selected one carefully, first offering the box to Frank.

"Well," Frank began, "I can't believe that Neal Mc-

Cune stabbed Bert Butler. He isn't that kind—to use a knife, and in the back. You feel that, don't you, Mr. Harrison?"

"I can't express an opinion, Frank," the prosecutor explained patiently; "though I trust you fully," he hastened to add.

"We can't talk it over frankly, then, as friend to friend—forgetting your official capacity for a moment?" The boy smiled nervously.

"No, I'm afraid not—exactly," the attorney answered, smiling slightly in his turn. His blue eyes were calm and friendly.

"Well, then—perhaps I'd better not tell you all I was going to. But I will say that I happen to *know* that McCune did not stab Butler. He knocked him down and left him. And the only other man who was there before you were was the brother, Bennie. I heard this morning that you had ordered Saunders to keep track of him. And I just now took the liberty of pulling him off the Detroit train and bringing him back to jail."

Harrison sprang to his feet. His face flushed. "You did? Did that damned Saunders—— Thank you, Frank. Come with me."

He swung into his coat and hat methodically, locked his door, and strode across to the jail. Saunders and Bennie Butler were sitting together in the living quarters of the jail. "Put this man in cell two," the prosecutor commanded. "He is under arrest. Hold on, search him before you put him in. And I will take the key." He glared at the sheriff, who hastened to obey. In five minutes Frank and Harrison were speeding westward in the attorney's car.

"We will go to the swamp and find Bennie's knife," he explained. "That is all that is necessary. I sus-

pected him from the first. He rode beside me both going out and returning yesterday, and I could feel his
knife against me as we were going out. When we came
back it wasn't there. That is why I had him detained."

Leaving the car at the head of the swamp, they followed the road to the little bridge where the struggle
had occurred. They soon located the place where Bert's
body had lain, by the blood spots on the sand and the
marks in the weeds. "It is my judgment that Bennie
would have thrown the knife away as soon as he withdrew it," Harrison explained. "He would have wanted
to get rid of it as soon as possible. He would have
thrown it into the swamp on the nearest side, as far
as he could. Then he would have thrown the sheath too,
probably more carefully. But since it was lighter it
would not go so far."

The attorney had brought a small wrench from the
car, and a hand-ax. Now he tied a handkerchief to the
wrench, which was of about the same weight as a
hunting-knife, and, holding it by the tip of the handle
between thumb and forefinger, swung it out into the
swamp. It caught in a clump of alders, about forty
feet away, and they could see the white of the handkerchief from the road. "Now I will go in to that point,"
the attorney said. "I will carry this pole, and you
watch it and tell me which way to go until I find the
handkerchief. The tangle is so dense that once in there
I can't see you or it, either one. Then I'll start clearing a space around the alders, and you follow me in.
Look before you take each step, for we mustn't crush
anything into the muck."

Frank watched the slow progress of the pole, shouting directions, until the attorney reached the handkerchief and set up the pole beside it. Then he entered the

swamp, taking a slightly different course, and guided by the sound of the ax. The search at first seemed hopeless, for the growth was dense and the ground soft and wet, water standing on it in many places. But they set to work after the attorney had explained his plan. "First we will clear a small circle around this bush. Then we'll cut radiating paths for a distance of twenty or thirty feet, and search each segment foot by foot. The knife must be somewhere in this circle. We must work very slowly, watching every move, and always throwing the brush back on the ground we have covered." They worked for fifteen minutes in silence. The gnats and mosquitoes were about them in swarms, and soon the attorney's sensitive face was red and swollen. But he worked on doggedly. Suddenly Frank, searching a space between alder clumps with head bent, felt a cold touch against his forehead, and, looking up, found that he had touched the metal tip of a knife sheath, dangling by a thong which had caught in the brush. "I've found the sheath," he shouted. "Come and see."

The attorney carefully marked the place he had been working with a blazed stick before he walked quietly over to look closely at the sheath and slip it into his pocket. "Let's see, that's nearly twenty feet nearer the road than the wrench," he commented. "Maybe we've been looking too far out. We must find the knife," he added. "This has no identifying mark."

They worked another hour, an hour and a half, two hours. Frank was sick with fatigue and discouragement, and sat down on a log to rest. He felt faint, and the swamp grew dim around him. Then he heard the attorney's voice calling, seemingly from far away. "Here it is, Frank. Come on."

He stumbled in the direction of the voice, but, standing beside the lawyer, he could not see the knife until Harrison laid his finger on it. It was buried to the hilt in the muck, between two brown roots of an alder clump, and only twenty feet from the road. "It must have slipped from his fingers," he remarked. "We were too far out." He withdrew it carefully, and pointed to the lettering on the brass banding of the hilt, scratched roughly with a nail or some dull instrument: "Benin Buter."

"That's all we need," said the prosecutor grimly, and without another word he led the way to the car. Frank followed wearily.

It was well after noon when they reached town, but Harrison drove directly to his office. "Have a chair, Frank," he directed. He placed the knife and sheath in a drawer of his desk, beside a large revolver, washed his hands and face at the little washstand in the corner, and sat down before his typewriter. After he had written for a few minutes he reached for his private phone, and called for Saunders. When that official appeared, perplexity and resentment in his jovial face, Harrison handed him the key to Butler's cell.

"I want you to bring Benjamin Butler to this office immediately," he said. "Handcuff him," he added.

In a few minutes the sheriff returned with his prisoner. Abject terror and misery contorted the man's small, yellow face.

"Sit down," Harrison commanded, placing a chair opposite his own. Bennie shrank into it.

"Benjamin Butler," the prosecutor began sternly when he had taken his seat, leaning forward, and looking directly into his prisoner's face, "you killed your brother."

The little man sprang up gibbering, wrenching at his

handcuffs. "Oooh, I never done it," he cried. "You let me be—I ain't done nothin'——"

"Sit down," the attorney thundered. He sank into the chair. "Hearing a shot, you ran up the road to investigate. Suddenly you came upon your brother, lying insensible in the weeds. You looked up and down the road. No one was in sight. You drew your knife and plunged it into his back, drew it out and plunged it in again and again. You saw the blood, and you were scared. You threw the knife into the brush, but it didn't go far. Then you took off the sheath and threw it more carefully, farther into the swamp. Then you ran back to call Saunders and me. You did it, Bennie. I know you did it." He leaned forward dramatically. The little man writhed and choked in his chair as though in a fit, and bit at his manacled hands.

"You did it, Benjamin Butler. I have the proof." The attorney drew open the drawer beside him, and lifted from it the sheath. "Here is your sheath," he said slowly, laying it on the desk between them. Butler stared with wide eyes, protruding like a rabbit's. "And here—is your knife." He laid it on the desk with a thump, and at the sound the little man collapsed forward, clawing at his throat and jabbering hoarsely.

"I never meant to do it—oh God—I didn't mean nothing. I hated him—he's done wrong to me—things that he hadn't ought to—ever since we was kids—oh God—oh, I never meant to kill him—oh God—let me go—let me go——"

Harrison clutched the shaking, clawlike hands and held them steadily.

"Benjamin Butler," he said clearly. "You have confessed the murder of your brother. Now you must sign this paper. Listen: 'I, Benjamin Butler, confess that on the morning of August 29, I found my brother, Bert Butler, lying insensible in the road in the swamp near McCune's farm, and that I stabbed him in the back with my knife, causing his death.'" The attorney dipped a pen and held it out. "Sign here," he commanded, indicating a place for the signature.

"I can't," Bennie gasped, "I can't—they'll hang me—I can't—I never meant——"

"Sign—you must sign it—now." He thrust the pen into the trembling fingers. The man leaned forward and scrawled his name across the sheet. Then, with a rat-like movement too swift for the attorney's quick grasp to intercept, he clutched the knife from the desk in both his manacled hands and drove it into his throat. Blood gushed over the paper, and he stiffened back into the chair, chuckling queerly. Frank sprang to his feet, but he went deathly sick at the sight of the blood, and reeled against the wall.

"Lay him down on the floor, Saunders," he heard the attorney's crisp voice. Then the telephone jangled. "Dr. Pratt? Come to Harrison's office. Rush!"

The prosecutor crossed the floor, folding a handkerchief, and laid it against the wound where Saunders had withdrawn the knife. Bennie's thin chest drew up convulsively, and then flattened as if trodden upon. The lawyer held the thin wrist, listened for the heart, and shook his head. "Guess I should have called the coroner," he remarked sadly. "That doctor's visit will be an unnecessary expense for the county."

Frank stumbled into the hall, and the attorney followed him. "Will McCune be freed now?" the boy asked.

"We may have to hold him on the liquor business—I don't know," the prosecutor answered cheerfully.

"The black posts of ruined piers ran out in straggling lines
from the grey shore."

.

"Anyway, he's a lucky man." He looked at Frank consideringly, as though about to speak further. Instead he held out his hand. "Thanks for your help, Frank," he said briefly, and turned back into the office.

As he passed slowly down the hall, Frank analysed that look. Manifestly he had done what he could for McCune. Had the attorney meant to warn him not to try to do too much? He remembered his decision to take the evening train. He had news for Rose, vitally important news. He must let her know what had happened. He looked at his watch. It was less than an hour till train time. Passing around to the rear of the courthouse, he found his car where he had left it in the morning, and drove to the depot, where he claimed his suitcase and bought a ticket to Detroit.

The beach was less than two blocks away. And noticing the agent's curious stare at his muddy clothes and sweat-stained, insect-bitten face, Frank drove down to the edge of the Lake. It was a deserted spot, out of sight of any dwelling. The black posts of ruined piers ran out in straggling lines from the grey shore. He undressed swiftly on the sand beside the car and plunged naked into the clear, cold water, swimming out a hundred feet before he turned back and came in with the waves. When he had dried himself with a towel from his suitcase and dressed himself in clean clothing, he felt immensely refreshed. He drove back to the depot just as the engine whistled; and he barely had time to arrange with the baggageman to see that his car was turned over to Finchburg (since it had been included in the sale of the plant) before the train pulled in.

He clambered aboard, found a seat, settled himself, and was filled with a musing thought of Rose as he had left her that morning, when the train started.

It ran slowly through the town, across the alley behind his home, and he thought he glimpsed his mother's
face at a window.

An uneasiness seized him, that mixed strangely with
his pain at seeing the limits of the little town slip by,
faster and faster, and his relief at the thought of Rose's
joy when he could tell her in the morning of her father's
vindication.

His uneasiness increased as the train went on, and
the familiar, lovely landscape hurried by: the hill-side
cemetery where his father lay, the rounded slopes
clothed with birch and oak; the Lake, blue purple now,
living and mysterious in the evening light. He found
that the vivid experiences of the preceding hours had
drained him of emotion, and he no longer felt the hot
and bitter resentment toward his mother which had
raged within him in the morning. But in its place had
come a vast lassitude and indifference, a sense of complete surrender and impotence.

He fought against this, telling himself that he should
make some gesture of reconciliation—that he should
not leave his mother thus, so irretrievably alone. He
knew that at the next stop his train would meet the
northbound local, and he thought that he should get
off and go back to Green Bush. But against this impulse came the thought of Rose alone in Detroit, looking for him in the morning, disappointed if he did not
come, and of how happy his news would make her.

Before he realized it they were slowing for Au Sable.
The local was already on the siding, and as they stopped
by the platform it steamed alongside. He grasped his
hat and suitcase irresolutely, peered out the window,
rose and sat down again in an agony of indecision. At
last he hurried down the aisle. On the platform he saw

that the cars of the local were moving, and before he could round the end of his own train they had passed beyond his reach. He found himself standing beside the open door of the café car, from which a white-capped waiter was staring at him curiously. He became suddenly aware of an incredibly violent hunger, and, grasping his suitcase weakly, he climbed aboard. As the train slipped swiftly away from the station, past the big sawmill and the stretch of Lake, he did not raise his eyes from the bill of fare.

CHAPTER XX

BRIEF snatches of sleep in the coach that night left Frank seemingly as tired as before; and in the morning doubts and uncertainties returned to torture him. Across his mood were projected black girders against screens of smoke and mist, through which were brief glimpses of bleak and oily water; foul smell of gas tanks, scream and clamour of engines, dimness and tumult of a train-shed, fetid air of a crowded waiting-room; then suddenly the cool sunlight of a wide street, where a sort of Sabbath calm prevailed over the swift passage of cabs and trucks. On one side were old brick residences, their stately, broad-windowed rooms degraded to the uses of "lodging by night or week." Across the street, behind the wide windows of a huge and beautiful stone building, workmen in black-streaked overalls were oiling gigantic presses. Drawn by their beauty as he always was, Frank crossed the street, to walk slowly the block's length of the newspaper building, and then briskly on to the post office.

A grimy, unimposing pile of stone, flanked by grotesque stone eagles, it crouched at the edge of Detroit's roaring business district—an overcrowded anachronism in a city of skyscrapers. Frank hurried through the entrance and around the teeming corridors, to find a pale, frightened-looking girl in a blue suit—Rose. She looked at him startled and fearful. He realized suddenly that he had not shaved for two days, and that he was dirty and haggard.

"I'm sorry to come looking this way," he greeted her. "I'm really all right."

"What about father?" she inquired eagerly.

He told her briefly of the events of the preceding day.

"Oh, Frank, I'm so glad!" She grasped his arm and relaxed against him, and tears filled her eyes. For the first time he realized the intensity of the anxiety which had racked her.

"Why, Rose," he soothed her.

"You saved him, dear Frank. I'll always remember."

Without answering her he drew her with him out of the building and down to the street. They walked slowly back the way he had come.

"What did your mother say, Frank?" Rose asked before he had time to speak. "Didn't she feel different after this happened?"

The lines of pain tightened in his face again. "I didn't see her. I just had time to catch the train." She was about to speak, but he went on. "I don't care anyway. I can't forgive her—for the way she treated you, and the way she's acted toward me all year. It's hurt me too much."

Rose looked keenly into his face. "It isn't right for her to make you suffer so," she said softly, her voice shaking.

"Don't let's talk about it now," he answered. "It's all behind us now, your father will be cleared, and we've ourselves to think about." He clasped her arm, then slid his hand forward to take her cold fingers in his. "Rose, I love you—more than ever now. I want you to marry me—now, this morning. I'll get a job here in Detroit and we'll live here together. All the other young fellows from Green Bush are getting jobs here—I guess I can."

She looked at him silently, with moist eyes.

"Rose, dear—please say you will. You want to do that, don't you?"

She looked away, and controlled her voice by an effort. "Not now, Frank—not now. We mustn't to-day —not this way. You must go on to Ann Arbor—didn't you tell me you had wired Mr. Steen that you were coming and wanted a job there?"

"Yes—but that doesn't matter. I don't *want* to go back to school. It's all a farce. I'll never be a professional man. I just want a good job, and a chance to be with you."

"You think that now. But maybe you would think differently later on, and be very sorry."

"Well, I could go back later as well as now."

She shook her head. "Now is the time, Frank. Maybe your mother was right——"

"She isn't! I won't——"

"Well, anyway, you must give yourself the chance."

"But I want you, Rose. I can't stand it away from you, now. I need you."

She looked at him tenderly, smiling a little sadly, and did not answer.

"Don't you care for that side of it, Rose?" he cried. "Don't you want to be with me? Don't you love me?"

"You know that I love you, Frank," she answered, meeting his eyes. "That is why I want you to go, now— because I do love you, and I think it's best for you. Besides—" she looked away with lowered eyes—"maybe a girl isn't ready to get married, just right off this way. Maybe she wants some nice clothes and— things she's never had. Maybe a little later——"

Frank caught at her words hopefully. "I don't more than half believe that—of *you,* Rose. You're not keen for a big wedding and all—like most girls, are you?"

"Well," she laughed at him, "most girls are."

He laughed in return, relaxing swiftly.

"You go on to Ann Arbor right away," she coaxed, "and see about your school work and a job. I'll stay here and do some shopping. And we'll see about it soon. Maybe you'll come to see me—and we'll write once or twice!"

Their slow walk had brought them back to the depot at which Frank had arrived. From the girl at the Travellers' Aid desk Rose secured addresses of two or three rooming-houses, and they took a cab to one of these. Rose engaged a small room for a week. Then they walked together to the Michigan Central depot, where a westbound train was almost due. A few moments later he left her standing in the centre of the big rotunda, her face white and smiling in its frame of tawny hair under the dark hat, clasping in her hand a slip of paper bearing his Ann Arbor address.

As he hurried to the train Frank had a feeling of intense physical suffering, and he could hardly force himself to mount the steps and find a seat. The mood persisted until the train had reached the country, and was flashing past fields and woodlands that streamed vividly by in the cool September sunshine. Then at last he relaxed, and fell asleep on the seat so soundly that the brakeman had to shake him violently to arouse him at Ann Arbor.

At the room he found Steen just preparing to leave for lunch, and they went out together. On the way back to the room and after their arrival there Frank told of the reasons for his telegram—the sale of the paper, the circumstances connected with the accusation of Rose's father, not omitting his conversation with

Rose that morning. Steen listened quietly, smoking and venturing an occasional question. Before his story was finished Frank felt drowsy, and presently he curled himself on his bed and fell asleep.

When he awoke, Steen was reading by a shaded light. There were sandwiches on the table, and an urn of coffee steaming softly on an electric grill. Frank's baggage had been delivered, and after a hot bath, a shave, and a change into fresh clothing he felt, as he told Steen, like a different fellow.

While they were consuming the sandwiches and coffee Steen inquired: "Would you consider a job as make-up man on the *Daily,* Frank—work from ten to two and sometimes later—fifteen dollars a week for six nights' work? Not very good pay, I'm afraid."

"That would be fine," Frank answered enthusiastically. "I could do it all right with a little practice, too, I think."

"Well, I guess you could have it. I spoke to Pettingill—he's the business manager this year—and he thought they would want you. We'll see him in the morning."

"That's fine of you, Steen," Frank began gratefully.

"Not at all—I wish you could have something editorial, but those jobs are all sewed up already. Perhaps in some ways this will be better, anyway. It won't conflict with your school work so much. You know, Frank," he went on, filling his pipe carefully and lighting it with a roll of paper applied to the electric grill, "I understand how you feel about this school business. You may look at it another way later on, or you may not. But why not try to arrange things so you can finish the work for your master's degree at mid-years, all but your thesis. You had a good start on that before you left. Then you might get a chance to teach the second semester, while you were finishing the thesis. You know the chief is keen for you."

"Do you really think so?"

"I know it. In fact, he's told me as much. He thinks very highly of you."

"But do you think I can clean up the courses this semester?"

"I don't see why not."

Frank sprang to his feet and thumped the table. "Great stuff, Steen, old man. You've sure got a head on you. That's just what I'll do."

"Well, it'll take some engineering. And it'll give you one hell of a load, Frank. Do you think you can stand it?"

"I'm sure I can. I was all in when I got here, but I'm really in better shape than I've ever been before. I know I can do it, Steen. I've got to."

"Well, we'll see Pettingill in the morning and cinch the job, then go after the other. But we must lie low about the job until your petition for extra hours is allowed—in fact, it had better not be known officially at all or it might make trouble. We can attend to that."

The next morning they found Pettingill in one of the railed-in divisions of the broad, well-lighted workroom of the *Daily*. He was a short, thickset man with a ruddy face and abundant reddish hair, whose brown suits and vivid cravats always seemed fresh from the clothier and haberdasher. Frank had known the man slightly when he was in Ann Arbor before, and after a few brusque questions, he and Steen were assured that the job was his. He could start work that night, as the initial *Daily* for the year would appear next morning. He sat down at a desk and scrawled a note on copy paper to Rose, to tell her of his good fortune.

The arrangement of the school work was a little more difficult. It involved the "seeing" of several deans, heads of departments, and chairmen of committees, in various parts of the campus and at conflicting or indeterminable office hours. Steen was ready with suggestions, and a word of recommendation once or twice where it was helpful (since he was this year a full-time instructor, continuing his graduate work also). Finally, by evening of the next day, Frank was ready to settle down to "cramming" on the neglected correspondence courses, with only the two examinations remaining between him and a registration that would complete his credit requirements for the master's degree by the end of the first semester.

Many times during the next week he regretted the evenings he had spent in reading or loafing during the preceding year. The work on the *Daily* proved fairly easy, and on the whole enjoyable. As a student and newspaper man he had been accustomed to late hours, and he easily adapted himself to going to bed at three or four—often five o'clock, and sleeping until ten or eleven, eating his first meal at noon, a dinner at six or seven, and a hearty lunch at midnight. The work of making-up, as rigid in its requirements and as varied in its possibilities as a chess game, he found usually genuinely absorbing, and always recreative. But it was hard to pin himself down to the correspondence courses. He was not especially interested in their content, and he was out of the habit of study. Steen helped him with quizzing and drill, and kept him at them. But it

GREEN BUSH

CHAPTER XXI

THE weeks that followed were crowded at first by the exorbitant demands of a heavy class schedule plus his four—often five or six—hours a night spent in the office of the *Daily*. He dispatched brief notes to Rose and received equally brief ones in reply, filled with her impressions of the city, of the big stores and the people. In one of her letters was the welcome news that the liquor case involving Neal McCune had been dropped, and he had been released. She would come to see him soon, she promised, if he could not come to see her. But she did not come, and Frank was too busy to wonder greatly.

More and more his brief periods of leisure were dominated by thoughts of his mother. He had no letters from her, and though he received the *Oscona County Gazette* each week and read it carefully, he found no news of her. He began to image her vividly: the memory of her shocked, grieved, and angered face, that morning he had left her so suddenly, would come to him first, and then he would imagine how she had spent the day, and the intervening days since he had left. He saw her going about her work in the big empty house, performing the regular routine with her accustomed thoroughness; and, if she sometimes broke down in her room and cried for him, facing the world proudly, and no doubt with a creditable explanation of his departure and his silence.

He counted up almost daily the time since he had

left home and in which he had had no word, and was surprised to see it reach five weeks—six weeks. Half a dozen times he began letters to her—letters of apology and contrition, letters of self-defence and explanation, letters of resentment for her silence. But each time before the letter was finished he encountered a positive inhibition which he could not overcome—his profound sense of wrong, both to himself and Rose, and his determination that he would not give in when he felt that he had been in the right. He watched the mail feverishly, day by day, for a letter from his mother, but none came; and as he sensed the strength of the resentful pride which kept her from writing to him, the inhibition to his own writing grew stronger. He began to worry over the matter, more and more, until the time came when he did not sleep at all between the end of his work on the *Daily* and the hour of his first class.

At this stage Steen interfered. He set himself a definite task of bringing Frank and Rose together; trusting to the girl, from what he knew of her indirectly, to find some solution for the situation in which he saw his friend. Accordingly, he secured a man to work for Frank one Saturday night, and that afternoon he accompanied Frank to Detroit. They went at once to the rooming-house where Frank had left Rose, but she was not there. "Yes, she stays here," the landlady admitted, "but she ain't here now." She was a stout, frowzy person with a black eye.

"Probably she's down town buying wedding garments," Steen suggested. "We'll tramp around a bit and come back in an hour or so."

When Rose had not returned by five o'clock, Frank became alarmed. "I'm afraid something's happened to her," he declared.

Steen laughed at him, and questioned the landlady. That person informed them that she thought Miss Mc-Cune worked down town—she didn't know where. "She's awful close-mouthed," she remarked. "Just tends to her own business. But she's away every mornin' by seven-thirty and back about seven—except Saturday night. She won't be home till 'bout eleven to-night."

Frank was wild. "Why didn't she tell me she was working?" he demanded of Steen. "She had plenty of money for this long, I know. How in hell are we going to put in the time till eleven o'clock? We've got to find her and make her quit this infernal job, whatever it is."

"You exhibit singular intelligence, my dear fellow," Steen remarked. "Do you realize that Detroit is a city of over a million souls, excluding the dissenting clergy, and that there are approximately ninety-two thousand, five hundred and sixty-nine girls and young women employed in her stores and industries? Our chance of finding the young lady——"

"Camp here on the steps if you want to, you damn fool. I'm going up town to hunt for her."

"In that case I shall amble gaily with you. We might appeal to the police—call all the local hospitals——"

"Steen, you *are* an ass at times."

"I have heard that the affliction you mention is contagious, which would amply account for my case. However——" Steen lit his pipe, and they set out.

At ten-thirty they were back at the rooming-house, Frank's nervousness somewhat blunted by fatigue. They found the small porch in possession of two amorous couples; but both men were so tired that, when satisfied that Miss McCune had not come in, they sat down on the steps regardless of resentful glances.

At eleven Frank saw Rose descend from a street car at the lighted corner half a block away and walk slowly toward the rooming-house. She carried her hat in her hand and her head was thrown back; but her gait and the carriage of her strong body suggested acute weariness.

She started as Frank spoke to her at the sidewalk, and, coming forward quickly, grasped his hand. Neither spoke. For a time Steen stood patiently, observing the pantomime. Then Rose dropped Frank's hand and took a step forward. "I believe this is Mr. Steen," she said.

"You are quite right," he agreed gaily. "And you are Miss McCune."

They shook hands, while Frank mumbled an apology for forgetting to introduce them.

"Characteristic and understandable, old chap," Steen commented affectionately. "And now, since the porch of Miss McCune's residence is occupied, suppose we find an ice-cream parlour and talk there a little while."

At the small drug store on the corner Steen gravely ordered soft drinks from the white-jacketed young clerk, who served them with equal solemnity. Frank and Rose were content to sit looking at each other. He forgot to ask her about the job, forgot all the questions and uncertainties which had beset him, in the great joy of seeing her.

"Did you wonder where I was this evening?" she asked gently at last. "Had you waited long?"

Frank roused himself. "Yes," he answered. "I was a little worried. You hadn't told me you were working, Rose."

She blushed. "I've been working since the Monday

after I came"—she hesitated—"at the five-and-ten on
Woodward Avenue. It was the only job I could get.
But it hasn't been bad. And I've got a better job now—
starting Monday—at Hudson's."

Frank appraised her closely. There was no change
in her clear blue eyes, with their steady, even gaze.
But her face was paler and thinner, her hair was combed
in a new way, and about her he sensed already a shade
of indefinable hardness and self-sufficiency.

"Rose," he pleaded. "Why are you working? You
don't need to, do you?"

Steen coughed slightly. "I'm wondering if I shall
see you to-morrow, Miss McCune," he began. "Could
you and Mr. Thompson have dinner with me—at Stryker's, we'll say? I really think I ought to suggest that
we go to our hotel now, Frank—after you see Miss Mc-
Cune safely home. She's had a tiresome day—and
you're tired too."

This arrangement was completed, and in addition
plans were made for a bus ride before dinner—for a bit
of air and a glimpse of the city. That night Steen noted
that Frank slept more soundly than he had for weeks.

Punctually at nine the next morning the two men presented themselves at Rose's door. She greeted them in
a new dress of sage-green silk, her glinting hair piled
high on her head. Frank realized that she had never
seemed so lovely to him before. She had a new coat
and hat of tan. He was very proud of her as they
walked down the street together, and was gratified to
note Steen's frank admiration.

At a little downstairs lunchroom, in an old residence
on Lafayette Avenue, they got coffee and rolls for breakfast. Then, down town, they took a "John R Street"
bus. The big vehicle, almost empty, rolled easily down

the broad, sunny street, meeting and passing motor cars continually—most of them small. It drove slowly past the enormous stone cube of the General Motors Building—"the largest office building in the world," Steen remarked, not without respect. Frank looked at him curiously.

Returning, the bus thumped steadily over the old pavement of John R Street, past the shaded lawns of fine old residences, past old brick churches where motors clustered thickly like shiny black flies at a syrup pan.

At last they alighted, and a few minutes' walk brought them to Stryker's, where walnut tables and woodwork, mirrors, painted walls, and florid Teutonic waiters in black tail-coats were reminiscent of the glories of a departed age. Steen ordered Stryker's famous "roast sucking-pig with sweet potatoes," with beer, and while they ate he discoursed quaintly of the good old days.

In the afternoon, still as Steen's guest, they saw the most promising motion picture on the day's bills. Then, proffering the urgency of work in Ann Arbor as an excuse, Steen left them, assuring Frank solemnly at parting that he approved his taste in matters feminine most unreservedly.

They did not protest too strongly against his going, but stood arm in arm in front of the theatre, watching his tall form hurry away. "Dear old Steen," Frank murmured affectionately.

"He is wonderful," Rose agreed, still flushed with her pleasure at his parting words. "And I think he's perfectly handsome—not a bit like his picture."

Frank laughed.

The hours that followed were ones of supreme relaxation and irresponsibility. They sauntered about the streets arm in arm, looking into windows, indifferent to

the hurrying crowds of dapper, sporty young men and
blatantly painted women. When the lights began to
come on they boarded a crowded street car for an amusement park, where they bought wiener sandwiches and
peanuts for supper, rode on a ferris wheel, and watched
from a bench the noisy ingathering of innumerable picnic parties with dirty, hilarious children and cross
mothers. Toward midnight they returned to Rose's
home. The little porch was empty now, quiet and vine-
shaded in the moonlight, and they sat together on a
bench. Frank's mood was one of complete surrender to
the quiet and the cool moonlight, the charm of Rose's
dear presence. He laid his head in her lap and closed
his eyes.

"Isn't it almost time for you to be thinking about getting back to Ann Arbor, dear boy?" she asked after a
little silence, smoothing his forehead with cool fingers.

He sat up and clasped her in his arms. "I don't want
to go back without you, Rose," he whispered. "Let's
be married in the morning and you come back with me.
I'm making almost enough for us to live on, and I
haven't touched the money I brought from Green Bush.
I don't want you to be working this way—and I want
you and need you with me, dear."

Her arms tightened around him, but she did not answer at once. Then she asked quietly: "How is your
mother, Frank?"

As he sensed the comparative calm with which he met
this question, even Frank himself realized the extent of
the healing which the day had wrought in him.

"I don't know," he answered truthfully. "I haven't
heard from her."

"Why, Frank," Rose drew away and faced him anxiously. "Haven't you written?"

"No, I haven't. I have meant to, but it has seemed I couldn't. When I started to write I would think about how she treated you—and me—and I couldn't finish. I have worried about it, Rose," he added.

She was silent a moment, understanding. "I know," she said at last. "That was what was the matter when you came. I was afraid for you. Don't you see, dear, that trouble has to be settled some way before we can really be happy together?"

"I am happy with you now," Frank protested, embracing her again.

"Yes," she met his lips with her own, "but we couldn't be for long. Frank dear, I want you to write to her, and try to set things right. She has been trying to do the best for you, always, even in sending me away—at least I think she has. And anyway, you can't dispose of things that way—not when you are you. It has been almost killing you—the worry—I can see that. She will be pleased that you are going on to school. Maybe if she knows I have wanted you to do that—she won't mind—your loving me—so much. And papa has been cleared now—maybe that will make some difference."

Frank caught the faint edge of steel in her voice. "But can things ever be really right again, Rose?" he urged.

"We must try to make them so," she answered positively. "Promise me that you'll write to her to-morrow, Frank. Remember that she is all alone. She has been suffering, too. She wasn't well, you know. Don't worry, though—dear boy—you've worried enough. But write to her fully, especially about your school work. And then maybe next Sunday you can come over and tell me what you hear."

"I'll write to-morrow," Frank promised. With the

decision a flood of relief filled him utterly, and he held her close to him, kissing her again and again. "Dear, dear girl," he whispered, "you have helped me so much to-day. I see now that you're right about it. I believe it will all work out. And I've had such a happy day, dear—I'm so happy now. It's such a relief to have the problem settled—and the right way too, I'm sure."

CHAPTER XXII

THEY stayed together on the porch, whispering or silent, until it was too late for Frank's last train to Ann Arbor. He decided, then, to go to his hotel, sleep for a couple of hours, and return to have breakfast with Rose on her way to work, taking an interurban car which would place him in Ann Arbor just in time for his late forenoon class.

The breakfast was a hurried but very happy one. "You can't imagine how good I feel to have that off my mind at last, dear," he told her. "I'm confident mother will meet me more than half-way. Anyway, I'll have done my part. And Sunday I'll see you again."

In the bright morning sunlight on the sidewalk in front of the restaurant he clasped her hand, then hurried to the interurban depot, turning once to glimpse her erect, blue-clad figure going steadily through the moving crowd, far down the block. On the car, as it hurtled swiftly westward, he busied himself composing his letter to his mother.

When the interurban car stopped abruptly at the busy intersection of Ann Arbor's drab, colourless down-town streets, Frank hurried down the steps. He was amazed to confront Steen, standing by the open door of a taxi-cab. His first thought was of some extraordinary and inexplicable interest in his making his class on time, and he framed a deprecating smile. But something in Steen's face, as he motioned silently toward the door of the cab, frightened him, and the smile chilled on his lips. Steen climbed in, closing the door behind him, and the driver started abruptly without waiting for directions.

"We are going to the hospital," Steen answered the question in Frank's eyes. "Your mother is there, having an operation."

Frank gasped, and felt a moment's sharp slowing of his heart. "When did she come?" he asked. A terrible apprehension gripped him, and he trembled.

"It seems they got here Saturday forenoon. The doctor from Green Bush is with her. . . . They went to the hospital first, and had an examination. Then they started trying to locate you through the regular channels, but offices were closed and it was late Saturday night before they got your address. Of course the landlady didn't know where we were. It seems the surgeons advised immediate operation—yesterday morning at the latest—but—they were prevailed upon to wait. . . . Unfortunately I fell in with Haller when I got back to Ann Arbor yesterday, and didn't get to the room until midnight. Then I tried to phone, but didn't know the name at Miss McCune's rooming-place. I expected you on one of the trains last night, or an earlier car."

"Have you been up all night meeting trains, old man?" Frank asked remorsefully.

"That is nothing," Steen answered. "But the surgeons wouldn't wait any longer—they were to operate early this morning. I suppose it's over by now."

"Did you hear what the trouble is?"

"No. But I know it is grave, Frank. You must be prepared."

Frank turned to the window and watched as they sped up to the entrance of the huge brick hospital building. On a side porch a patient lay on a wheel chair in the sunshine, under a grey blanket. The uniformed young woman at the central desk recognized Steen. "Mrs. Thompson has been taken to a room on the second floor in the east wing," she told him. "I will call the nurse there." She made a connection on the little switchboard beside her desk, meanwhile looking at Frank. "Is this Mr. Thompson?" she asked Steen.

"Yes."

Frank stood by, miserably silent.

"The nurse says you may come up," the young woman told Frank.

Steen hesitated.

"I guess there's nothing I can do, Frank," he said. "I'll be back later. Is there any report as to her condition?" he asked the attendant.

"She hasn't come out from the anæsthetic yet," she answered.

Frank gave his friend a look of pain and gratitude, and walked nervously down the corridor which the attendant indicated. He caught glimpses of white-walled rooms, with high, narrow beds and white enamelled tables. Rosy-faced student nurses in blue and white uniforms passed and repassed him, looking at his distraught face. He asked one of them for directions, and finally reached the right corridor. Half-way down it a door opened suddenly, and he was face to face with Dr. Pratt. The big man's strong face was filled with pain, in which reproach, questioning, and sympathy fought for mastery. He clasped Frank's hand without a word, and drew the door softly shut behind him.

"How is she?" Frank gasped.

"Pretty bad, Frank. The operation was successful, so far as that goes. But she shows no sign of rallying.

She was not fit for it at all—but it had to be done—it would have killed her in a day or two—and now the shock may."

Frank dropped the doctor's hand and turned away. The corridor swam greyly before his eyes, and he knew that he was crying. The doctor's hand closed on his shoulder and turned him round, but he could see the grave, reproachful old face only dimly through his tears. "Frank, where have you been?" the doctor was asking, a world of pain in his voice. "What has been the trouble between you and your mother? She had let on to everyone in Green Bush that you were in school and doing finely, and that she was hearing from you. But on the way down here she told me she hadn't heard from you, and didn't know your address—wasn't even sure you were here."

"We quarrelled," Frank answered weakly. "It was mainly my fault, I'm afraid."

"Before you left home?"

"Yes—the day I came away."

"Well, that explains some things. She has gone downhill so fast this fall—gone all to pieces. I knew there must be something preying on her mind, but she wouldn't tell me. You know she hasn't been well for years. Several times I've advised a trip down here, for examination and possible operation, but she wouldn't come. She has had an unnatural dread of hospitals and operations. Then what I had been fearing came all at once. I rushed her here, and they should have operated yesterday. But she wasn't fit. She wanted you, and we thought if we could find you the improvement in her nervous condition might compensate for the delay. But this morning we had to go ahead."

Pain drove into Frank's whole being, tearing horribly.

He leaned against the wall. "Was she—still unwilling?" he chocked.

"Yes," said the doctor bluntly. "She was hysterical."

Tears filled the boy's eyes again, and he fumbled for his handkerchief. He felt the doctor's hand under his arm, and there was a kinder tone in the brusque voice as he said: "Steady now, Frank. Steady down. You'll want to go in and see her soon now. There's no use worrying about it now. And there's a chance that she may rally, even yet."

"Only a chance, doctor?" the boy gasped.

"Only a chance, I'm afraid. She was debilitated, run down—her system was badly poisoned—and her nervousness made shock almost likely. Still, there is a chance."

A few minutes later they entered the room.

A white-uniformed nurse sat by the bedside. She had ruddy hair like Rose's, but was smaller than Rose and very pretty, with a hard, crystalline remoteness. On the narrow bed by the window Mrs. Thompson lay supine beneath a sheet, her whole form inert, motionless; her face, hollowed and worn by pain, was somewhat distorted and discoloured; her lips were parted. Frank could not perceive her breathing. She looked incredibly older, frailer than he could remember her; and as strange, remote, as though she were already dead.

"There is no improvement,' the nurse remarked softly to Dr. Pratt, in an even, impersonal voice. He crossed to the bed and bent above the impassive form, his ear to her chest, then laid his fingers on the limp, wasted wrist. He seemed even more grave when he turned away and with a glance at Frank led the way back to the corridor. They sat on a bench and waited. The doctor was silent. Frank felt dazed, incredulous.

Presently the doctor left him and returned to the
room. There was a brief, agonizing period of loneliness. Then the doctor returned and sat down without a
word. Almost immediately the nurse appeared at the
door and signalled to him. Moved by a premonition,
Frank followed. He found the nurse holding his
mother's wrist, and the doctor bending over her with a
stethoscope. He listened for a long time, applying the
instrument to her wrinkled breast. Finally he straightened up, and dropped the stethoscope in his pocket.
Gently, with a precision that indicated powerful restraint, he composed the passive limbs and straightened
the arms. Then, holding the sheet as though to place
it over her face, he turned to Frank.

The boy stared incredulously. He could see no
change. "She has died," the doctor said.

An impulse to fling himself by the bed, to cry wildly,
fought with his habitual self-control. He crossed to
the bedside and stood looking down into his mother's
face. As he watched, it seemed to sharpen and assume
definiteness of outline. It grew sculpturesque—a mask
of dulled ivory against the pillow. There was no
triumph in the face, and no bitterness. But to the
boy it seemed an epitome of pain and disappointment.
Groping, he found the chair which the nurse had left,
and, sinking into it, covered his eyes with his hands.

In the hours that followed, his mind swiftly built de-
fensive walls of numbness against the sharp wound of
pain. The doctor arranged the details of the journey
back to Green Bush. Steen packed his clothes, found
a substitute for him at the *Daily,* arranged excuses from
his classes. On the journey he was almost inert, listless—drugged with emotional fatigue. The doctor did

not try to talk or question him, but his manner was increasingly sympathetic.

At Green Bush there were moments of acute suffering, as when he entered his home and saw the kitchen in the neat order in which his mother had left it, or when he met Mr. Steele and clasped his hand silently. They reached the town in the evening, and the funeral had been arranged by telegraph for the next day. The Reverend Strout had been removed from Green Bush by the conference, and his place had been taken by one Hadley, a wholesome, outdoor-seeming fellow whom Frank found at least tolerable. But the service at the house seemed endless, and Frank was shocked to find himself almost asleep. The conventional music and prayers, which caused the women to sob all through the crowded rooms, seemed puerile and insignificant to Frank. They had no relation to real sorrow, he reflected bitterly. Then came the long ride to the hill-side cemetery, under a grey sky heavy with sleet and rain. Leaving the few attendant carriages outside the cemetery, the hearse crawled cautiously up the hill to a point near the Thompson lot. A pile of yellow sand marked the open grave. The pall-bearers scrambled and strained with their burden. There was a moment of pause and whispered direction. Then the minister began to intone a burial service. Lifting his eyes, Frank saw at his feet the open grave, below him the hill-side, marked with mounds, and beyond them the road, the shore, the Lake—grey water crashing dully on the beach, rolling, massive, under the clouded sky, in a heavy wind that strained the pines along the hill-side and drove stinging sleet against his face.

As he looked, the whole structure of protective numb-

ness and indifference in his mind sloughed away, and
Frank knew that beneath his consciousness pain and
remorse had been eating his very soul. His body trembled, and he could barely restrain himself from breaking
from the group and dashing shrieking down the hill.
An intolerable agony of loneliness and self-reproach assailed him. In that black casket lay his mother—his
mother, soon to be covered by the yellow sand, never to
know that he regretted all his harshness, never to know
that he loved her. All the suffering and sacrifice of her
life for him—the pain that had bought his life almost at
the cost of her own, the tenderness that had sheltered
his fragile, sensitive childhood, the self-denials that
had sent him to the University, summed themselves
swiftly and relentlessly against him. It was in violent
agony that he saw the coffin lowered, and the first handful of earth thrown upon it. In piteous anguish that
he could not bear to share or reveal he crept down the
hill alone, found a seat in a waiting carriage, and rode
back to town. He locked himself in his room until almost train time, and departed without talking to anyone,
leaving only a note for Dr. Pratt stating that his job
required his immediate return.

CHAPTER XXIII

IT was a dull and altered Ann Arbor that met Frank's eyes as he crawled from the train next morning. The colours of trees and houses seemed curiously disturbed and unnatural. Motors and street cars either passed him noiselessly, or grated and roared so horribly that he almost cried out in pain.

The room was empty, and he tumbled into bed half undressed, and slept. It was twilight when he awoke, and Steen was smoking quietly by the window, looking down the grey street.

Frank crawled stiffly from the bed and walked into the bathroom. There was hot water in the taps, and clean towels hung above the tub. "Steen's thoughtfulness," he reflected unconcernedly. Half an hour later they set out together for supper. Characteristically Steen asked no questions: and Frank, while planning vaguely to tell Steen something of his trip, postponed any reference to it. The mass of pain that lay about his heart seemed better left unprobed, guarded.

His substitute was glad to turn over the job at the *Daily* to him, and for a time the work eased him, with its swift, concrete decisions, its feel of definite achievement as the pages grew beneath his hands. When he was through he felt no sleepiness, and he walked for almost an hour through the chilly, deserted streets. Only one or two houses showed lights in upper windows. The late moon glowed faintly, low in the west. Finally, still broad awake, he went to the room and lighted his

193

study lamp, shading it so as not to disturb Steen, who
rolled over in his bed and muttered something in Dutch.
He sat for a while, thinking of Rose; but he could not
think of her without remembering their last hours together; and the ghastly irony of that happiness
haunted him.   He must wait a few days before he wrote
to Rose, he decided.

He pulled his books from the case where Steen had
put them, and set himself vigorously to the task of writing a note-book in one of the courses.   He had to record
his personal reactions to a number of volumes of modern English and American poetry—Masefield, de la
Mare, Sandburg, Masters, Frost.   He wrote his criticisms rapidly, in a vigorous, dogmatic manner such as
he knew the instructor liked.   He was still working
when it was time to go to breakfast and then to class.
The note-book was almost finished, and he read some
of the criticisms to Steen, over their sweet rolls
and coffee; but they seemed empty and childish.   He
went to class with a strong bitterness in his heart.

The days that followed were ones of increasing emptiness.   He speedily exhausted the possibilities of his accumulated assignments.   He attacked the thesis with
renewed energy, and in addition undertook some reading which he had long planned to do—certain novels of
Cabell, the early works of Thackeray—odds and ends
from his "books to read" list.   But Thackeray he could
not read at all, and Cabell, devoured rapidly, left him
unsatisfied.

The recurring thought of Rose brought him only pain.
His agonized remorse for the circumstances of his
mother's death gradually transformed itself into a perverse sense of guilt in the thought of his relations with
Rose, and of Rose herself.   He longed to go to her, to

write to her, and yet he was withheld by this obsession which he could not master. It seemed to him that he had never known suffering before.

The nights gave him a few hours' respite, when he worked in the print-shop and could surrender his mind to the demands of what he was doing. He deliberately prolonged the task as much as possible, labouring over the final pages until the waiting pressmen cursed him. When at last he left the office he would be physically fatigued, but his mind was as active as ever. He would sit fidgeting in his room, trying to read; and twice when the first colour of dawn appeared he left the house again, to tramp out to the east edge of the town and watch the sunrise. But he found no pleasure in it—only increased bitterness.

The Sunday after his return was a long hell to him. He had fallen asleep when he got back from work Sunday morning; he awoke in a couple of hours, dressed, and tried to read. He walked about the room, stared out the window. Finally Steen suggested that they take a walk.

It was one of the rare warm days of early winter, when hazes of Indian summer hung over the hills around Ann Arbor. The winey reds of the oaks were dusked and dulled by greys and browns. The long rolls of land were warm with dull greens of frosted pastures and heavy brown of ploughed lands. But the walk proved an agony to him, for it invited him to confidence, and he found that he could not bear to talk to Steen of his mother or her death. He walked rapidly and silently, a few paces ahead. And Steen followed patiently, drawing on his pipe.

Frank was glad when they got back to the room. He read a Sunday paper for two or three hours before, at

Steen's grave, sympathetic suggestion, he went to bed, since there was no paper to get out for the next day. He could not sleep, however. Long after Steen's quiet breathing announced that he was sleeping, Frank lay awake. His mind went over and over the events of the week before: the ghastly irony of his happiness with Rose, his assurance that everything would be all right, while his mother waited in the hospital for some word from him before she died. Acute physical longing for Rose filled him as he thought of her: but, fighting and conquering his desire, came the sense of repulsion, the feeling that he could not bear to see Rose or to let her know his agony. The sense of treachery toward his mother, of acute remorse, filled him, and he writhed, silent and dry-eyed, on his bed. At last a whiteness filled the eastern sky, dawn approached, and he slept fitfully until Steen awoke him in time for his class.

Each day that followed was a growing torture. The desire to see Rose and try to find surcease from his sorrow in her presence grew stronger and stronger, but with it increased also his sense of guilt, and the perverse, only partly conscious desire for expiation which kept him from her.

Tuesday brought him a note in her fine, clear handwriting, telling him she was sorry not to see him Sunday, and hoped he could come the following Sunday: it was evident she had not yet heard of his mother's death. His first impulse was to board the next car and go to her. But he waited, and presently her ignorance of his suffering seemed to make her altogether external to it, and it seemed to him indivisible, never to be shared with anyone in the world.

Memories of his mother haunted him: countless little things he had forgotten, incidents of his boyhood when she had comforted him or reproved him or been proud of him, times when he had disappointed her or had found her a sufficient refuge and source of courage. His father, too, came vividly before him, always with a strange look of sorrow and reproach in his eyes. Frank felt a sense of disloyalty to his father that complicated his grief: a feeling that his father had sacrificed so much for her, and all so willingly, while Frank himself had been impatient and selfish. Always he came back to the irretrievableness of it all, the futility of any gesture of penitence or regret, until it seemed that he could not bear his suffering.

He grew haggard and white. As he looked at himself one morning in the glass he realized suddenly the resemblance to his father's face of the reflection that looked out at him, and was startled and at the same time conscious of a faint sense of the dramatic which shamed him.

He knew that Steen was watching him closely, and sometimes longed with his whole heart to unburden himself. But the wall of silence he had built up would not be broken down, and instead of confiding in his friend, Frank met his few cautious advances rudely, even brutally. For the most part Steen pretended to ignore his evident mental unrest, and spoke only of commonplaces.

The week dragged on, each day a hideous interval made bearable only by the few hours of manual and mental labour at the print-shop when his mind found rest and he relaxed in jokes and banter with his fellow workmen. When Sunday drew near, with the long void of hours it represented, it seemed to Frank that he could not endure the day.

He secured a typewriter, and set himself the task of copying a note-book. But midway of the morning his

mind suddenly and completely rebelled.   He sprang up
from the table, trembling with nervousness.   Steen sat
by the window, smoking and reading.

Frank rummaged in the closet for an old hat and
coat.   "Come on, you dirty Dutchman," he remarked
thickly.   "Let's go to Detroit and get drunk."

Steen got up at once, looking at him sharply.   "Always glad to oblige in that regard," he agreed.   "I'm
right beside you."

They rode in silence, broken only by Steen's cautious
suggestion that they eat before seeking out a dispenser
of liquors.

The hot, highly seasoned food at a down-town restaurant subtly blunted and transformed the raging current
of Frank's desire.   As they strolled slowly down the
avenue toward the river, they passed a burlesque theatre, the entrance flanked by a photograph of a row of
girls in tights.

"Let's go in," Frank suggested abruptly.

They paid a greasy, black-moustached cashier for bal-
.cony seats and entered the dimly lighted theatre, filled
with the smoke of cheap cigars.   In a little while the
orchestra of five or six pieces began to bang out an old
march tune, the footlights flared on, and the show began.

The audience, composed entirely of men, was attentive
and appreciative.   The antics of the comedians were
greeted with shouts of laughter.   And when the well-
fleshed, vivid woman in ruffled silk dress and under-
things danced a fast, voluptuous dance with her skirts
lifted to her thighs, the big barn-like house shook with
clapping, whistles, and stamping of feet.   The woman
seized a slender, awkward girl from the "bathing-suit
chorus" which was supporting her dance, dragged her

to the front of the stage, and went through her dance again, forcing the girl to accompany her. The girl hid her face and tried to pull away, and the audience roared and shouted more loudly than before.

Frank rose to his feet, his face white, and clambering over the feet of indignant neighbours, left the theatre, followed by Steen.

"I've been a fool, Steen," he said abruptly, when they reached the sidewalk. "This sort of thing isn't what I want. I'm going out to see Rose."

"I'm glad, Frank," Steen told him.

They hailed a passing taxi and directed the driver to Rose's rooming-place. "If she's there I'll go on back to Ann Arbor," Steen proposed, and Frank did not dissent.

Steen watched from the car until he saw Rose coming quickly down the stairs, beyond the broad door of the old house. Then he motioned to the driver to go on.

When Frank saw her coming, her face infinitely tender and filled with understanding, such a weakness of relief seized him that he almost fell. He leaned against the doorpost, and his eyes filled with tears. He felt her guiding him to the seat behind the vines, let her draw him down beside her.

"Don't, Rose, don't," he protested. "I'm soiled, and guilty—my mother died in Ann Arbor before I got back," he broke off, and deep sobs racked him. For the first time since his mother's death he cried freely, unrestrainedly.

She held his hand tightly, drew his head against her shoulder and smoothed his hair. Little by little he told her, in broken sentences, the story of his return to Ann Arbor, the trip to Green Bush, and of the torturing days that had intervened; and learned that she had heard only the day before of his mother's death, in a letter from her mother, and had spent the night and all the day in waiting for him, hoping and expecting he would come to her.

"If you had not come I would have come to Ann Arbor to see you to-morrow," she told him simply. And as he looked into her grave, clear eyes, Frank knew fully that he had found now the only salvation from the horror which had possessed him. "I think my mother would have forgiven me," he said at last, stroking her hand. "Anyway, there's life to live, for a little while at least. I've grieved enough, I guess. And now —we won't talk of that any more."

Strange healing flowed from her to him. His taut nerves relaxed, and he grew dumb, content to sit close beside her through the long, cool twilight, feeling the touch of her body against his, tasting the fragrance of her hair, listening to the quiet music of her infrequent speech. Only when the night grew late, and the prospect of being separated from her came before him, was he moved to active response. It seemed he could not bear to leave her for a moment. A vast need of her possessed him. Horror and emptiness seemed ready to lay hold upon him if he were alone. She was his only defence.

"I need you, Rose," he told her. "Truly I cannot live without you. It sounds foolish, I know. But I was almost insane before I came to you to-day—I have been for a week. I realize it now. But with you I'm safe. Please, please, let's be together from now on. Come with me to Ann Arbor and we'll be married in the morning, and then we'll decide what to do. You know I need you, Rose."

"Yes." She pressed his hand. "I'll stay with you, dear," she promised softly. "But marriage, now—are

you sure you want that? Think of all it means. You
want to marry me now, because you need me. But
won't you regret it afterward?"

"You know I wanted to marry you before," he reproached her.

"Yes, I know," she answered softly. She looked long
at him, her love for him speaking in her eyes. "I'll go
to Ann Arbor with you, anyway," she decided at last.
"Let's go to the station now, and wait there for a train.
I'll be back in a minute."

He waited placidly. In a little while she came softly
down the stairs, carrying a bag. They walked slowly
to the station, where the yellow lights of lamp-posts
were dim in the pale moonlight. The big waiting-room
was almost deserted. Frank bought their tickets, and
they found a bench at one side and sat down to wait for
the early morning train. Physical weariness and relaxation settled upon him, and at last he laid his head
against her shoulder, half reclining in the seat. She
had to wake him when the train was called.

They drew out slowly through the environs of Detroit,
filled with noises of early morning. Frank stared curiously at the factories and workshops. "There's where
I belong," he told Rose suddenly, "not in school. I'm
coming back here and get a job." The short sleep had
refreshed him immeasurably, and he felt a vast renewal
of confidence as he sat beside her in the rushing car, her
bag between his feet. "That life would suffocate me
now," he went on. "I know it would be bad for me. I
want work and lots of it, and *you*. Then I'll be happy,
and save my soul." He smiled grimly, but Rose did not
smile, and was silent.

"Let's consult Mr. Steen about it all, Frank," she proposed finally. "If he thinks we ought to be married,

I—guess I won't object. But I think we ought not to announce it now—people in Green Bush would not understand."

"I don't care if they don't," Frank said shortly.

"Well—shall we talk to Mr. Steen?"

"You know he likes you," he rallied her gently. "You know he'll be favourable."

She blushed warmly. "I know he's your best friend," she protested.

"Yes, indeed he is," Frank agreed. "We *will* talk to him. That's a good idea."

Frank called Steen from the station, and they met for breakfast. Frank explained the situation with a quiet gaiety that seemed like his old self, and Steen approved instantly.

"That's good stuff, Frank, old boy," he remarked. "I say go ahead. Of course," he added whimsically, "my chief motive is my desire to get rid of a singularly annoying room-mate. But nevertheless, I say go ahead. May I arrange the—er—formalities? And are you going to Niagara Falls for the honeymoon, or will you be content with some less stupendous natural phenomenon?"

"We're going back to Detroit to get a job," Frank announced.

"Two jobs," Rose corrected him. "If you work I'm going to too—for a while anyway. If I don't get fired for absence I'll still have a job when I get back."

"Well, we'll see about that," said Frank. "Yes, Steen, you engage a representative of the cloth, and see that the news *doesn't* get out. You can go with me to get a licence, too."

They were married that evening, with Steen and Haller as witnesses, by a young student pastor, a pale, serious, near-sighted little fellow who was vastly disturbed when Steen, who had been clowning all evening, announced solemnly that no wedding ceremony was binding until the presiding clergyman had kissed the bride. During the day Frank had packed his few belongings for shipment to Detroit, and had called upon such of his instructors as he cared to warn of his departure. Some of them he left to wonder and fill in absence reports. He did, however, arrange for a substitute in the job on the *Daily*, and wrote a letter of explanation to the head of his department. He had decided with Rose that the wedding should be kept secret for a time: word could be sent to Green Bush later on, they felt, though of course Rose wrote to her mother and father about it.

At early sundown they took a train for Detroit, accompanied by Steen and Haller. There was a wedding supper at the Cadillac, where Frank had the thrill of registering for "Mr. and Mrs. F. Thompson" for the first time: a supper of which he remembered nothing afterward except that Steen smoked an unaccustomed cigar, and forced one on him. At last the two friends departed, already a bit hilarious, for certain rendezvous known to them before they should return to Ann Arbor. "We must do our best suitably to celebrate the events of the day," Steen had announced solemnly. Frank and Rose took the elevator to their room and were alone together, in a new intimacy of comradeship that was already assured, and filled with a deep sense of sacredness and peace.

CHAPTER XXIV

THE next morning they spent in finding a place to live. They studied the advertisements of "furnished rooms for light housekeeping" in the Sunday paper, and rented the second place they looked at—a little suite of two rooms and bath. Its chief claim to consideration was the fact that the worn furniture and rugs were clean, and that one window of the small livingroom-bedroom looked out into the branches of a tree—grey and bare now, and shaking in a snowy wind on this morning. Behind this room was a tiny kitchenette with a gas plate—a dark, musty little hole; and to one side was the cramped, old-fashioned bathroom. The price for these quarters was one which surprised even Frank, accustomed as he was to high rentals in Ann Arbor. But they decided to pay it rather than to look farther. It was near the down-town district, on a wide street of old mansions that ran down into the heart of the city. Frank had determined to seek work in a print-shop, instead of going into the factories as had been his first impulse; and from this location they could both walk to work.

The high rental, and the evident impossibility of Rose's keeping happily busy in these narrow rooms all day, helped to make Frank agree to her going on with her work in Hudson's basement—selling children's stockings, she explained it was. They would get their breakfasts together in the rooms, they decided, and their evening meals together down town. Lunches would be hurried at best, and they would be apart unless he found a place near the store where she worked.

The first printing-office at which Frank applied hired him, however—a big commercial plant near the depot at which he had so often arrived from Green Bush. It was a year of rapid expansion in Detroit, and a season of especial pressure in the printing business as well; and a man of all-around experience such as Frank had, who was promising in appearance and not too ambitious in the matter of pay, was readily given a trial.

The shop was a big one. On one large floor were a score of composing-stands and tables, flanked by a battery of linotype machines on one side and of presses on the other. The presses were of various types—big bed presses for calendars, compact high-speed presses, a long row of jobbers. Upward of fifty men worked in this one huge room. Above were the binding and hand-colouring departments, whence scores of girls and women came trooping down a steep, worn stairway at noon and evening. In the basement below were the stock-rooms, piled with tons of paper of all sorts and colours.

Frank liked the work in the shop. He fitted readily enough into the rough *camaraderie* of the workmen— partly because of the fact that he suppressed all reference to the fact that he was a university graduate, inventing instead a nebulous mythical past of printing experience. He discussed with his fellow compositors the plant, the foreman, the pressmen, and the girls from the bindery who came into the press-room occasionally to help in some way. He talked with them, too, about the moving pictures and vaudeville performances which were most popular, and pronounced on the relative merits of various near-beers. He liked the roar of the big presses, the smell of ink, the continual bustle of many workmen, the pressure of work. When he first entered the plant certain delayed calendar orders were being completed at the eleventh hour, and the presses were working day and night. Later on, catalogues and college annuals were the main part of the work.

Gradually the job palled on Frank. He realized one day that, although he got more and more of the work which required intelligence and skill on the part of the compositor, almost never did a piece of work pass through his hands in which beauty, or genuine excellence of printing, was a primary consideration; and when this did happen, the designing was all in the hands of other men—he was only a tool in the performance of the task. He had no personal contact with the customer, and he never printed the forms he composed— he seldom even drew proofs of them. He realized at last that printing was not a craft under such conditions, but an industry, and he a cog in the machine almost as completely as the factory worker who spends his day repeating one minor operation.

It was not until the college annuals came to occupy most of the time of the plant, however, that Frank's growing discontent found concrete material for its development. The manufacture of these pretentious and expensive volumes, with their elaborate, tasteless engravings, their crass and ribald cartoons, and their bold advertisements of sweaters and fraternity jewellery as the most important things in college life, appeared to him suddenly as a stupendous and unmitigated folly. He saw quite clearly how fatuous it was that this army of men and machines should be busied for many days in the manufacture of such monuments of ugliness and vulgarity.

He tried to talk with some of his fellow workmen about this, cautiously and at odd moments. But he discovered that to most of them the work of the shop was all alike—just so much to be done and got out of the way, so that they could be free for the bowling-alley or the movies or the dance-hall. They did not care what they were doing, but they would discuss vociferously the need for better wages and new equipment in the plant.

From only two did he get a spark of response to his veiled suggestions. One was a young German, who confided his longing for a shop of his own, where he could do just what he liked. The other was an old man in the proof-reading room, a dry little man with sandy hair and moustache, whom Frank surprised one day studying a catalogue of incunabula. Their acquaintance progressed slowly until one night the old man invited Frank to call on him: and, accepting on an impulse and leaving Rose at a movie, he climbed the stairs to a third-floor room near the plant, where he found a mellow oil light, a little stove, and a collection of beautiful books which amazed and delighted him.

Of Rose's work he learned little. He knew that she was almost exhausted, night after night, during the weeks preceding Christmas; and that she was not laid off, as many of the "basement girls" were, when the holiday trade was over. On Christmas day he sent to the Green Bush paper a note to the effect that "Frank Thompson and Rose McCune had been married in Detroit, where Mr. Thompson is employed at present." They had planned some simple Christmas festivities, but Rose was so tired that they spent the day at home. She was most pleased by one of his little gifts to her— a blooming primrose in an earthen pot.

Their life went along methodically with a growing

coldness of routine which the brief physical intimacy of their nights together at the rooms failed to dispel. Many evenings they spent at vaudeville or motion-picture theatres, and a few at more pretentious plays. On other evenings they stayed at home, Frank reading while Rose sewed. But the rooms were likely to be cold and the light was poor, and it was pleasanter down town. They liked the noisy, brightly lighted streets, the hurrying, rosy crowds in their furs and heavy coats, the clatter of street cars and rush of motors.

They tried various cafeterias and restaurants for their evening meals, and made little expeditions into foreign sections of the city, for new sights and strange cookery. They had agreed not to break into the savings which Frank had brought with him from Green Bush. But their combined incomes left little to be added to these, after the expenses of each week were paid.

On a night soon after New Year's, they sat tiredly in a cafeteria, eating a tasteless, meagre supper. About them were the banging of trays and the clatter of heavy dishes, the noises of rapid eating.

"This is a hell of a life," Frank observed. "I've been making up sheets of Junior pictures for the *Walleye* all day: 'Carl E. Goof, Sigma Digma Thigma, Freshman Track Team, Sophomore Party Committee'—and then a supper like this."

"I don't know that it's any worse than trying to sell stockings to dowdy, snuffly women that paw them over and don't know the size they want," Rose answered coldly, a sharp edge in her voice.

Frank stared at her, then pushed aside his unfinished dish of rice pudding and waited nervously until she rose.

"I'm too tired to go to even a movie to-night," he announced, as they stepped from the swinging doors into the cold, snowy street.

"All right, we'll go straight home then." But she drew him around a corner to pass the lighted windows of Woodward Avenue, and paused again and again to study the clothing and jewellery they contained, while he shivered and hunched his shoulders.

She stopped before a rich grey coat of heavy, fur-like cloth, marked as a special post-holiday bargain at $118. "Do you suppose by the time we're fifty we can afford things like that, Frank?" she asked.

He winced, and did not reply.

In their rooms at last, Frank stretched his feet to a radiator. Relaxed and comfortable, he began unthinkingly to talk again about the work of the shop. "It's the limit," he declared. "On my feet nine hours a day without a minute's rest, running back and forth with that cursed junk. If it were something——"

Rose interrupted harshly. Her eyes flashed in her pale face. "Oh, I wish you'd let up on that," she told him. "You talk as though you were the only one that's on his feet all day, or has to do things that are stupid. I've heard enough about it for to-night."

Frank jerked to his feet. His face flushed hotly. A sharp rejoinder crowded to his lips, but he bit it back. He picked up his hat and coat quietly, closed the door behind him, and walked steadily down the stairs.

He felt hot all over. Rose had been needlessly harsh and inconsiderate—oh, well! He felt sick and cheated. He looked back at the long agony of the fall which had preceded his marriage with Rose, and at his present life, and saw little to give satisfaction. He wondered what the future could hold worth waiting for. A mood of

desperate recklessness filled him, and he turned a corner and walked swiftly toward the lower part of the
city.

Blaring music assailed him. He paused before a
large photograph of girls in bathing-suits. He was at
the entrance of the burlesque theatre where he and
Steen had gone the fall before.

The memory of that night rose vividly within him.
Shaken, he stepped into a doorway beside the theatre
and stood quiet for a moment. From the corner near
him the avenues curved away like long golden talons.
He saw hurrying thousands, and it seemed to him that
he and Rose like all of these were caught and impaled
in a huge and torturing trap. His eyes burned.

He crossed the street swiftly, and at a candy store
which he found open bought a little box of chocolates.
Then he took a short cut toward home. His way led
through a dark street of small frame stores and tene-
ments. The biting wind blew snow along the deserted
sidewalk. Behind frosted windows of hash-houses and
pool-halls were noisy voices.

In the wind came a whining cry. On the steps of a
tenement, with dim lights in the upper windows,
crouched a little girl, huddled in a man's ragged coat.
Frank paused beside her, and on an impulse thrust the
small package of candy into the child's lap. The cry
stopped suddenly, and her thin, stupid face, drawn with
cold and bleared by crying, stared up at him.

"It's all right," Frank assured her. "It's candy—
good candy. Eat it."

He hurried on. What a foolish thing to do, he reflected. Everything he had done that night was foolish. At the rooms, he crossed directly to where Rose
was sitting, darning stockings. She looked at him ques-

tioningly. "I'm sorry that I went away, Rose," he told her. "I was a fool. Please forgive me."

She rose and took him in her arms, the stockings dropping to the floor between their feet. "Oh, dear," she said, "it was my fault. We were both too tired——"

"And I was foolish again," he went on. "I got a little candy for you, and then there was a little girl crying down here on the street, and I gave it to her. I'm sorry."

"Oh, don't worry about that, dear. It's you I want." She held him close, his face against her shoulder.

As the winter advanced, Frank found that he was losing weight, and became increasingly tired at the end of each day. Rose, too, was pale, and sat listless and unresponsive while they ate their supper at some noisy cafeteria, and watched a motion picture, or the varied numbers of a vaudeville performance, afterward. Frank was inclined to ascribe these changes in them to restaurant fare, and spoke often of getting a better place to live, where Rose could really keep house and do their own cooking instead of working at the store.

"Wouldn't you like that, dear?" he asked, one evening in February as they were walking home because the night was bright and not too cold. "I ought to get a raise this spring. And anyhow there'll be money coming to me—my money from the estate, you know. We can use some of that."

"I don't know as we ought to use any of that money," she answered dully. "How much will there be?"

"I don't know. Guess I'll write to Henkel about it."

He did write, and received in reply the suggestion that he come to Green Bush for a settlement very soon.

Henkel added the information that as executor he had sold the Thompson home to Finchburg.

"Shall we go, do you think, Rose?" Frank asked that night, after reading her the letter.

"Can we?" she asked, a slight eagerness in her voice. "What about our jobs?"

Frank frowned. "Hang the jobs," he said suddenly. "We can get them again, or something else. Anyway, you ought to get home awhile. You've been needing it."

She turned a tired face toward him. "I would like to see the folks, Frank," she answered simply. "But I'm happy with you, dear. Only, I don't like to see you so tired, and you're getting so thin." She rubbed her hands across his shoulder-blades, and bent his head down for a quick kiss. "I'd like to get you out home and feed you up," she told him.

"Well, we'll go," he decided. "We'll buy a new trunk for our stuff, and give up these rooms at the end of this month. Only three more weeks of stockings and annuals, girlie!" She smiled at him wistfully.

CHAPTER XXV

TO eyes accustomed to factory smoke and the grey streets of Detroit, the country was inexpressibly free and refreshing. Frank and Rose had not confessed their home-sickness to each other. But they sat side by side, watching eagerly, as the little train hurried northward from Bay City. The first, earliest signs of spring were in the land: bloom of willows, touch of green on yellow pastures. Small fields of winter wheat gave here and there strong tones of green. At one little town a child stood on the station platform with a fist full of arbutus. At another a spindle-legged colt followed solemnly after the buggy drawn by his mother down the muddy street. They caught glimpses again and again of the Lake, something almost intolerably alive in its fresh vividness of blue.

As they neared Green Bush, and the first hills they had seen since they left Ann Arbor crowded the track close to the Lake, Frank and Rose turned to each other with shining eyes. "It *is* home, isn't it?" he whispered, and then looked away with sudden, lingering pain as the train rushed by the hill-side cemetery.

At the hotel in Green Bush they were met with a curious, hesitating welcome by the proprietress. To relieve her uncertainty Frank hastened to sign "Mr. and Mrs. Frank Thompson" on the register, where one of her boys had been scrawling a pencil picture of a rooster. A few minutes later he was on his way to the drug store to see Mr. Steele. There was no mistaking his welcome here. The old druggist was busy in his prescription room, and peered through the door a moment before he recognized Frank. Then he limped forward as fast as he could, not saying a word, but his broad hand held out and his fine dark eyes shining with pleasure. "I'm glad to see you, Frank, glad to see you," he said finally. Then he dropped Frank's hand suddenly, turned away, and went behind the counter. He fumbled a moment under the shelves, found an unopened box of cigars of the kind Frank's father had smoked, and pried it open with trembling fingers. "Have some, Frank—take three or four." He had nothing more to say, waiting for Frank to tell what he chose of what he had been doing and of the reason for his being in Green Bush.

As Frank had hoped, Dr. Pratt chanced into the drug store. He hustled past Frank at the counter without noticing him, holding out a prescription blank to the druggist. "Could you put this up while I get some supper, E. J.?" he demanded. "I've got to drive out to Hurt's again to-night. And the clay roads out that way are simply—well!"

He turned, and peering at Frank for the first time, held out his big hairy hand. His grey eyes behind the gold-bowed glasses lit up, and he squeezed Frank's fingers. "How are you—how are you? Why, look at him, E. J.—I'd say it was his father!"

"Yes, I noticed that," said the druggist huskily; and Frank knew why he had turned away so suddenly a few moments before.

The three men chatted a few minutes, the doctor inquiring about Frank's experience in Detroit, and his plans. Frank felt at first a little reserve in the doctor's manner, but it thawed rapidly.

"How is Mr. Finchburg making it, with the *Ga-*

zette?" Frank finally asked, addressing the druggist.

"Why," Mr. Steele answered hesitatingly, looking out the window, "fairly well, I guess."

"He's no newspaper man, Frank," the doctor interjected bluntly. "He's lazy, and people don't like him. He even ran against E. J. here for secretary of the school board—wanted it himself. Of course he got licked, but it didn't make him any friends. It's good you had the paper built up as well as you did, or it would be clear run down by now."

"He puts out a pretty good-looking paper," Frank hazarded; "better than most." The news the doctor had given troubled him more than he liked to admit.

"Yes, he does that," Mr. Steele agreed.

"Well, that kid you had in there before you left does most of the work—that young Dale," the doctor maintained. "He about lives at the shop."

That evening, as Frank and Rose ate their supper in the bare dining-room of the hotel, under the frankly observant eyes of the waitress, Frank was called to the telephone. He heard Mrs. Steele's sweet-toned, quiet voice, inviting him to spend the evening with her and Mr. Steele. "And be sure to bring your wife," she finished. Rose was delighted by the invitation. She dressed with unusual care, and punctually at eight o'clock they started for the Steele home. A clear yellow moonlight filled the sky, and a crisp, clattering rush of waves from the Lake sounded through the quiet town.

It was three hours later when at last they walked briskly away under the budding branches of the maples down the narrow street, empty and silent save for the constant voice of the Lake. "I don't know how much of my estrangement from my mother the Steeles are ig-

norant of, and how much they know and have forgiven,"
Frank remarked.

Rose did not answer. Frank had scarcely spoken of
his mother or his relation to her since that Sunday
night, months before, when he had come to her, and she
had respected his reticence.

"At any rate," he went on, "they are our friends.
They are wonderful people—two of the finest in the
world. I think they would forgive me, even if they
knew it all; and they would hold nothing against you.
Of course, I suppose there aren't many people in Green
Bush who would be so broad-minded about it—possibly
there aren't any others at all. But that doesn't lessen
the significance of these two."

The next morning Frank made a satisfactory beginning at his business arrangements with Mr. Henkel.
From the banker he heard more definite and disquieting
news of Mr. Finchburg's lack of success with the paper.

"He's not a likable man, is the whole trouble,
Frank," Mr. Henkel told him. "He can't get along with
people—has trouble with everybody. And of course
that has a big effect on the business. He's had difficulty
in meeting some of his payments, though the terms were
favourable enough. He seems to be able to get money
from somewhere—his wife's people, I guess—or we
would have had trouble with him before now."

When Frank returned to the hotel, late in the forenoon, Uncle Marion had just driven up with the spring
wagon, and Frank and Rose with their suitcases were
loaded for the trip to the McCune farm.

Uncle Marion was the same hale, jolly old man, with
the nut-brown face fringed with white hair, and his
pleasure at seeing Rose was a delight to Frank. He
kissed her and held her in his arms a moment, then

turned to Frank with a confidence and cordiality which was only a foretaste of the family's welcome to him. From the moment he stepped inside the McCune door he felt that he was at home. Rose's mother embraced him warmly, her eyes bright with tears of happiness. Then the big Scotchman took his hand and squeezed it tight; and there was a moment's silence as they looked into each other's eyes, remembering the summer before. The boy greeted Frank shyly, but his face was shining with happiness.

Dinner was waiting for them, and in a few minutes they were eating. Frank had developed a prodigious appetite during the long, cold ride, and he ate with a heartiness that almost alarmed him. Rose rallied him laughingly, while her mother and Uncle Marion reproved her and heaped his plate again.

After dinner he felt drowsy, but followed Rose at the boy's invitation to see his pet rabbits, one of which had young, in the pens behind the house. Soon he was tramping about with the men, looking at the stock— small, scrubby milk cows and fine, fat horses—and watching the feeding and the early milking. Before he went in for supper he split a big armful of maple wood at the pile near the house, and went staggering into the kitchen under its weight.

The evening was spent in talk, much of which was cryptical to Frank, as it concerned neighbours and affairs of the settlement of which he knew nothing except the little that Rose had told him. Mrs. McCune and Uncle Marion were equally voluble, and Rose surprised him in her capacity for eager, light-hearted talk. Her father and the boy listened silently. Only once did McCune vouchsafe a comment. Uncle Marion had just remarked: "The Moore place's for sale again, Rose."

"Is that so?"

"Yes, I heard about it on the way out to Green Bush to-day. The old lady's died, an' that young Moore's no shakes at all. It's that place over beyond the clay knolls," he explained to Frank, "with the house partly built. You an' Rose better buy it an' go to farmin'," he added jokingly.

There was a moment of silence, in which the eyes of Frank and Rose met swiftly in a brief, intuitive exchange of emotion. Into the silence came McCune's quiet voice: "Well, it's a pretty fair piece of land."

When Rose and Frank were alone that night in the little blue-walled room with the walnut bed and the gay-blocked quilt, Frank found himself prodigiously sleepy. But the sleepiness was only a part of a completely released and happy peace of mind, a warm joyousness that enveloped him. Rose was at once gay and tender as he had never seen her before. "Do you know, Frank," she told him softly, "I feel as if we had just been married, an' this was our honeymoon."

There came to him with sudden biting pain the tragic intensity of their first night together, the maddened sensitiveness which he had brought to her for healing, and the spareness and hard artificiality of their life in the months that were past. He realized all at once how she had been cheated—they had both been cheated —of the accustomed irresponsible surrender to the love and joy of life together.

"We'll pretend it *is* our honeymoon," he told her. "We'll forget all these months that are past, and really begin to live now." He took her in his arms.

The next morning they talked about the Moore place while they were dressing in the frosty room. "Let's go over and look at it this morning," Frank suggested.

"It's a great morning for a walk. I'll have to go back to town to-morrow to settle up with Henkel."

They walked briskly down the sandy road in the cool sunlight, past the little lake, deep blue and ruffled with waves that were tipped with brightness, and up a short, steep hill to the edge of the old clearing. The grey walls of the unfinished house bulked sharply against the azure sky. The clean, carefully laid logs were all of a size, and the door and window openings had been framed with clean dressed lumber. Evidently the plan had been for three rooms—a large kitchen and living-room, and two smaller sleeping-rooms. All stood open to the sky, and clean dead grass was long between the sills.

Frank and Rose explored the unfinished dwelling, then turned their attention to the land itself. The house stood back some hundred and fifty feet from the road, near the centre of the small clearing which was the only part of the farm that had ever been ploughed. This clearing, some two or three acres in extent, was spotted with big pine stumps, black against the dun of the grass, and fringed with the brush and saplings of second growth. It, and the thirty or forty acres of "the Moore place" adjacent to it, were of a light, sandy soil on the surface. But the presence of the large stumps of white pine, and the abundance of poplar and birch in the second growth, indicated that a clay subsoil was not too far down.

Farther back, as Frank and Rose advanced from the road, the character of the soil changed suddenly and surprisingly. On one hand a gentle even slope, clothed with second growth of increasing size and density, swept back to a ragged fringe of big hardwood trees against the sky-line—the sure sign of rich land. On the other hand a deep glen with precipitous clay sides led down to a little lake—a tiny gem of bright blue water, fringed by young trees of cedar, birch, swamp maple, spruce and tamarack, and enclosed by steep, wooded slopes.

Frank uttered an exclamation of surprise as they came within sight of the lake, and stopped abruptly. "What lake is that?" he asked.

"Some call it Lost Lake," Rose answered, "because it's so hard to find. I used to call it Jewel Lake," she added. "I used to come back here after the cows."

"Your place is right over there?" Frank pointed to the south-west.

"Yes—only about a mile across. Spruce Lake is just over the hardwood ridge there—the larger lake you saw last summer. It has a big swamp at the north end, you know. But the cows come around the south end." Her face clouded, then cleared. "You know, Frank," she declared, "I don't believe papa will ever get into such trouble again. And he'll never forget what you did for him. My, the folks like you, Frank," she added. "I'm so glad."

He smiled at her. "I'm glad too," he answered, "because I like them." He turned toward the lake. "I like your name for it," he said; "we'll call it that. It's a beautiful, beautiful thing. It's deep, I suppose?"

"Oh, yes—and fed by springs. There's a spring right down in this hollow. Let's go down to it."

She ran down a faintly marked cow-path, and he followed exultantly her sure-footed, buoyant progress. In a cedar thicket near the foot of a huge live pine they found the spring—a shallow basin of perfectly clear water that shone like topaz in a narrow band of sunlight against the brown leaf-mould.

Rose knelt and drank, lifting the water to her lips in cupped hands. "It could be cleaned out and curbed and make a fine spring," she suggested practically.

"I wish it were up by the house," he answered earnestly. Then both laughed at their seriousness. "Shall we buy this place and go to farming, Rose?" Frank challenged her.

"What do you think of the land?" she parried.

"I like the looks of that." He waved his hand toward the gentle slope which led up to the fringe of hardwoods. "There must be great soil there. And that where the house is would be productive if it were properly handled." His face grew grave, and Rose, watching him, knew that he was thinking of his father.

"Do you think you *want* to farm, Frank?" she asked gently. "Seems as if there are so many other things that you could do—big things, out in the world. Would you be happy here?"

"I'd be happy anywhere with you, dear," he answered impulsively, as his eyes turned to her tender, serious face. He caught her hand and pressed it against his lips. "And I have a suspicion that I'd be happiest here. *You'd* be happiest here, wouldn't you, Rose?" he added.

"We mustn't think of that," she answered—"not first of all. I would be happy here—I like it here. But I will be happiest wherever you are happy, dear. You know that." She laid her hand on his arm, and looked up steadily into his eyes.

He turned away after a moment, and they walked together down toward the edge of the little lake. The stream from the spring fell into the lake with a low, pleasant purling, and near it was a sandy place, marked by hoofs, where the cattle had come down to drink.

"Let's see if I can find the way home across this way," Rose suggested—"or would you rather go back by the road?"

"No, I think it would be fun to go this way." They skirted the lake by a trail that ran now through thickets of poplar and alder as tall as a man on horseback and now came out by bits of open marsh where they could see the lake beyond the brown band of grass. Presently Rose turned up a hollow which ran back away from the lake past the end of the fringe of hardwoods, and after an easy climb they came out suddenly within sight of the McCune clearing. Rose laughed triumphantly. "Of course I knew the way," she said. "It's only a couple of years since I drove cows here. But it seems so much longer than that."

Dinner was ready when they returned. When the meal was finished and McCune was filling his pipe, Frank addressed him. "What do you think of this Moore place? Rose and I are thinking seriously of buying it." He caught Mrs. McCune's surprised, delighted look before the Scotchman answered.

"Well," he said, "of course the one forty is rough—all cut up by the lake. And so is part of the other back forty. But there's a fine strip of land running up to the hardwoods there—thirty or forty acres of it, I'd say. The front of the place along the road is pretty light."

"I'd guess it nearer fifty acres of clay, Neal," Uncle Marion began argumentatively. "The plains don't run back over twenty rods on the west line, does it? I remember when we brushed through there for Moore."

"It ain't rightly plains anyway, Marion," Mrs. McCune interposed. "I've heard you say yourself there wa'n't a foot of plains on the Moore place."

Frank smiled to himself.

"What does young Moore want for it, did you hear?" he asked Uncle Marion.

"He asts fifteen hundred for the quarter-section," the old man replied. "But he'd shade that a good bit—specially if he got consider'ble ready cash in the deal. You know'm, don't you?"

"Yes, I've seen him around the pool-hall." Frank remembered the fellow's pale blue eyes and pimply, vacant face.

"Well, Rose, what do you think?" He turned to her questioningly.

"I'm afraid Frank might not like farming, if he really got into it," Rose answered, speaking to the others rather than to Frank. "He hasn't really farmed. And he has such a good education—it seems like he ought to use it."

McCune rose and began to draw on his heavy jacket. "Would you care to see the corners of it this afternoon, Frank," he asked—"run the lines roughly? Then you could see exactly what it is."

"Yes, I would like to," Frank answered.

McCune got out his surveying instrument with its buckskin hood, and Uncle Marion brought a bag of red-flagged metal stakes from the woodshed. The three men and the boy set out together. "Don't you want to go along, Rose?" Frank asked her.

"No, I know the land anyway. I'll visit with mamma."

"Neal can carry the chain as well as anyone," his father remarked, as the boy ran on ahead. "You can follow along with me. We'll just run the west line through the hardwoods. That will show you how much

clay land there is. And I know where the line on the
other side is. It runs about fifteen rods from the east
edge of the lake, back to the section corner."

They walked around the road to the corner of the
Moore place, and McCune soon found the stake he had
left when he had surveyed the place before. He set up
his instrument and in a few minutes was able to point
out to Frank a faint groove in the even surface of the
second growth running back to the edge of the hardwoods. "That's the line we brushed through before," he
explained. "You couldn't see it, probably, when the
leaves are on. We won't need to chain through there,
Marion," he added, consulting a little leather-bound
book of field notes. "That big beech is right on the line,
and it's fourteen chains four links to this edge of it.
We'll set up again there and then go through to the corner." He hooded the instrument, slung it over his shoulder, and set off briskly through the second growth, the
others following. The boy and Uncle Marion seemed a
bit disappointed, Frank thought.

When they reached the big beech Frank could see
the blaze clearly on its smooth grey trunk, some ten
feet up. McCune set his instrument beside the tree and
sighted into the woods ahead. He indicated a tree some
distance away, and the boy and Uncle Marion began
chaining toward it. When he was satisfied that they
were proceeding in a line straight enough for his purpose, McCune took up the instrument again, and he and
Frank followed slowly.

The second growth gave place suddenly to larger
trees, and a few rods brought them into a bit of the original hardwood forest. Great trunks ran up straight
and clean to vaulted boughs and a delicate tracery of
twigs against the sharply blue sky. Beneath their feet

was a heavy matting of fallen leaves, rich umber and cinnamon, sodden now with the moisture of the recent thaws and holding still in a hollow here and there a bit of snow. The ground was almost free of undergrowth, and they moved easily through a spacious calm that had something religious and mystical about it. Frank was silent. "It's nice up here, eh?" McCune said quietly, as he paused to shift his instrument to the other shoulder.

"Yes, it surely is." Frank paused for a moment and let the older man precede him, until the soft footfalls died away, and he stood for a moment in the utter hush of the woods.

There was no doubt in his mind when he returned to the house that night. "I think we should buy it," he told Rose when they were alone after supper. "It is worth the money as an advertisement; and I'll have at least three thousand in cash when I settle up with Henkel. We can buy it for twelve or thirteen hundred probably, complete the house, build a barn and stock up, and still have a little to go on besides the payments from the paper. I feel it would kill me to go back to Detroit or Ann Arbor now, Rose. A year or two out here will put me on my feet and give us a chance to decide what we want to do. I believe we'll want to stay here."

Uncle Marion took him to town in the buggy the next day—a slow drive over muddy roads, for it had rained in the night. When he returned in the evening he brought a deed to the land.

CHAPTER XXVI

SOMEWHAT to Frank's surprise, Henkel had seemed favourable to the purchase from the start. He knew the land; in fact, his bank held a mortgage on it. And Frank wondered if the chance for the collection of this debt had anything to do with the banker's attitude toward the deal. Moore was summoned, and consented readily enough to part with his hundred and sixty acres for twelve hundred dollars cash. In accordance with his practice in dealing with such gentry as Moore, the banker gathered those to whom he knew the fellow owed money, and saw that their claims were paid before the money was handed over to him. Among these was Dr. Pratt; and his pleased surprise at Frank's investment was a great encouragement to the boy. "A year or two on the farm will be the best thing in the world for you, Frank," he declared. "And anyway we want you to stay around here." When the deal was completed and the land was his, Frank still had nearly two thousand dollars of the money which had been left from his father's life insurance and had accrued from the payments on the paper and the house which Finchburg had bought. And there were still some three thousand dollars to be paid by Finchburg, in instalments over a term of years.

When Frank and Uncle Marion got home, almost at sundown, the old man could scarcely take time to unhitch and stable the team, so great was his eagerness to get in the house and tell the news. They met McCune at the door, coming out with the milk-pails. "Neal, he's bought it!" the old man cried.

McCune set down the pails and wrung Frank's hand. "I'm glad," he said gruffly. "We'll be glad to have you here." Behind McCune in the door were Rose and her mother, and the deep joy which Frank saw in their faces drove away the vague doubts which had assailed him on the homeward drive. For the first time he sensed the strength of the bond which bound Rose to her kin and her home. And he felt ready to surrender himself to the same ties.

The boy capered spontaneously about the living-room, shouting shrilly: "Hooray, hooray, hooray! Rose and Frank is going to live here by us!" Frank! It seemed good to have a brother, even a very noisy and irresponsible one.

After the supper, that was like a banquet, Frank recounted the details of the purchase to his eager audience, and then asked for advice as to what to do first. Should he buy stock, machinery, order seed?

"Oh, we want to fix up the house the *first* thing, Frank," Rose cried.

"You can just as well stay here," her mother protested. "It'll soon be seedin'-time, an' if you go at the house Frank can't get ground ready."

"Rose is right," said her father decisively. "They're welcome here, of course. But it's some distance to go back and forth. And your work never seems to count till you're really on the land. We can get La Forgue to help with the plastering, and if we all go at it we can have that house ready in a few days. You'll want a cellar under it, won't you, Frank? That would be the first thing——"

McCune's plan was carried out. The next day the

three men set out in the McCune wagon with spades, shovels, axes, and a wheelbarrow. The digging was easy in the sandy soil, except where a little frost lingered along the north wall. At noon Rose drove over in the buggy, bringing them a hot lunch in covered vessels packed in a box of hay, and tin plates from which to eat.

As they worked, Frank marvelled at McCune's strength and Uncle Marion's dexterity. In a short time they had made an opening under the sill at one end of the house and placed an incline so that the barrow could be used, and the earth went out rapidly to lie in yellow piles ready for the subsequent "banking" of the house. At a depth of about four feet they struck a hard, greyish sand, and some eighteen inches under this the tough red clay. This Uncle Marion declared to be rare good luck. He showed Frank how by tamping the clay with a slight mixture of sand a smooth hard floor could be produced, resembling cement, but resilient. "That will keep the cream cool for Rose," he declared. "She can set her jars right on the cellar floor."

That evening and the next forenoon, at the McCune place, Uncle Marion set about squaring and dressing cedar posts for the walls of the cellar at "Frank's place," as they called it. Frank was set at hauling these with the McCune team and wagon, and he welcomed the change, for the work of the preceding day had exhausted him. The cellar was soon completed. McCune secured from a neighbour, at a low price, the rough lumber which would be needed for rafters, joists, and sheeting, and he and Uncle Marion put up this part of the building while Frank made two trips to the sawmill at Wilberville for flooring and shingles. The windows, doors, and hardware he hauled from Green Bush, together with lime for the plastering, and brick for a chimney. La Forgue was secured to help with the building of the chimney and the plastering, and he also assisted in fitting the doors and windows and laying the floor. In a few days the house was completed. New white plaster filled the chinks between the clean grey logs. Mrs. McCune and Rose polished the windows and scrubbed the new floors.

Then came the day when Frank and Rose drove to Green Bush to buy supplies for their new home: staple groceries, a kitchen table and two chairs, a broom, plain dishes. "We can get fancy things later, Frank," Rose insisted. When Frank suggested buying a cheap "bedroom set," Rose said that her mother wanted to furnish the bedroom. Their only extravagances were the best kitchen range the stores in Green Bush afforded, and a shining kitchen cabinet. Rose was delighted with the cabinet, and kept looking back as they drove slowly homeward to see that no accident befell it.

The trading had taken a long time, and it was dark when they reached the new house. Frank was surprised to see a light in the window. "We'll drive in," Rose said, suppressed excitement in her voice.

They found the McCunes and Uncle Marion there— and a bright lamp and a new clock on the shelf, woven rugs on the clean maple floors, and, in the bedroom, the low walnut bed and washstand Frank had liked so well, a splint-bottomed chair made by Uncle Marion, supplies of hand-sewed linen, and pillows filled with goose feathers. On shelves in the cellar were scores of jars of canned fruits and glasses of jellies, and hanging from the beams were home-cured hams and sides of bacon.

In a bin at one side were potatoes, carrots, turnips, and onions.

Frank did not know what to say. "You—you are too good to us," he stammered.

"We hadn't much chance to do for you when you were married," Mrs. McCune told him. "So this is really just a wedding present. We're *so* happy to be doing it!"

It was the work of only a few minutes to unload the new things and pile them in the kitchen. Uncle Marion had kindling ready, and in a little while a fire was burning brightly in the new stove. The blacking made an abominable smell as it grew hot, and drove them all out of doors, choking and laughing. But they soon returned, and presently they sat on improvised seats around the new kitchen table to eat the first meal in the new house—composed chiefly of fried chicken, cakes and pies brought by Mrs. McCune, but with tea and potatoes prepared on the new stove.

Finally the McCunes drove away in the dim moonlight, the boy curled up on a pile of blankets in the back of the wagon and Uncle Marion smoking placidly beside him. Frank and Rose were alone in the new house. They worked for a while arranging things in the kitchen —putting groceries and cooking-utensils in their proper places in the kitchen cabinet, washing the dishes. But Rose was very tired, and soon Frank urged that they wait until morning to do more.

The little bedroom was sweet with the fragrance of new lumber. Through the open window, when the light was out, they could see under the dim moonlight the outlines of their clearing, and vaguely the contours of their land beyond, clear to the line of hardwoods, shadowy and lovely.

"It's ours, our own," they whispered to each other; and they fell asleep warmed by the emotion bred in them by hundreds of generations of home-loving, earth-loving men and women.

CHAPTER XXVII

THE next day was Sunday, and Frank and Rose spent the forenoon in walking about the clearing, deciding on locations for stable, chicken-coop, kitchen garden, orchard, and potato patch, and planning their work for the week to follow. At noon they walked to the McCunes' for dinner. They borrowed seed catalogues and lists of nursery stock, and with Uncle Marion's help Frank made out a list of the tools and implements he would need to buy. Some of the more expensive machines, which would be needed only for seasonal work, he could borrow from the Mc-Cunes—as mowing-machine, grain drill, and so forth. But he must have a plough, a harrow, a wagon, and a supply of axes, chains, spades, grubbing-hoes, and similar tools for clearing.

"But first of all you must have a team," Uncle Marion concluded. "And before you buy a team you must have a place to put 'em. Neal and I'll come over in the mornin' an' help you rig up some kind o' a stable. There's a sale in by Wilberville the day after to-morrow, 'n some horses advertised. You might pick up a lot o' this stuff up there. We'll take you in if you like. Then you can go out to Green Bush for the rest."

That evening Frank and Rose spent poring over seed catalogues, with their alluring pictures and glowing descriptions. They ordered seed of peas and beans, radishes and lettuce and sweet corn, and a dozen other vegetables for their garden. And Rose wanted petunias

and calliopsis, zinnias and marigolds and portulaca—
"annuals that will grow fast and give us flowers this
first year," she explained. She added pansies for a bed
by her kitchen window.

The next morning McCune and Uncle Marion were on
hand before Frank had finished breakfast. They led
the way into the swamp adjacent to the little lake and
cut a score of large dead cedar and tamarack trees,
which were close enough to the edge to be dragged out
with a long chain. By noon these were at the site
chosen for the barn; and by nightfall they had been cut
into lengths, laid up for the rough walls of a small
square stable, and the enclosure partially roofed with
some old lumber which the men had brought with them
in the wagon. Enough was done to provide a shelter
for a team until Frank could build something better.

Bright and early the next morning Uncle Marion and
Frank, with Rose and her mother, started for the sale
near Wilberville. They took the large wagon rather
than the "democrat" in which such trips were usually
made, in the thought that Frank might buy something
which could be brought home.

The morning was cool and bright. A boisterous wind
blew over the blue hills beyond Wilberville and drove
shouting through the brush and timber, sending last
year's leaves scuttling before it. "It will be warm before night," Uncle Marion prophesied. "Spring will
open up fast now."

Frank had never before attended one of these country auctions, and he found it of very keen interest. It
was a social event of considerable importance, he per-
ceived. Farmers from miles around, with their wives
and children, gathered around the bleak little black
shanty by the edge of a swamp, where the sale was to

take place. Children scuffled on the yellow grass under the budded apple-trees. Men stood about in little groups with their hands in their pockets, talking briefly, or examined the implements and animals which were to be offered for sale. The women crowded into the house; but they were all out again, clustered about the auctioneer on the narrow back stoop, when the selling began, for kitchen utensils and household articles were sold first: a bracket lamp without a chimney, for ten cents; frying-pans for a quarter; a granite tea-kettle for fifteen cents; and so on.

The auctioneer was a tall, stooped man, with a narrow weather-beaten face, a scraggly neck, and protruding china-blue eyes one of which was half shaded by a drooping lid. His ordinary voice was a slow, nasal drawl; but he conducted the selling in a high, piping sing-song which was monotonously musical in effect. He interspersed the selling with a constant flow of banter and repartee.

"Here, now, everybody, here's a nice chiney wash-bowl an' pitcher, with flowers on it—how much am I bid? How much for the chiney wash-bowl and pitcher? *Waal, Sal McAlpin, don't you never wash yer face?* Start it, somebody, bid somethin', I don't care how much or how little jist so it's somethin'; nice chiney wash-bowl and pitcher; *come-on-an' bid on it, Penny, the women likes these sort o' things—maybe you can get a woman to match*—ten cents from Penny Rohrbacker— ten cents I'm bid——"

He stopped with an expression of complete surprise at the roar of guffaws which greeted this joke on the confirmed bachelor of the neighbourhood.

When the tools were offered, Frank bought a post-hole auger and a pitchfork, and was about to bid again when Uncle Marion drew him aside. "Just wink me off what you want, Frank," he whispered, "an' I'll buy it cheaper'n you will. Some o' these fellers likes to run things up on a new feller." Frank had noticed this himself, in bidding for a log chain which he had finally let go, to the chagrin of his opponent. The rest of his buying was done through Uncle Marion, to considerably better advantage. The old man was a shrewd bidder, well known to the auctioneer and to most of those present, and was able to buy things at the lowest possible prices.

Somewhat to his surprise Frank acquired a wagon for thirty dollars, a set of harness for twenty, and, finally, the team of old horses, one for thirty dollars and the other for forty-five. He had liked one of the horses from the moment he saw him—a spirited fellow for all his years of hard work and harness-galls, with wideset, prominent eyes and small, pony-like ears. The other horse, larger and older, seemed stolid and dependable. The young man who was selling out—a renter who was going to work at Flint—seemed to feel some little real affection for the team. "They're good an' true, both o' 'em," he told Frank. "I've worked 'em hard an' they've never laid down on me a minute!"

At last the sale was over. Rose had bought a crate of miscellaneous hens and three ducks, and Frank had secured a small quantity of seed oats. They paid the bill, loaded their new possessions into the wagon Frank had bought, and drove away behind Uncle Marion, the chains and tools rattling, the ducks quacking loudly, and the old horses stepping out briskly as if glad to be setting forth on a new adventure. When they were out of sight of the small crowd left at the sale-ground, Frank drew Rose to his side and kissed her. It was a happy ride home together, through the chill dusk over the winding miles of trail.

The next day there was a chicken-coop to build, a bin to fix for the oats. Other small, important tasks followed. But within the week Frank had brought a new plough and harrow, with a load of other supplies, from Green Bush, and was ready to begin the preparation of the ground for the garden.

This first ploughing of the new land was a noteworthy experience for Frank. They had chosen for the garden a plot of ground west of the house, part of which had been included in the original clearing, but most of which was virgin soil. Second growth had covered this unploughed part, but a brush fire the spring before had run into it for a little way here, and the dead saplings were standing leafless, while amongst them the bronzy shoots of new sprouts were beginning to appear.

Frank had found that these dead saplings were easily knocked over with an ax, and that their trunks made excellent firewood, while the twigs and smaller branches were useful as kindling. By the time he was ready for the ploughing, the space for the garden was cleared of the second growth. There were some large pine stumps in the space they had set apart, but it seemed better to leave these and work around them for a year than to take time to remove them.

The first furrow went well enough in the old clearing; but in the new soil the roots of the fire-killed saplings, still alive in the ground, caught the plough and made it jerk unevenly, or tumbled the soil back into the furrow behind it. Sometimes the point of the plough would catch under a root of one of the pine stumps, and then it was necessary for Frank to wrench and drag its weight back, and press down on the handles until the root was passed. It was hard, heavy work, demanding the utmost strength of every muscle of his body. But the old team, accustomed to work in new land, was patient and careful; and in spite of aching back and arms and blistered hands and feet, Frank got through the job. He drove out of the garden when sunset was flaming beyond the hardwoods, and turned with a strange, new pride to look at his work: crooked, uneven furrows, bits of tenacious brush sticking up here and there; but ploughed, ready for the harrow and the seed, ready for use. He looked at the plough, its brave red and green splotched with earth and marred by stumps and brambles, but its share and lay and coulter polished, smoother to the touch than silk, brighter than silver.

Earth and the plough: an exultant sense of kinship with elemental things—of self-sufficing strength and conquest—filled him as he drove the horses to the barn, unharnessed and fed them, and walked stiffly to the house where Rose's lamp shone from the window. And she, seeing the firm set of his tired mouth and the light in his eyes when he entered, understood without the need of words; and crossing swiftly to him, kissed him before she poured warm water for his face and hands and placed their steaming supper on the table.

CHAPTER XXVIII

WITH a swiftness almost incomprehensible, summer followed the slow spring into the land. Trilliums and dog-toothed violets succeeded the arbutus and hepaticas where Frank was working at his clearing. The three cows he had purchased found abundant pasture on the marshes and slopes around the little lake. Frank was incredibly busy—building fences, clearing and ploughing more land for a crop of peas and oats for winter feed—sowing the seed, following the harrow back and forth, back and forth over the uneven ground.

As he came in from the field he would find Rose working in the garden. She spent long hours in smoothing the ground after the harrow left it and raking from it the remaining bits of root so that it would form a comparatively firm and even seed-bed. Then one evening after an early supper she and Frank planted most of the garden seeds together—he making drills in the soft soil with a hoe, and she following to plant the seed, one knee on the earth, her hand tracing the furrow. Above them august colours of sunset brightened and faded. The budded hardwoods were outlined sheerly against the west. When the work was finished Rose straightened herself wearily enough, and smiled at Frank. They walked slowly toward the little house, their earth-browned hands clasped firmly.

On a warm morning in early May, Frank came in

from the clearing to find Rose standing beside a little coop which she had placed in the sunshine near the house. On the board at the front of the coop, yellow fluffs of chicks squatted and blinked at the light, or tottered precariously into the shallow water dish. "What do you think of our first young live stock?" Rose greeted him as they went into the house together.

The meals of these days were important and much enjoyed events. The food was simple—bread and cured meat, vegetables, and canned fruit given them by Mrs. McCune, with milk from their own cows, and butter Rose made with her own hands. But the food was well cooked and abundant, and Frank experienced a simple, fundamental joy in it such as he had never known before. They would eat slowly, with much talk of the day's work and of immediate hopes and plans. From week to week Frank's body grew stronger and more robust; and it seemed to him that he grew in other ways as well.

Rose developed too, subtly and profoundly. Frank found in her new depths and richnesses of personality, new capacities for fun and tenderness and endurance. And they were both happy, in a way that made all their earlier association seem as remote and fabulous as an evil dream. On Sundays they made excursions to the woods and swamps, finding strange new flowers—twinflower and pitcher-plant and the glorious showy lady-slipper—and marvelling at the variety and beauty of moths and butterflies and birds. For the rest of each week they were utterly absorbed in the demands of the season, pitting their strength day by day against the soil and the sun and wind and rain for the making of food for themselves and their own; and they gloried in it. They rose at sunrise and worked till dark or after;

ate largely, slept soundly, laughed much; and grew brown and strong and sound.

"I wish Steen could see me now," Frank remarked one day in early summer, when the rural mail-carrier brought them a card in Steen's writing from Stratford-on-Avon.

"Don't you wish you were with him at Stratford?" Rose asked him.

"Not for one minute. This suits me. Well, what's for dinner to-day, old Rosy girl?"

With his team and wagon Frank helped the McCunes make hay, receiving hay in payment for his services. Late in the summer he hired Uncle Marion to mow for him the marsh near the road, where he had first seen Rose and her father working; and he and Rose hauled the fragrant, sharp-bladed grass to their barn. This marsh, on land belonging to a lumber company, was regarded as common property, and sometimes one neighbour cut it, sometimes another. This year no one else cared for it. "It will feed our horses this winter," Frank told Rose. And he enjoyed loading and hauling the sweet-smelling stuff; it was heavy to handle and difficult to keep on the wagon, but by this time Frank had developed strength that surprised him, so that he could pitch big forkfuls with comparative ease. And Rose was expert at building the load.

They talked or were silent, as the mood fitted, in this work together, for there was no need of talk between them. Sometimes as they drove slowly with a load from the marsh toward home Frank looked consideringly at Rose sitting at ease on the hay beside him, and wondered of what she was thinking as she gazed off toward the distant blue hills in the west. She remained essentially mysterious to him, for all her nearness. She was

daily more beautiful and more dear, but at times inscru-
table, filled with a maturing and tender wisdom in which
he had no part.

On cool and cloudy days in August, when the foretaste of fall was already in the air, Frank went into the
big second growth near the hardwood timber to clear
land for a large field which he meant to plough the next
year. He would rise early, to milk the cows while the
cold yellow sunlight was level across the barn-lot. He
would turn them out and hear the bells go jangling
slowly away toward the lake while he carried the milk
to the house and strained it. Then he would grind his
ax, the squeaking stone clattering against the hard steel,
while the smell of pancakes and coffee from the kitchen
window sharpened his hunger. He would enter, drink
deeply of the fresh spring water in the tin bucket,
and sit down to his meal with Rose—cool and bright
and lovely in a fresh dress, her blue eyes richly alive
in her brown, full-blooded face, as she talked and
ate.

There was the brisk walk to the slashing, past the
garden, opulent now with its bright tomatoes and
squashes, its rows of beets and carrots and beans, and
the stream of colour down the middle where Rose had
planted her flower seeds; past the field where the peas
and oats he had sowed were growing luxuriantly, the
oats in dark green head, and the peas with pods full-
formed at the bases of the vines, but sprinkled with
white and purple blossoms at the tips.

In the slashing the dew was still heavy on leaves and
twigs, and came spattering down in big drops as he
struck his first blow at the base of a young poplar.
Birdcalls rang through the stillness, butterflies and
moths hovered over bronzed leaves in the cool sun.

Rhythm of ax-blows filled the space of the slashing—
flash and sweep of blade, crack of yielding wood. There
was tremble and hush of the young tree severed, swoop
and crash of its fall. Poplar, basswood, wild cherry,
maple, beech and ash and ironwood and birch, he cut
them down, trimmed out the straight poles for firewood,
threw the tops, with brush and undergrowth and fallen
logs of the older forest, into huge heaps to burn.

As he worked alone through the long forenoons,
Frank thought of the significance of what he was doing.
He seemed the sole variable factor in a vast equation of
natural forces, swinging the irresistible productive force
of this fragment of the earth from one channel over into
another, more useful for mankind. He saw himself as
at once the destroyer and the creator, ending now life-
chains of tree and fern that had held this soil since the
glaciers left it, and putting in their place another chain
—of legume and cereal and grass, and sheep and kine,
that might last there for other untold thousands of
years. Memory of poems he had loved came into his
mind: bits of Whitman—The Song of Occupations,
Song of the Broad Ax—and he saw how all the work-
ers of the earth—farmers and artisans and mechanics—
joined in a stupendous harmony of productive labour in
which he had a part. He remembered Moody:

"Jill-o'er-the-ground is purple-blue,
Blue is the quaker-maid,
The alder-clump where the brook comes through
Breeds cresses in its shade.
To be out of the moiling street
With its swelter and its sin!
Who has given to me this sweet,
And given my brother dust to eat?
And when will his wage come in?"

And his heart was filled with a bitter and generous grief for the millions of the cities, for his fellow workmen in Detroit and in all the vast, complex modern world of industry, and a wish that they could know the joy of this work, under the blue of sky, with bird-song and fragrant winds from the hardwoods, their own land beneath their feet and their own food to reward the labour of their hands.

Beauty was all about him, he well knew, and hourly he slew beauty—the crushed wing of moth or butterfly, the uprooted fern or flower, the felled smooth trunks of little trees. He loved them all, and yet he destroyed them. As he worked he made a little song for these trees he sacrificed.

> "I remember
> Virginal birches—
> Sweet white trunks and twinkling leaves,
> Dancers in sunlight, in rain and wind.
>   Withered, brown,
>   Ready for the dance of fire.
> I see wide fields,
> I hear the murmur of bees in clover,
> And the laughter of brown children."

As he worked on and on, he came at last to realize how small and transient were all the effects of this so painful and exacting labour of his hands. He saw himself as but the earlier agent of a destruction which wind and lightning and decay must otherwise have wrought at last. And he realized that if his hands or other hands that might follow his should be stayed soon or late, trees would grow here again, and the wilderness would cover all the traces of his labour. He saw that to him as to the trees he slew there was but one law—the law of earth, ancient and inescapable—live, and destroy to live, and be destroyed to make other life.

He worked more soberly and steadfastly, and paused sometimes to contemplate the beauty that he squandered.

September came, a season of gorgeous profusion of colour—gold and crimson spilled in infinite prodigality over the wooded hills. The new clearing that Frank had done had opened the land from their house to the westward, so that now they could see beyond their field to mile on mile of rolling woodland, fold on fold of colour, bounded against the sky-line by a long low line of hills. Evening after evening they watched the sunset there, the swift passage of a world of coloured light; not without exaltation of spirit, though their shoes were stained with the dung of stable and cow-lot and their hands were rough and hard with toil.

Frank had made one acquisition which Uncle Marion had not approved. He had taken "on trial" from a neighbour who "could not make it work," a large cable-and-drum stump-puller. If he liked it, he was to pay the owner half what the machine had cost. If he did not, he was to return it without any payment.

"Them things is dangerous," Uncle Marion told him. "Pete's afraid of it—that's why he don't want it. You'd better 'a' built yerself a tripod, like ours." But Frank had read of the cable machines in his farm magazines, and was confident that they were better for his work.

By October he had finished the slashing and piling on the five-acre patch he meant to plough the next spring, and had burned the brush and hauled the firewood into a huge pile by the house, ready for sawing. Then he dragged the stump-puller into the land and set to work. He "anchored" the puller to a large pine

stump with a short, heavy cable, hitched the old team to
the long braced sweep which turned the drum, and attached the draught cable to a smaller poplar stump.
It came out easily—the horses hardly tightened the
cable. A young birch gave the same result. An ash
offered more resistance, and finally broke at the ground
line. By this time Frank's new strength was almost
exhausted by the labour of dragging the excessively
heavy cable, and his hands were rasped and bleeding.
Rose came out to see the work.

"I don't believe you need the puller for these stubs,
Frank," she suggested kindly. "Just hitch the team on
them with a chain."

Frank tried this plan, and found it a much easier way
of disposing of the smaller stumps, knee-high and as
large as his arm. Soon he had the clearing dotted with
piles of these, each with its spreading roots. A few he
was compelled to leave in the ground, as they broke
where the chain was attached. Others broke at the
ground line. The young trees had been thick: it seemed
to Frank that he wrested his new land only yard by
yard, even foot by foot, from the wilderness. And he
was still leaving the largest of the green stumps and the
huge pines—the worst of all.

Finally he was ready to hitch to the puller again for
this final task. The machine was a powerful one, and
pulled some of the large stumps unaided. And with the
smaller ones out of the way, he made better progress
than he had anticipated. But moving the machine
from one place to another was a laborious process, and
each time he dragged the heavy cable out to its full
length he swore at the weight of the thing.

He found that some of the stumps required chopping
of certain bracing roots, and that this could be best ac-

complished while the cable was taut, with the strain
on the stump. There was a ratchet on the drum of the
machine which was designed to catch and hold it in any
position, as the horses could not be expected to stand
and hold the excessive strain of the cable while the
driver left them to do his chopping. But this ratchet
did not work properly, and, though he had been warned
to stay away from the machine while it was pulling, he
found it necessary repeatedly to go in behind the sweep
to set the ratchet.

On a warm, still morning in mid-October, when the
air was rich with the smoky smell of autumn and frost
lay thick in the hollows, he was working on a slight
slope, about half-way across the clearing, pulling a
large pine stump. The horses, pulling downward on
the slope, had more than the usual strain on the sweep
when he decided that he must chop a brace root; and,
holding the lines and speaking to the team to make them
hold their position, he started in behind the sweep to
set the ratchet. Out of the tail of his eye he saw the
horses suddenly lunge forward, as though falling. And
at the same instant a crashing, intolerable pain filled
his side and back, and blackness swept over him.

When he regained consciousness he saw Rose's face,
blanched and frightened, above him, and knew that he
was lying on the ground. He was aware of prickling
discomfort in his back and hip, and moved slightly.
Instantly he lost consciousness again.

Hours later he opened his eyes to the familiar walls
of the bedroom in the little house. Rose was beside
him, her face tragic and determined in the lamplight;
and he saw Dr. Pratt's unmistakable thick shoulders
and cropped, silvery head in the doorway behind her.

He moved his lips.

"Hush," Rose told him. "Doctor!" she called softly.

"What happened?" Frank inquired thickly.

"Well, so you're coming out of it, old fellow," the doctor greeted him quietly. "We were a little worried about you. You've taken quite a nap. Your stump-puller kicked you, and you've been twelve hours thinking about it."

Frank saw that Rose did not smile, and her face grew grey. The doctor saw it too. "You go and lie down now, Rose," he ordered swiftly. "They've got a bed ready for you in the next room. This beggar's all right now—we'll soon have him as good as new. You get right to sleep now," he directed. "I'm going to stay all night, so you won't need to think about your husband. There's no danger now—but I don't want him to crawl out of bed."

The next day Frank heard the story. The clevis which attached his team to the sweep had broken, letting the full strain of the stretched cable back against him. The iron brace of the sweep had caught him on the point of the hip, injuring the bone to some extent and jarring his spine. Rose had chanced to see the team grazing near the puller, and, running out, had found him doubled up over the sweep, with his head down. She had laid him on the ground, bathed his face with cold water, and brought him temporarily to consciousness. Then she had mounted one of the horses and ridden frantically over the cow-trail to the cornfield where her father and Uncle Marion were working. Uncle Marion had gone the three miles to the nearest telephone, to call the doctor, while McCune and Rose had carried Frank to the house, and made him as comfortable as they could.

"You'll have to stay in bed for a while, Frank," the

doctor told him. "That hip is badly injured—how much so, we can't tell. But there's no paralysis, and I think you'll come out pretty luckily."

For a time Frank's apprehension for himself was swallowed up in his anxiety for Rose; for months before she had told him that she was to bear a child, conceived in the joy of their first weeks together in the new home; and he feared that the fright and exertion might have serious consequences for her. But instead she seemed to draw from some hidden source strength and self-reliance proportionate to his weakness. She assumed the active management of their affairs, with a decision and efficiency that he almost resented. McCune or Uncle Marion came to the place every day at first. The big Scotchman had little to say, but Frank felt his sympathy and concern. "Don't let anything worry you, Frank," he would remark when leaving.

Uncle Marion was more talkative. "You should 'a' let that thing alone; you know I told you it was dangerous," he reminded Frank.

"Well, you can tell Pete to come and get it, and we'll pay him for hauling it away—can't he, Frank?" Rose asked. And Frank agreed.

When he was able to sit propped up by the window, Frank saw the tripod stump-puller from the McCune place hunched over a stump in his clearing, the old man busy around it. "We ain't usin' it to home, so I tipped it on to the wagon and brought it over," he explained. All through the weeks that followed until the ground froze he worked there, occasionally with McCune's help but usually alone, slowly but steadily widening the clearing which Frank had commenced, and making necessary preparations for the coming of winter—digging the potatoes, banking the house and barns.

"The tripod stump-puller . . . hunched over a stump in
the clearing."

"I ain't needed to Neal's now," he explained. "If Rose'll board me an' keep me in baccy I'll putter around here for a spell." And Frank was too badly hurt to protest; he could only half express his gratitude. "Why, that's nothin'," the old man told him. "Ain't you one o' us, an' Rose my own girl? An' I'm an old man, nothin' to do but work an' no one to work for but you an' Neal's. I like to stay here—Rose's a good cook, most as good as her mother." And he pinched her firm arm, and went out to finish his job of roofing the cow-stable.

CHAPTER XXIX

A S winter came on, Frank was able to get about the place and attend to the stock. The first heavy snowfall occurred on Christmas day, and the next morning the whole landscape was covered with a dense, even blanket two feet thick. A few days later McCune and Uncle Marion both departed with their teams for a lumber camp at the far side of the county, where they had secured work for the winter. Mrs. McCune and the boy, Neal, came to stay with Frank and Rose. There was room for the McCune milk cows in the shed which Frank had built before his accident, and the young cattle were permitted to shift for themselves at the McCune place, between haystacks and stream, with an occasional visit from the boy to make sure that feed was in reach. The four of them were very cosy and comfortable in the little house. Rose insisted on looking after her chickens and doing most of the housework—it would be better for her, she said. And Mrs. McCune busied herself day after day piecing quilts, and sewing clothes and blankets for the baby. But to Frank the days seemed interminable. There was little to do, but even less that he could do. Every evening he read for three or four hours. Steen, tardily notified of his accident, had sent on a box of recent books and magazines, and Frank went through the preceding year's more important novels and books of criticism at a rapid pace. More satisfying were some books which Dr. Pratt brought him—a set of Burton's "Arabian Nights."

In the mornings Frank lay in bed until breakfast was ready, then dressed himself painfully, his bedroom door open to admit a little warmth from the kitchen. He would eat heartily of the fragrant cakes and yellow honey, drink two cups of coffee, and go out into the cold, clean world, where the wooded hills were grey-blue beyond miles of tree-dulled snow.

In the little stable the milk cows awaited their breakfast impatiently. The wild hay which he fed in the mornings from stacks near the stable was tough and refractory. He would wrench loose small forkfuls at the cost of grinding pain in his hip, and carry them to the mangers for the hungry cows. Then he would clean the flanks and udders of the cows with wisps of hay and sit down to milk, steam from the manure of the stable floor rising around him. By the time he had finished, driven the cows outside toward the stream, and done a little perfunctory cleaning of the stable, he was tired and sick. Returning to the house, he would lie down for a while, until the noon meal was ready.

Rose seldom came into his room at such times. A strange self-sufficiency seemed to invest her—in the strength with which she had made the work of the farm go forward in spite of his accident, in the importance attached to her approaching confinement. She seemed to find enough to do in the kitchen, or at her sewing, or in feeding and caring for the few chickens. Frank often wondered what she felt and what she thought about the ordeal that lay before her with the coming of the baby—about himself, and about everything. But he did not try to ask her: she was withdrawn, adequate. He wondered sometimes if she were pretending, for his sake, a strength she did not really possess. But he became convinced that her strength was not assumed.

She was growing, developing, that was all: life had been and was hard for her, and she was meeting and conquering it, beside him, but without him. She was more and more herself. Gradually a vague bitterness of resentment and loneliness crept into his heart.

In the evening there was the same dreary round—the feeding in the dark stable; the smells of the breath of cattle, the hot milk, and the stable floor. As he crouched on the stool, his cold fingers pumping thin streams steadily into the slippery bucket, he would think of Steen. How was the old boy? he would wonder wistfully. His mind would build swiftly and lovingly the scene around their study-table in the old days—Haller's eager face thrust forward through a haze of pipe smoke, Dutton's drawling, luxurious intonation of some golden ribaldry. Acutely he longed for Ann Arbor, for that comradeship, that freedom. With a shock he would come back to the dim stable, the uneasy noise of feeding cows.

In the evening, the books were unsatisfying. He wanted conversation, companionship. But he did not try to talk to Rose and her mother, interested in their sewing or in housework, or in bits of news about the neighbours. They seemed strangely and increasingly alien to him. He would sit staring at the stove for an hour at a time, brooding, lonely. Sometimes he roused himself to help the boy, Neal, with his school work, or to join him in a game of checkers. But always the sense of isolation, and a vague feeling of injury and injustice, were at the back of his mind.

In February the supply of wood which Frank had secured began to run low, and on bright, calm days he made trips into the hardwoods for more fuel. He felled dead and crooked trees and sawed them into lengths

which he could load, sometimes working all of the short
day at a single tree; for the snow was very deep now,
and his hip was still so sore that he had to move very
cautiously. Rose protested against his doing this work
at all, but he insisted that he enjoyed it.

One day in late February he went to the woods a little earlier than usual, having harnessed the team and
prepared the sleigh before an early dinner. He had
opened a road to a very large dead maple near the centre of the woods, and he meant to have most of it in the
woodpile by nightfall. The trunk would be too heavy for
him to put on the sleighs alone, but the top and branches
would make a load and would be the best of firewood.

He attacked the chopping at once, sending the keen
ax ringing steadily against the hard wood in a deep,
smooth kerf. As he paused to rest, the silence of the
winter woods settled around him—the profound, solemn
hush broken only by faint callings of chickadee and nut-
hatch, or the scramble of a squirrel. How complete the
pause which held the yet-breathing earth, he reflected,
how strange and deep the sleep of trees and plants. He
leaned against the great grey trunk for a little while to
ease the soreness in his hip, and wished for himself such
peace.

The slowly mounting discouragement of weeks filled
him utterly. He seemed drained of incentive and emotion, dulled, inert. The cold, lucent calm that surrounded him found him as impersonal as the dead tree
against which he leaned. He closed his eyes, and for
a moment his blood seemed stilled, his senses swallowed
in complete inanimation. He was defeated, lost—left
only the power to endure, as wood and stones endure.
Stiffly he turned to the chopping again, glancing up
from time to time lest a limb of the dead tree should jar

loose and fall upon him. Then he got his big saw from the sleigh, and worked on steadily.

At last the cuts met. There was the long pause of the upright, shuddering trunk, the wide, breath-taking arc of the falling top, and the echoing crash that came back in a muffled boom from across the lake, as great branches snapped and were driven into the snow.

As Frank worked at the trimming and loading of the wood, he became aware that the sky had grown pallid, and the sun, still high in the west, was wan. Before he had completed the load the sun had disappeared altogether, and the whole sky was overcast with a low cloud of darkening grey that swept in faster and faster from the great Lake to the east. "Big snow coming," Frank muttered to himself. Before he gained the barn the first flakes were coming slowly down—huge, wet masses that clung to his clothing and to the wood so that his back and arms were wet before he had finished unloading.

He sank wearily into his chair that night after he had eaten supper. He was very tired, and the ache in his hip was insistent. "You mustn't go to the woods to-morrow, Frank," Rose admonished him, as she moved slowly from table to stove, clearing the supper dishes.

" I don't think I'll need to," he answered. "We'll have wood enough now when we get it sawed. And there's still quite a lot of the other. I'm tired to-night—guess I'll go to bed."

"Aren't you going to read to-night?" she asked, surprised.

"No, I'm tired, I told you," he answered shortly. Taking his candle, he walked stiffly into the cold bedroom.

He was roused when Rose entered the room, an hour

or so later, and heard a curious steady tapping against
the slightly open window. "The snow has turned to
sleet," Rose told him. "It's coming fast."

He was awakened in the morning by Rose's pressing
of his hand. "Look," she said. He sat up and peered
out the window. It was just sunrise, and the sky was
clear. The level light streamed cold and yellow along
a world of ice. There was ice on the woodpile, ice on
the stables and chicken-coop, a broad band of ice on
every twig and branch of the little trees outside the window. Frank started from the bed, but Rose drew him
down beside her and buried her face against his shoulder. "It's come," she whispered, drawing him tight.

He stared at her uncomprehending, and she lifted
her head and looked at him, courage and pride filling
her sober face. "The time has come," she repeated
softly. "For the last hour or two I've been sure. Listen, dear." She drew him down as he started to
rise again, and held him close. "I don't want you to
worry—I'll be all right. And don't expose yourself—
you're not well. I'm sorry it has to be so hard for you
these days, dear—oh." She gasped and he felt her body
grow tense beneath the blankets. "You can tell mamma
now," she said after a moment.

Frank called Mrs. McCune, then dressed in the kitchen
while he was starting a fire. He pushed the door open,
breaking the ice and snow which had lodged against it,
and started toward the barn. He found himself walking on an uneven sheet of ice which covered the drifts.
It supported his weight until he chanced to step on a
sheltered spot behind a stump. Then the crust gave
suddenly and his leg plunged thigh-deep into the soft
snow below, wrenching his sore hip horribly. The pain
sickened him for a moment, and the glare of sun on the

ice swirled redly before his eyes. When he recovered himself, he crawled on with the utmost caution, feeling his way foot by foot and keeping to the most exposed places, where the ice was thicker, but slick and treacherous.

Reaching the barn, he fed the team and milked hurriedly. When he returned to the house, he found the boy eating porridge and cakes at the kitchen table. "Neal must go to Osborne's to have them phone for the doctor," Mrs. McCune explained. "You mustn't walk on this ice, and a horse could hardly get through. He can go on foot."

"I'll take my little sled," Neal proposed quickly. "Then I can slide half-way."

"Well—but you must hurry, not stop to play."

"Oh, I will, mamma."

He was off in a few minutes, running lightly over the ice with the little sled zigzagging behind him. "He'll make a quick trip," his mother commented.

However, it was fully noon before the child returned. "Telephone won't work at Osborne's," he reported. "The line's all down. We went on to the next place to try from there, but it's worse the nearer you get to the Lake. They say the doctor couldn't come anyway—a team can't get through—the ice'll cut their legs all to pieces."

Frank and Mrs. McCune stared at each other helplessly. "Can I have some dinner, ma?" the child requested. "I'm awful hungry."

"Why, sure, sure, of course you are. An' you're a fine boy, too, to make that trip for us." She set food on the table, while Frank stared out the window at the unearthly brightness. Presently he felt a hand on his shoulder, and turned to look into Rose's face.

"Mamma told me," she said simply. "We'll just have to get along without the doctor—lots of women do. Mamma has everything ready the best she can. Don't worry, dear." She pulled his head down to kiss her pale, strained face.

The hours that followed were intolerably long. The boy did the chores at the barn so that Frank could remain at the house. But nervousness drove him outside, and he fed and cared for the poultry with utmost care, then split wood steadily for an hour or more. A slight breeze had come up, sharp and penetrating, which clicked and rattled the icy twigs. Occasionally an overburdened sapling in the hardwoods, bent double under its weight of ice, gave way under the strain with a sharp report, and the loaded branches shattered on the icy floor of the drifts with a crackling roar.

Finally Rose called for Frank to come in and read to her. He found a volume of Kipling—"Traffics and Discoveries"—and read with enthusiasm and feeling but with a curious unconsciousness of what his lips were saying. His wife sat in the still brightness of the little living-room, a shapeless mass in her robes and blankets, her face ivory-white against the braids of tawny hair, her eyes dim and remote as though she had withdrawn into some fastness of herself. At nightfall she dismissed him tenderly, and signed for her mother to come.

Frank prepared supper for the boy, who soon went to bed. He sat on by the kitchen stove, feeding it occasionally with the maple wood which he had heaped high in the wood-box. Cold crept into the room. He hunched feverishly over the stove, sipping hot tea. He did not feel sleepy.

Soon after midnight Mrs. McCune came into the room, closing the door softly behind her. "Frank," she told him quietly, "we'll have to get to the doctor. I'm afraid—it seems like it's not going right—I can't manage alone. The best way will be to take her to Green Bush in the sleigh—right away. You can't walk it, and anyway we'll get the doctor sooner that way—and she'll be at the hospital. The horses will have to suffer, I guess," she added sombrely. "You might wrap their legs in sacks. You get the team, and I'll wake Neal and tell him to look after things until we get back."

In an hour they were ready to start. Frank had harnessed the team by lantern-light, chained the wagon box on the sleigh, and made a bed of hay and blankets in the rear end. On this the two women lay down together, covered warmly with quilts and robes. Frank stood in front to drive. The boy watched them go, standing in the lighted doorway, his young face soberly proud with his responsibility, and a little frightened.

As they started, the rear part of the sleigh swung alarmingly to one side, and Mrs. McCune told Frank to wrap small pieces of chain about the runners to keep them from slipping sideways.

They set off under the starlight, for it was a moonless night—down a long hill, across a swamp, and up the slope on the other side. In a few places the crust was so strong that it supported the weight of the horses. But most of the time their feet broke through, dropping them suddenly almost to their bellies in the drifts. Frank had wrapped their forelegs in grain bags, tied on with heavy cord. But before they had gone a mile he saw dark spots on the edges of the tracks the horses left, and found that their legs were bleeding and the bags were cut and frayed. He stopped on a firm place and tore long narrow strips from the end of a horse-blanket, lashing these around and around the animals' legs like the bandages he had seen used on race-horses. Before he climbed back into the sleigh he bent over Rose's face. Her eyes were closed, but she opened them and looked up at him. "Don't worry," she whispered. "It's going to be all right. Just go on."

When the horses stopped again, panting and bleeding, they had covered half the distance, and the stars were paling in the swiftly growing light of dawn. "I guess I'll try it sitting up awhile, or on my knees," Rose said faintly. And Mrs. McCune arranged a seat for her while Frank rebandaged the dripping, lacerated legs of the team. Again they started bravely, but the bandages would not hold. At last Frank pulled off his duck-and-leather coat and with his knife cut four boots from the sleeves, which he bound on with thongs pared from the lines. He drove on in his shirt-sleeves, and Rose laughed faintly at the spectacle of his spindle arms protruding from his thick-clothed body. "Isn't it awful cold for you, dear?" she asked. Then he saw her face contract with a spasm of pain.

They were paralleling the telephone line now; the wires hung in loops and festoons like great white cables. Half the posts had broken off, and fallen or mutilated trees were everywhere. The ice was thicker as they neared the lake, and the horses broke through less frequently. Suddenly they swung out on the well-graded gravel highway, where the snow had not drifted, and there was firm if slippery footing. Frank urged the almost exhausted team to a hazardous slow trot, and they slipped steadily past the last farm-houses, past the dark pine groves on the bluffs, and down the long slope that led to the little town.

From the icebound Lake a grey band of vapour had followed the sun, and spread over the whole sky, seem-

ing to warm and soften the air as it came. The horses
were staggering when they drew up at the door of the
hospital. It was the work of only a minute to help
Rose from the sleigh, and she climbed the steps on the
doctor's arm. Frank drove around the corner to the
livery barn, threw his lines to the proprietor with a hurried injunction to "do your best for 'em," and stumbled
back to the hospital.

Behind the closed door of an inner room he heard
quick steps, the creak of bed-springs, and sharp low
voices. The nurse appeared suddenly from the doorway, smiled at him reassuringly, and disappeared again
with a bundle. Once he caught a glimpse of the doctor, strangely altered and fearful in apron and gloves.

He sat humped by the window in the doctor's little office, his mind apprehensive and yet vacant. The room
was warm, and drowsiness crept over him. Ashamed,
he straightened up and turned the pages of a magazine.
But he was dozing when the doctor entered quietly and
laid a hand on his shoulder. He looked up, shamefaced
and terrified.

"Well, Frank," and his heart gave a great leap of
joy at the doctor's tone, "fine new girl in there. Rose
has had a hard time, but it's all right now. Want to
come in and see her a minute? Then I guess we'll put
you to bed too," he added, noting keenly the twinge of
pain that crossed Frank's haggard face as he straightened up.

Rose lay relaxed on the high, narrow bed, her tawny
braids bright on the pillow beside her pale, drawn face.
She turned to Frank eyes luminous with such pride and
joy as he had never imagined before. "Look at her,
Frank!" she whispered.

In a basket on two chairs beside the bed was a small

red object, swathed in a blanket, wrinkled and grotesque. Frank gulped and stared in consternation.
"Is—is it all right?" he asked.

"Of course, silly. All babies look that way when
they're just *new*."

He looked back at her face, drawn and white and
shadowed, to her still, relaxed form under the sheets, to
her eyes, so tired and so joyous, and knelt suddenly by
the bed, the tears running down his cheeks.

"Dear, dear man," she breathed, and moved her hand
so that her fingers touched his face.

CHAPTER XXX

FRANK did sleep all day, and well into the night. When he awoke, the nurse brought him water and food, assured him that Rose and the baby were "fine," and told him that the doctor had commanded that he should by no means get out of bed.

In fact he stayed there almost as long as Rose did. As a result of the exposure and exertion of the trip to Green Bush an inflammation developed in his hip, with some swelling and an alarming degree of soreness, and the doctor prevailed upon him to remain quiet until it subsided. Mrs. McCune returned home when the baby was twenty-four hours old, explaining that Rose did not need her and that she was worried about the boy alone at home. She got a ride part-way with a neighbour, and walked the remaining miles over the snow.

A marked rise in temperature followed the sleet storm, increasing from day to day, and the liveryman soon was able to take Frank's horses home, their legs still bandaged, but otherwise none the worse for their trip. The ice went out on the Lake one night with a stiff offshore wind, and next morning the loud voice of the blue waters filled the little town. Frank was soon able to walk about a little, visiting the drug store and the bank and the post office. He called at the *Gazette,* but was received by Finchburg in a surly silence broken only by disparaging references to the "deadness" of Green Bush and the "poor pay" afforded by certain advertisers.

264

Frank wrote a long letter to Steen, telling him in detail of the events of the fall and winter—for he had not written for months—inquiring rather wistfully about affairs at the University, and waxing enthusiastic over the charms of his new daughter. He received by return mail an ironic but most sympathetic note from Steen, expressing the hope that the necessity of affording the young lady in question the advantage of a liberal education might persuade him to return to civilization, when all other arguments and appeals were unavailing.

The baby already seemed beautiful to Frank, and her tiny being inexpressibly dear. She filled out rapidly, revealed rich blue eyes and a down of yellow hair, and her tiny fingers grew plump and soft. She was the "best baby," as the nurse put it, sleeping diligently most of the time and seldom asserting herself vocally except at mealtime. Rose's progress was also satisfactory, and at the end of two weeks she was able to walk across the street with Frank to participate in the purchase of a baby carriage—"something plain and substantial," she told the unctuous dealer, "that I can wheel her out to the barnyard in when I do the milking." He seemed startled, but led the way to the rear of the store.

The same day, seemingly by accident, a stranger appeared at the hospital whom Dr. Pratt introduced as "Dr. Hoffman, from Detroit. I want you to tell him all about your trouble with your hip, Frank," he added, "how you got hurt, and all the progress of the trouble."

Frank shook hands with the thickset, keen-eyed young man, with his heavy, blunt nose and hands and his peculiar silvery hair. In a few minutes he was answering simple, lucid questions, one after another. Then there was a prolonged examination, in which the strange doctor's thick fingers revealed a marvellous deftness and precision.

"We must have the photographs," he decided.

"Then we'll go back with you as far as Bay City tonight," Dr. Pratt suggested, "and use the machine there."

"Do you think I am in for serious trouble, Dr. Hoffman?" Frank asked.

"We'll know better when we have the photographs," he replied quietly.

The trip to Bay City and the hour at the big hospital there were to Frank hideously reminiscent of the incidents of his mother's death; and he spent a bad half-hour while the doctors were examining the negatives. Finally Dr. Pratt came into the room where he was waiting.

"Well, Frank," he began, his hand resting in almost fatherly affection on the boy's shoulder, "your hip looks pretty bad. Dr. Hoffman says we must operate. He's a specialist in such things—that's really why I had him stop in Green Bush—to see you. He'd been up to Cheboygan for an operation. Would you rather stay with us in Green Bush or go to the big hospital in Detroit?"

"I'd much rather stay with you," Frank answered.

"Well, we'll do our best for you," the doctor's tone was pleased. "It will cost a bit more for the operation, of course, but less for the hospital fees; and you must realize in advance, Frank, that you're going to be laid up a long, long time—eight or ten weeks at least."

"But my farm work," Frank protested—"Rose—can't it be postponed? Spring will be coming soon."

Dr. Hoffman had entered the room, and answered quietly in his rich, precise voice. "It is already dangerously tardy, Mr. Thompson. If we are to have even a moderate chance of succeeding in the operation it must be prompt."

"What are the alternatives?" Frank asked unsteadily. "This is something of a shock to me."

"Yes," Dr. Hoffman nodded understandingly. "I know quite how you feel. The alternatives are probable loss of the limb, and injury to the spine of an extent not easily estimated—perhaps fatal."

"Well," Frank wavered, "can I afford the operation?"

"We will see that you can," Dr. Pratt interposed quickly. "Don't worry about that."

"Mr. Thompson naturally wants to know the extent of the obligation he is assuming," Dr. Hoffman remarked a little sharply. "You prefer to remain at Green Bush?" he asked Frank.

"Yes, I do, very much."

"In that case I shall charge two hundred and fifty dollars for the operation. Dr. Pratt can tell you about the hospital fees. Well, gentlemen, I shall bid you good day. I must go to my train."

On the return trip to Green Bush, Dr. Pratt explained to Frank the nature of his malady and its dangers, and the treatment which would be attempted. "Tuberculosis has attacked the joint and the adjacent surfaces," he explained, "and perhaps the base of the spine. Dr. Hoffman will remove the diseased tissue. In the after-treatment we will try to prevent stiffening of the joint. If you were younger or older the prognosis would be more grave. As it is, there is a chance of failure."

For nearly a week Frank was kept in bed on a light diet, in order that the inflammation might subside as much as possible. Rose remained in town at Dr. Pratt's suggestion, securing a room where she could care for

the baby, but spending most of her time with Frank.
She would want to be there at the time for the operation,
he said, and the roads were uncertain at this time of
year.

Finally the day came. Frank had a nervous dread
of the operation, particularly of the anæsthetic, which
he was unable to conceal. "Would there be any way of
doing it without the ether?" he implored Dr. Pratt at
the last minute.

"Of course not, Frank. You're foolish. You'll
withstand the anæsthetic all right—thousands of people do daily." His face tightened as he saw the fear in
Frank's eyes, and knew how his mother's death haunted
him as he faced the ordeal himself. "Don't worry,
Frank," he added kindly. "You're in fine shape, everything is hopeful. Anyway, we take a chance every day,
old man. This is just one more."

"Yes, I know that." Frank rallied himself to speak
encouragingly to Rose and press her hand before he
walked into the operating-room. "Don't worry, dear,"
he urged her. "I'll see you in a little while. I'll be all
right."

"I'm going out to wheel baby in the sunshine," she answered. "It's so nice down by the Lake. I'll be thinking of you."

As the nurse adjusted the mask over his face, he heard
the click of the screen-door below and the soft thump,
thump, thump as Rose eased the rubber-tired wheels
of the baby carriage down the cement steps. And he
had a moment of keen regret that he had not insisted
on buying the more attractive cab which she had thought
too expensive, but which he had known she wanted.

His first consciousness was of the noise of waves, ap-
pallingly close and loud; and it seemed to him that he

was swimming furiously after Rose and the baby cab,
which were hurled and battered, and disappeared in a
cloud of spray. The room sprang into a moment's brief
clarity, with the face of the nurse staring at him curiously, very large and putty-coloured, and the walls sagging queerly. Then he was blind again, and very sick.
When he really came to himself Rose was sitting tran-
quilly beside him. She seemed withdrawn and grey.
But there was immeasurable peace in her presence, and
he relaxed himself to sleep.

CHAPTER XXXI

THE operation had been successful, he was told next morning; and in spite of himself the words held for him a vivid premonitory ring. But he would have to be very quiet for a long, long time.

He remained in bed for weeks and weeks. Spring opened up fully, and Rose went home to attend to garden and poultry and cattle. She was restless in town with nothing to do, and her mother could not stay away from home. She came in to see Frank often, and wrote to him nearly every day. Mr. and Mrs. Steele, too, were frequent callers, and the doctor spent an hour or so with him nearly every evening. But through the long afternoons and the wakeful nights he lay alone, listening to the little noises of the hospital and the village street, and more often to the voice of the Lake which, below or above all other sounds, was an ever-present rhythm in the background of his thought.

It came to seem akin to the rhythms of his blood and breathing, a thing as elemental and as fully a part of himself. Day after day he visioned the miles of deep blue water, on the brink of which the village clung at the foot of the hills. Stronger and stronger grew his sense of the kinship between Lake and land, and of the frailness of man's tenure of them both. Ships crossed and recrossed the line of his vision, when he was propped by the window—blots of smoke or gleaming points of white against the horizon—leaving the water pathless as before. But almost as transient was the trace of man's going on the earth. He knew how swiftly the wilderness reclaimed deserted clearings, how rapid and complete the triumph of wind and rain and growing things over fences and dwellings, barriers and roads.

Even the skyscrapers and vast towers of cities, the hollowed hills and canals and bridges—he remembered tales of great cities which the jungle had swallowed, and monoliths fallen in the sand. Momently he seemed to hold his universe in uninfringed perspective: and to see himself as infinitely obscure and tiny, one of the swarming hordes of a brief race, a child of earth; moving, but unseparated from her, and soon to slip back, quiet, to herself. And he knew how little is man's strength in the face of the destiny that he inherits.

Hour long he lay in the narrow hospital bed, bearing the steady pain of the slow, slow healing of his hip, and pondering, solving the meaning of this busy, self-absorbed microcosm, this village of five hundred souls, between the unsubdued and unsubduable Lake and land.

The weeks of delay seemed unbearable. He read a great deal; tried writing—outlining a series of brief stories of the region; sent long letters to Steen, who supplied him with books and magazines. Each day was a problem in the disposition of time, not always satisfactorily solved. The hip healed with incredible slowness, and the hospital bills mounted alarmingly in spite of the low rates Dr. Pratt charged him. At last he was permitted to walk to the drug store for a chat with Mr. Steele, and then to hobble about the village or walk down to the old pier and look out at the deserted warehouse and the grey Lake. His hip was slightly stiffened, and the affected leg seemed shorter than the other. He moved only with pain. Still, it was a prodigious relief to be out in the spring sunshine. Finally, but not until June, the doctor took him home in a new car he had bought for his practice.

There was a strangeness about the familiar place which secretly appalled him. He stared at the little rooms, which seemed strangely altered in the coolness of the June evening from their close warmth in the winter days he had last spent in them. The little trees had put out new growth, the garden was marked by bright, clean rows of young vegetables, the clearing was covered with the grain Uncle Marion had sowed there— a rich green in colour, and already ankle-high. The baby had grown astonishingly, and was persuaded to smile at the doctor when Rose exhibited her proudly. Even Rose seemed strange, though he had seen her every few days. She seemed taller, more positive in her move-ments. And he sensed a degree of self-assertion in her that had been developed through these months in which she had managed everything in his absence.

The doctor stayed for supper at Rose's invitation, and talked jovially as he ate. "You'd better get to bed now, young man," he remarked as he was leaving. "You look tired. And take it easy, now, take it easy. Don't get out and try to lift the earth. Rose, I'm trusting you to see that he behaves himself."

"I'll try," she agreed brightly.

Frank's strained nerves rebelled at the lightness of her tone. "I *am* tired," he told the doctor. "Guess I'll get right to bed." He hobbled into the bedroom while Rose escorted the doctor to the car, and undressed without a light. Warm, misty moonlight lay on the garden, the young orchard, the slope of the field. Its beauty seemed alien and withdrawn. He crept into his bed and pressed his face against the pillow.

Next morning Uncle Marion appeared bright and

early at their kitchen door, carrying a shining tin bucket on his arm. He welcomed Frank warmly, then squinted judicially toward the garden.

"I see the bugs is startin' in on them potatoes o' yours," he remarked. "Thought I'd come over an' pick 'em. If you git the old ones right on the start they don't never amount to much."

After breakfast Frank followed the old man out to the potato patch, where the neat, clean rows of sturdy young plants covered almost half an acre with their leafy yellow-green foliage. On the tops of the leaves or hidden along the stems were fat black and yellow beetles, as large as the nail of one's little finger. Uncle Marion was walking slowly between the rows, his thick body bent above the plants, dexterously grasping the beetles with his fingers and dropping them into the pail. Occasionally he gave the pail a sharp shake to dislodge the insects which were crawling painfully up the smooth sides. At the end of each "round," as he reached the end of the patch nearest the house, he emptied a pint or more of the beetles into a jar containing kerosene, where they kicked frantically for a moment and then were quiet.

The sun smote the gleaming pail in flares and shafts of light that hurt Frank's eyes. This seemed a rather sorry and sordid business to him—ugly in its details, and futile, since half the time, spent in spraying the plants a little later, would be far more effective. He turned away, and walked slowly back toward the buildings. For the first time his home smote him as inexpressibly bare and ugly—the squat grey house, with black tar paper covering the cellar door, the crazy, patched stable, flanked by a huge manure pile and the trampled and scattered remnants of hay stacks. He was seized with an almost intolerable sickness of disgust and discouragement at the thought of his last weeks here—the cold and darkness and pain, the work at the stable with the noisy, stupid cattle about him and the filth on his hands and feet. Abruptly he turned aside, and took the cow-path which wound past the edge of the clearings toward the lake. Clover was blooming in the small clearing he had made the first year, its rich, honeyed fragrance blown to him strongly in the warm sunshine. Beyond, in the larger field where he had met the accident with the stump-puller and where Uncle Marion and McCune had toiled on to complete the clearing in his absence, the young oats and peas were almost knee-high, and rich black-green in colour. At the brushy boundary of clearing and timber, wood was ricked up and logs were piled. He looked with wistful eyes at the beauty of the field, its gentle slope covered with the rich, even growth. He wished that he could have completed the work, so that it would seem all his own.

He walked slowly on into the uncleared land, feeling his way cautiously through the tangle of sweet fern and brambles that covered the ground between the blackened stumps, under the young trees.

Suddenly he came out upon an open slope above the little lake. It lay below him there, a mirror of grey and green and blue in its circle of balsams and cedars, as virgin and primitive as though he were the first man to look upon it. Half-way down the slope he paused in the sunlight. About his feet was a dance and flutter of little moths—brown, black, blue, and pink, wing-barred and veined. In the drowsy, fragrant warmth of the southern slope they circled close to the ground in silent, delicate swarms, over the clover and through the broad bronze and silver leaves of poplar shoots.

"At the brushy boundary of clearing and timber, wood was ricked up."

He sank down among them, watching fascinated. Beauty, beauty called to him, from the little lake and the life of earth. The longing seized him to be one with the earth, absorbed and lost in the silent maze of growth and decay. He turned on his face, lay prone in the grass, steeped in the warmth of sunlight, drowned in the many-tongued voice of the ground. He was inert, passive, a piece of the untilled soil.

He lay there a long time, motionless. Slowly the unacknowledged rebellion against poverty and disease, which had burned in him all these months, seeped away. A breeze stirred his hair. The very smell and taste of sun-warmed earth were in his face. A moth lit on his hand. All urgency and pain had left him, all terror, all desire. He did not cling to the earth or grovel—he was a part of it. As he lay there motionless he felt the touch of rain and snow, the blows of storm, but they did not chill or bruise him. An unspeakable calm possessed him, a peace deeper than any he had ever known or dreamed. Child of the earth, why should he fear or question? The certainties of defeat and death came clear at last, known, held within his life, no longer dreadful. Strength flowed into him from the sunlight and the soil.

He rose to his knees, and a strange lightness of heart filled him as he studied the quiet flutter and dance of the moths, the questing flight of bees and hurry of ants, the intricate loveliness of the plants beneath his hands. He rose and walked slowly toward his home. Half-formed and tentative, a creed of courage came to him, born of his conflict with disaster and pain: a courage holding together and as one the dearness of life and the nearness of death, the sureness of defeat and the joy of the fight.

CHAPTER XXXII

IN the days that followed, Frank found things that he could do. He would rise early in the morning, and build the fires while Rose went directly to the barn to milk. In the cool, moist sunlight he would walk stiffly to the chicken-house, carrying a measure of grain, and swing open the door. The fowls would tumble out and eat greedily, a few trailing after him as he returned to the house. He would prepare cereal, coffee, and eggs, and have the breakfast ready when Rose came in with the milk. Later he would churn, perhaps, a book propped on his knees as he rotated the heavy barrel slowly and steadily. Or he would work for a while in the garden, hoeing very carefully, and stooping painfully now and then to pull a weed from the row of lacy-leaved carrots or grey-green salsify. Soon he began to go to the clearing for a little while each afternoon, chopping and trimming saplings. He was still unable to carry the heavy pieces of log and stump to the piles for burning.

The work tired him, and there were many hours of profound discouragement, when he surveyed hopelessly the straits to which his venture on the land had brought him. But, in spite of the pain, he began once more to relish the work itself. When he was tired he would sit on a log and rest, watching the clouds, or the flight of insects, or the work of a squirrel or birds in the near trees. And the slow hours in the clearing, alone with the miles of sky and hills and the multitudinous life of

the wilderness, seldom failed to bring him a renewed ori-
entation of himself, and to send him home at night with
a sense of healing and of strength.

The summer discovered for him new meanings in his
relationship with Rose. He had come now to rejoice in
her strength instead of resenting it. She was adequate,
ready for the emergency, and yet steady and whole-
hearted in her allegiance to him. The old spontane-
ous tenderness for her had grown into something more
assured, born of respect for her strength and appreciation of the finely reticent sympathy with which she
treated him. Slowly, as he worked more and more in
the open, pleasure in his food came back to him; and
their simple but abundant and well-cooked meals, with
the accompanying talk of daily tasks and the constant
interest of the droll and lovely baby, were a recurring
quiet joy. In the evenings he read briefly. Steen sent
him current magazines and new books, but he exhausted
most of these in an hour. He opened a box of old texts,
and read "Hamlet," Spenser, and North's Plutarch
with a strange new glow of interest. His mind seemed
stronger and more alert than ever before. And as, with
August, the first signs of early autumn appeared in the
land—bright flags of swamp maple along the little lake,
long cool days in which the wind was filled with a smoky
tang—a deep and reasoned satisfaction in living arose
within him, which the thought of the depletion of his
means by his illness, and even the persisting pains and
stiffness in his hip, with their continual menace, could
not destroy.

It was a great event when, one evening in mid-August,
he felt able to scramble on the back of one of the old
horses, with a stump as stepping-block, and ride after
the cows. At sunset he heard their bells in the hollows

beyond the little lake; and he drove them slowly back along the winding trail, between the hardwoods and the water. He rode between alders and young balm-trees as high as his head, where late moths fluttered, and past bits of open marsh across which the still lake, veiled with thin grey mist, mirrored the soft colours in the west. Filled, the cows filed home, a winding line of broad slow backs, black and brown and dun. To creak of crickets, croak of frogs, the cowbells sang, a silvery, jangling music, pastoral, world-old. Stars came into the pale sky. Against the pure evening light, trees on the near horizon were silhouetted clearly, in perfected beauty of outline of trunk and twig and leaf. As he followed the cows into the yard Rose came toward him from the house, pushing the baby in her cab and carrying a pail. She helped him to dismount, and, turning, he pressed her in his arms, and held her close. "Why, dear," she whispered, and kissed his lips.

There was a noise of a motor on the hill below their gate, and a car turned into the yard. Frank limped forward to meet it, and saw Henkel's small, thin form climbing out.

"Thought I'd better drive out and see you awhile this evening, Frank," the banker began directly. "Let's just stay here by the car. Finchburg was in this afternoon, and said he's going to throw up the paper—can't make it go. There's a payment due the end of this month, you know, and he has nothing to meet it with. I told him he'd have to stay until he got a buyer, or you made some other arrangement. But he's crazy to get away, now he's decided to go. I thought I'd see what you wanted to do about it?"

"What would you advise, Mr. Henkel?" Frank asked quietly, his heart thumping.

"Well, Frank, the only thing I can see is for you to take hold of it yourself, for a while anyway. The paper's run down awfully, Frank—I don't believe you realize yourself how bad it is. The books make a bad showing—really bad. We couldn't hope to sell at any advantage now—we'd have to give it away. But if you could take hold of it, that would be different. People liked you, and trusted you. Advertisers would come back. And I should think you could do it, Frank. You can do that better than farming. That young Dale does most of the real printing, as it is."

"What is Finchburg willing to do?" Frank inquired.

"He would take a thousand dollars cash for his equity in the paper and house both—that's less than half what he's put into it. Otherwise, I suppose he'd try to sell his contracts outside—might tie things up worse than ever."

"Well, I don't know," said Frank slowly. "I'll have to think it over. That would take more cash than we have. I don't know about leaving the farm. I'll talk it over with Rose, Mr. Henkel, and come in and see you to-morrow."

"All right, Frank. We'll be glad to carry you for as much as you need or all of it, as far as that is concerned. Well, I'll be getting back. I thought you ought to hear about it." He climbed into the machine.

"Yes, indeed. Thank you ever so much for coming out."

"Oh, that's all right. I hope you'll decide to take it up, Frank. Well, good night to you." He waved his hand and drove away.

Frank stood silently in the yard while the big car coasted down the hill and purred smoothly up the opposite slope toward Green Bush. Then he walked slowly into the house and sat down by the kitchen table, beside the unlighted lamp.

Rose found him there when she entered. "What's the matter, Frank?" she asked quickly. "Who was it in the car?"

"It was Henkel. He came out to tell me Finchburg is giving up the paper. He wants to sell out to me for a thousand dollars—his interest in the paper and the house. Otherwise he'll sell to someone else for anything he can get. He's going to leave."

She strained the milk, and carried the baby, who had fallen asleep in her cab, to her crib. Then she drew a chair beside Frank's in the cool darkness of the little kitchen, and touched his hand.

"What do you think you'll do, dear?" she asked.

"I hardly know. I'm happy here, I'm not anxious to get into the paper again. But if we let him sell out to someone else, we may lose everything. On the other hand, if we buy him out we'll have to go in debt. It seems a good deal of a risk to run, either way." He paused, and was silent for a time. "What do you think, Rose?" he asked finally. "I know you would hate to leave our home here."

"I could—if it seemed best," she answered softly. But in the vibrancy of her tone he read the intensity of the emotion which opposed her speech. "I like it here," she added simply, turning her face toward him in the dimness.

"Yes, I know. So do I." Their hands touched and held lightly, on the table between them. "I've been thinking I might manage the paper and we could still stay here. I could go into Green Bush for two or three days a week, and the rest of the time leave it to Dale.

A little later I ought to be able to drive a Ford, and then I could come home nights and go in as often as there would be any need. In the winters perhaps we could move to town and live at the old place. It wouldn't be so satisfactory, of course, as being here the year around. But it need be only for a year or two, until I can get the paper built up again. Then we can sell, for cash, and come here to stay—if I—am able to farm."

"That's what I'm afraid of, Frank—that's what I want to consider most of all. Would it be better for your chance of health to go back into the paper, or not?"

"Well, Dr. Pratt seems to be more afraid of my working outdoors too much than not enough, right now. The rides back and forth would be good for me. Of course if it were a question of staying cooped up in the office and doing all the composition and presswork myself it would be different. Really, Rose, I believe the chances for my health are as good one way as the other. Don't you believe maybe this plan would be a good one?" He spoke wistfully, hesitant.

"Well, I'd like to keep the farm, even if we couldn't be here all year—if it wouldn't be too hard for you, going back and forth. We could go in for berry-raising and fresh vegetables—there's some market at Green Bush—and you could take things in with you, if you didn't mind. And we could milk through the summer and have one cow and some chickens in town in the winter, couldn't we?"

"Yes, we could haul feed in for them. It wouldn't be so bad. Well, let's sleep on it, and to-morrow we'll see what we can do." His voice was unsteady, doubtful. Rose looked closely at him, then rose suddenly, and, lighting a lamp, set about some final tasks in the kitchen. Frank stepped out of doors into the quiet yard. A moon just past full had risen, and the night was cool and still. A whippoorwill called intermittently from the edge of the clearing. He could hear the breathing of the cattle in the yard, and the snuffling and trampling of the old horses in a small pasture below the barn. All these familiar sounds came to him keenly, sharpened with a suddenly renewed sense of his weakness, of the imminence of defeat.

He walked slowly through the garden, brushing the moisture from the dew-wet potato vines against his ankles, and crawled through the fence into the field where the peas and oats had been lately cut. Moonlight silvered its soft contours into dim loveliness. Against the sky filled with faint stars the long vague mass of the hardwoods was mysterious and beautiful. He crossed the field slowly, and felt his way along the path beyond, down to the little lake. A sickness of discouragement and despair mounted steadily within him. He felt that he could not distort and complicate his hard-fought life with these new tasks and problems. The assurance he had wrung from his life with the soil was for the moment broken. He felt weakness, impotence, a renewed keen and bitter sense of frustration and defeat.

At the edge of the lake he paused. Then he crept out on a fallen cedar that lay above the water, drawn irresistibly by the calm splendor of the moonlight on its stillness. Kneeling on the log, he peered beneath him. The lake dropped away sharply from the very edge, and the water where he knelt was black and deep. He stretched out his arm and touched the surface with his fingers. It was warm. He let his hand hang motionless below him, and the little ripples of its coming died away. Peace, stillness drew him—to plunge the arm down, down to the elbow, the shoulder, to press his face against that clean and silent warmth—to be lost, forgetting, part of the lake's beauty, part of the lake's peace.

As he looked steadily into its motionless depths, it seemed to open beneath him that black void of the numberless unknowing years of nothingness. And for a little while, steadily and calmly, he saw clearly the time and space that make a toy of man, and faced at once the presence and the meaning of death.

Then, slowly, the world swung into being around him again. The log was hard beneath his knees. He saw the wooded slopes, the sky filled with moonlight and pale stars. A red planet glowed dully below the moon in the east.

He crept back along the log, climbed the bank, and walked slowly toward the house. A curious calm exultation filled him, a sense of mastery.

Rose was already asleep, her calm face turned toward the open window, pale glints on her braided hair. He bent above her, his whole being flooded suddenly with passionate tenderness. She was one fact in a universe of lies: a fleeting, evanescent fact, to be sure, as fugitive as all the dreams of earth. But for the moment true and his, bound to him by their common fate. Their child, their home, themselves, he saw as brief dissolving links of the chain of earth; and piercingly dear to him became their days together, sunlight and food and words, the touch of hands.

CHAPTER XXXIII

WITHIN a week Frank had taken Finchburg's place in the office, to the vast delight of Dale and the quiet jubilation of Henkel, Mr. Steele, and Dr. Pratt. Within the month the Finchburg household had left Green Bush, bag and baggage, and Frank had fitted up a room in the old house where he could sleep and cook his breakfast when he stayed in town.

Frank was puzzled by his response to the experience of returning to the old home. The Finchburgs had moved, rearranged, and destroyed or mutilated many things. The place seemed more strange than familiar. And the poignancy of grief and remorse which he had expected to feel did not visit him. Instead there was, in all his memories of his mother and his father, for the most part only a wistful, resigning sorrow.

Soon he felt again the quiet pleasure of dealing with the life of the community, chronicling the small events of village and country-side or wielding his slight influence for improvements: "Pioneer Called Home," "Stork Visits Green Bush," "Road Meeting Held": the whole banal and yet absorbing business of the country paper. He found a richer and more far-reaching pleasure than ever before in his contacts with such people as Mr. Steele and Dr. Pratt, and devoted himself to learning to know his other fellow townsmen more fully and understandingly, probing his way toward the inarticulate, defeated dream which he believed to be at the heart of every man. He listened patiently to maundering, inconsequential plans for the improvement of stores and farms and settlements, lent an ear to talk of oil, of reforesting, of piers and summer hotels, watched gravely and with inward quiet mirth the political discussions and violent, unsignificant arguments at the courthouse. There were contacts, in the daily necessity of his business, that irritated and exasperated or disgusted him; others that were beneficent and rewarding. Always there was the Lake before his office window, and the land to which he returned after each publication day, to help him keep poise and sanity, and to enable him to remember that, after all, the *Oscona County Gazette* was not quite the sole thing of importance in the universe.

The drives, to and from the village, were the finest part of his whole experience. He still used the old horse and buggy, even after he might have driven a car, and stayed in town two or three nights of each week; partly because he needed these evenings in Green Bush for his work, and partly because he enjoyed the leisurely contact with the country-side which an automobile would not afford. Usually he drove in to the village Sunday afternoon, or early Monday morning, and returned Wednesday, after the paper had been mailed, leaving things in charge of Dale for the rest of the week. Occasionally he made a further drive, to Wilberville or another of the inland towns, in these intervening days. He saw grain ripening in the small fields along the way, grain harvested and in shock. In old orchards fruit was white or red on the trees and on the ground, and from the road he caught the musty smell of apples as he passed. The young birches and poplars and maples of the abundant second growth, that edged and surrounded the orchards and the fields, turned gold and crimson, and the rich green of grassland and pasture gave way to umber and russet.

With the first snow, Frank and Rose moved some of their household goods and a few hens and a cow to the old home in Green Bush. Uncle Marion had volunteered to stay on their place and care for the rest of the poultry and cattle, as there was no work in the lumber woods this winter—the last big timber in the county had been felled: an arrangement which they found particularly desirable. They were beginning to prosper modestly, for Rose had continued to meet most of their small expenses with the proceeds from her poultry and butter, and the paper was picking up steadily. There was money enough for a new silk dress for Rose at Christmas time, in which she might appear at church as befitted the editor's wife, and for a new suit for Frank, and innumerable gifts for the baby, now able to stand on her feet with the help of a supporting finger, and becoming amazingly if unintelligibly vocal at times.

The winter passed swiftly, and with the coming of the cold, tardy spring Rose and the child returned to the farm, and the weekly drives began again. The poultry-house was enlarged to make room for hundreds of baby chicks, ordered from a hatchery. Berry plants and bushes were set out in long rows. Two milk cows were added to their herd. On his part, Frank made a determined effort for additional subscriptions and advertising, seeking to bring the paper to the point it had reached when he had turned it over to Finchburg. There was steady work for both of them, exacting, tiring work that left little time for recreation, even for talk.

Frank was occasionally conscious of the irony of their lives. He smiled grimly at himself sometimes as he set out for the long drive on a cold, foggy May morning, when the country-side was dulled and hidden in banks of grey. To accompany an old horse on such a morning over some miles of lonely road, in physical discomfort accentuated by the soreness in his hip which chilling always induced; to fuss and hurry and sweat for three days so that a few hundred people might read, with difficulty if at all, certain wholly unsignificant words; to come driving back to toil for three more days planting potatoes or building chicken-coops or cleaning cow-stables: the spectacle was not wholly delightful. But Frank could not condemn the man whom he saw preoccupied with this trivial and futile round. He saw other men and other deeds and dreams, all in the last analysis equally futile, equally trivial; but he was not disturbed. After all, it would be something to be free from debt, to plant the peonies and fruit-trees they would like by their little house. It was much to live half of each week's life with Rose and their child, and part of the other half with Dr. Pratt and the Steeles. And it was, perhaps, most of all to see, to think, and to be grimly happy on these slow, crawling journeys back and forth between the Lake's edge and the land.

On a morning in early August, nearly a year from the time he had taken the paper again, Frank found in his mail an unusually slender letter from Steen. He opened it curiously.

"I have decided to make a journey which I have long promised myself," he read. "I am coming up to visit you. I have just finished teaching in summer school, and feel the need of the healing which you claim is to be found in bucolic surroundings. Hence I am availing myself of the invitation you have extended so often. I can stay only a few days—but look for me Wednesday morning. Yours, Steen."

With an exclamation of delight Frank thrust the letter into his pocket and hurried across the street to his office. "Whoop her up, Dale, old man," he shouted. "We've got to get the paper out early this week. I've got company coming Wednesday morning—a fellow I knew at Ann Arbor." He sent a note to Rose by the rural carrier, to give her the news of the impending visit, and then set about the task of getting the paper out and things off his hands so that he would be ready to take Steen directly to the farm when he came in.

The greeting between the two men was quiet but affectionate. Frank led the way to his buggy and put Steen's suitcase beneath the seat. "This is my Cadillac, old fellow," he announced. "Think you could stand it?"

"I haven't *seen* a horse for an age, until I came into your woods up here," Steen answered. "I'll enjoy the novelty. But—can't you drive a car, Frank?"

"Yes, I guess I could." Frank had been aware that Steen had noticed his limp. "My game leg has become so much a commonplace to me that I forget I have it," he remarked. "Sometimes it's worse and sometimes better, but never very bad and never quite well. Dr. Pratt says it may flare up again at any time, or may stay this way for years. I guess I could drive a car, all right. And we might afford a second-hand flivver. But the fact is I haven't cared for it. You know we move to town in the winter. And the rest of the year I like the drive. This is our place here," he added, indicating the old house as they drove down the deep-shaded street under the arching maples.

"This is a beautiful street," said Steen. "It must be lovely in the fall."

"The smooth trunks of giant beeches shone dimly in a
shadowy stillness."

"It is. Oh, this is a great place, old man, a great country. You'll like it."

"Perhaps I shall," Steen agreed indulgently.

They drove slowly out the gravelled pike, pausing to look back from the hill-top over the town to the Lake, glittering under the forenoon sun; past fields of beans and ruddy-silvered buckwheat, past orchards heavy with green fruit, and meadows freshly mowed or brown with seeded clover, and fields of low corn bright with tassel and silk. The highway gave to the sandy country road, past tangled swamps of hemlock and cedar, slopes of luxuriant second growth, a deserted clearing; and so to the pole bridge over the swift stream, and up the slope to Frank's home.

Rose welcomed Steen warmly and performed promptly enough the necessary rite of exhibiting the baby—a plump toddler, now, with blue eyes of perennial brightness and good nature, and abundant silky yellow hair. Steen greeted the child gravely, a little embarrassed, Frank thought. "How do you do, Miss Thompson?" he asked, holding out his white, slender hand. Little Rose smiled at him, clinging to her mother's skirts.

Almost immediately Frank led Steen out of doors to "see the place." Rose joined the expedition as far as the poultry yard and the garden, then returned to the house to prepare dinner while Frank led the way on into the clearings. He talked of his plans for this field and that, indicating the dimensions of his proposed ultimate clearing, and pointed out the place at which he had had the fateful encounter with the stump-puller. They reached the margin of the original forest, where the smooth trunks of giant beeches shone dimly in a shadowy stillness.

Turning suddenly, Frank surprised a quizzical look in Steen's eyes, and noted lines of fatigue about his mouth. With a sense of shock, he realized that his friend was tired.

"Come on back to the house, old man," he said apologetically. "You're all worn out with this traipsing about the farm. I ought to be ashamed of myself."

"You're merely the perennial fond landholder, Frank," Steen rallied him. "But I didn't sleep well last night, and I *am* a bit tired."

He was ready to walk with Frank after the cows that night, however, and was held for a time by the beauty of the little lake beneath the sunset. "It *is* beautiful, Frank," he agreed solemnly. "I'm glad I came up here to see it—and you. We can understand each other better in what I want to talk with you about."

"What is that?"

"A plan I want to propose to you. I'll tell you when we get back to the house, so Rose can listen."

They gathered about the kitchen table, after the milking was done and the lamp was burning, and Steen filled his pipe and began to talk. "I've been thinking about you folks a great deal lately," he began. "Of course I have thought about you ever since you came up here. As you know from my letters, I've hoped you would come back to Ann Arbor, and I've thought of urging you to from time to time, but it has never seemed quite feasible. Now, I believe the opportunity has come. As you know, I've been a full-time instructor this past year, with a fair salary. I've been reappointed for next year. But I've decided, just this summer, that I want to go east for a year. I've talked with my chief about you, and he wants you. You know he has wanted you in the past—and he isn't a man whose interest in one he likes will wane in a year or two. He's agreed to take you on in my place for the coming year, if you will come, and make me an assistant professor when I return next year, so that you could stay on. I know from what you've written that you've brought the paper back to where it would sell advantageously, now. And I want you to come. What do you think of it?"

Frank glanced swiftly at Rose. "It's awfully good of you, Steen," he said promptly. "Of course we hadn't thought of anything of the sort."

"No, it's not good of me at all. I want you there. I know you can do good work and enjoy it; and I believe that eventually in teaching you would find leisure for the creative work that I've always held you ought to do. I know you haven't thought of it, Frank," he went on understandingly. "That's why I'm springing the thing on you right away, instead of waiting till later in my visit—so we can talk it over fully, and you can have time to decide."

"When must you go back, Steen?" Frank asked.

"Saturday morning, I'm afraid," he answered. "I must hurry back to Ann Arbor," he explained, as they both started to protest. "It's a short stay, I know. But the chief has someone else in view for the place if you don't take it, and I must let him know. And then I must get home for a few days before I start east. I want to work in the libraries awhile before school opens at Cambridge."

"Well, we'll think about it and talk it over," Frank told him. "I don't know what to say, to-night."

"Yes, I know. Well, I feel true rural sleepiness creeping upon me. I'll bid you good night."

"What do you think of the plan, Rose?" Frank asked as soon as they were alone together. "Would you be happy at Ann Arbor?"

"I would be happy anywhere with you, Frank, truly, you know that. It seems like a fine chance for you; if you want to teach ever, this is your chance, I should think. And we have a good many years to think of, I expect. We must decide wisely." She clasped him suddenly in her arms, pressed her firm body against him strongly. "Whatever you decide will be all right with me, dear," she whispered. "Oh, my husband, I love you so much!"

The next day the two friends walked and talked, while Rose was busy with her work in the house. "I can't help feeling that you're burying yourself up here, Frank, with your work with the farm and the paper," Steen urged him. "You can't really be satisfied with what you are doing, are you?"

"Well, I don't know. There are little things that seem worth while. We have a project for a village library on foot—more books for the youngsters. And there is to be a lecture course——"

"But, Frank, you don't think those things are really *important,* do you—that they count for much against the inertia of the community?"

"Do you think this dissertation on Anglo-Saxon inflections that you're going to do is really important, Steen," Frank countered, "or that you're saving the world teaching Freshman English?"

"Scarcely," Steen admitted with a grimace.

"The point is, old man, that it isn't what a man *does* that counts—to him. It's what he thinks and feels that make his life."

"Well, suppose I grant that. Can you think and feel

here to your utmost capacity? What do you have to compensate for the intellectual contacts, the discussions, the plays and concerts? Don't those things attract you?"

"They do, I admit. I suppose I would get rusty here. Still, there are books; they mean more here, for I have time to read them slowly, and to think about them as I work in the fields. And I have a few real friends to talk to—almost as many as I ever found in the football-ridden multitude. Dr. Pratt—the Steeles—I want you to meet Mr. Steele."

"But what of your life on the farm? There's no development there, is there? If there is, where are the men to show for it—the enlightened, broad-minded farmers? In the farm bureau and third-party movements?"

"Hardly. Collectively the farmer, like the public in general, is a 'hass,' as Dickens put it. Individually he is less avaricious and bigoted than poor rural schools, a nondescript or non-existent rural clergy, and wretched venal journals like the one I have the honour to own might lead us to expect. Some of the very finest men I know are farmers—great-hearted, courageous, clear-minded men. I suspect that for elemental decency and achievement the settlers along this road would stack up pretty favourably with a like number of professors, at Ann Arbor or anywhere else. Of course there are sneaks, bigots, morons, scalawags, on farms as elsewhere. It isn't farming that makes them so."

"You always could phrase a thing, Frank," Steen told him. "But men live courageously and tolerantly in cities, don't they—some of them?"

"Of course, and more honour to them. But I don't know that I could. Look at that field, Steen. Half of it, over to where I got hurt by the stump-puller, I made

with my own hands. It was waste land—beautiful—
and worthless. I made it into a field, beautiful—and
useful. Look at the curves of it, the gentle slope and
the hollows. I know them all, for I cut the brush,
cleared away the stumps, from every foot. There is
something I have created. True, a few years may see it
wilderness again. The generations may reject it, as
they might a book or a picture. But something from it
has entered into me. It has fed and sustained me. I'm
stronger because of it."

"I can feel that," said Steen slowly. "You have
changed out here, matured mightily. There is something I envy in you."

"Steen," said Frank suddenly, "are you afraid to
die?"

"Why," Steen answered dryly, "I prefer to postpone
the event. Are you subject to attacks of homicidal
mania? Or why do you ask?"

"Because I am not afraid, Steen," Frank answered
earnestly. "I know I sound like a fool. But these
years with the land have taught me something about
myself and all that I might do. I have learned to live
much more richly than ever before, because I am not
afraid to die. I wonder if I could keep hold of that, if
I left the land?"

"I think you could," Steen answered soberly.
"That's perhaps why we need you at Ann Arbor."

Rose invited Dr. Pratt and the Steeles to drive out
for supper on Friday evening, the last of Steen's visit,
and prepared for the guests a meal of especial elaborate-
ness. It was really a memorable feast, with fried
chicken and gravy, new peas and potatoes, lettuce and
green beans, and a sherbet made with the juices of wild

fruit, with a masterly cake, for dessert. Steen ate with an appetite for which he felt frequent need of apology. In the evening Steen and Dr. Pratt engaged in a brief argument about the merits of Burton, and there was quiet talk of events in Green Bush and the neighbour-hood, and a generous cutting of Rose's flowers for Mrs. Steele to take home with her.

CHAPTER XXXIV

IN the morning Frank had the horse ready before the early breakfast, in order to drive Steen to the train. It was a grey day, and the hills were remote and austerely lovely as the two men drove rapidly toward town.

"What have you decided, Frank?" Steen asked affectionately. "Are you coming down with us; or haven't you decided yet after all?"

"It's hard to know, Steen," Frank answered simply. "I'll write to you within a day or two, if that will do."

"Yes, surely. We'll say no more about it now."

They chatted quietly as they drove along, and while they waited for the train. "I'll see you next year in any case, Frank," Steen told him at parting. "If you're not at Ann Arbor, I'm coming here again. But I hope you'll be there."

He waved his hand as the train pulled away. Frank climbed into the old buggy, gathered up the lines, and drove slowly back to the office. Dale greeted him in surprise. "There's a feller just in about his subscription," he began.

"Never mind now, Dale, old fellow," Frank interrupted. "We'll see about it later. You can lay off for to-day, if you like. I'll keep shop." When the boy had gone he locked the door and pulled down the shade until from his desk just a narrow strip of grey street, green grass, and grey water was visible. He sat for a long time quiet, staring blankly into the deserted shop. At

300

last he took paper and pen from a drawer, and slowly and thoughtfully wrote his letter to Steen—pausing, rewriting, with erasures and corrections, until he had finished.

"DEAR STEEN: I have decided to stay here. I shall go on with the paper for a time, with the farm as long as I live. Perhaps when I sell the paper we can spend some weeks of each winter with you in the city there—possibly not. I am choosing, not because Rose will be happiest here—though I know she will; but because my own life seems to me likely to be richest and fullest here on the land.

"I will try to tell you how I have thought the thing out many times on my long drives. I think I see that prolonged contact with the earth has brought me finally the power to confront my life, my fate, and myself at once with clearness of vision and with peace of mind. I do not say that this is unquestionably fortunate or desirable. Perhaps they are happier who in the din of cities so successfully cloak the essential mystery of life with the glitter of achievement, and of pleasure. Yet even such must know moments of heart-stopping agony when briefly through the shams that crowd their days they glimpse annihilation. Of this alone I can be certain: that love and knowledge of the earth, which means daily observation and acceptance of the facts of birth and death, of the puniness of man's efforts and the little meaning of his life, has brought me happiness: compounded of joy in simple things—pleasure in food, in wife and children, in beauty of flower and tree, of sky and water and the forms of earth, in the dependence and faithfulness of beasts, in freedom that comes from knowledge and acceptance of my weakness and of death.

"The earth has maimed and broken me, perhaps, as ultimately it will defeat every effort of my life. But also it has given me strength to bear disaster and defeat, and death.

"To me death is not a strange or fearful thing. I see it all about me daily, hourly—myself the agent of a million deaths as I reap or mow or plough my fields. All day long I slaughter little trees—slender grey-trunked maples, green-barked poplars, silvery birches—that my cattle may have a place to graze, or that my plough may turn the soil to raise food for beasts and men. I know death as common and simple—a part of life.

"I shall regret it—yes. I have loved beauty, and in this land beauty is about me hour by hour. I have loved men and women and children—my neighbours, my wife, my child. Not gladly shall I leave the sight of leaves and sky, the taste of berries and of bread and meat, the fragrance of the smoky wind of autumn, the sound of bird-song and of running water and of wind in trees, the touch of long-beloved lips and hands. But I am not afraid to die.

"I could not always live happily with you in the city there, hurrying from class-room to club, and from dinner with guests to the theatre. Sooner or later I should lie awake listening to the wind and rain, and realize the unutterable futility of all that I was doing, of all that men can do. I would see the house about me, clothing, books, the campus halls, railroads, skyscrapers, for what they are—brief devisings whereby to mask oblivion. And because I was one with these things, caught and enmeshed with them, their maker and their tool, madness and despair would seize upon me, and I would be afraid to live or die.

"No, I shall stay here, where it is easy to remember

that I am no conqueror of earth, but brief and frail; and this remembering, to find enough of happiness in every day, and to live free and unafraid.

"You say that I might write a book if I came to the city to live. Perhaps I might. And perhaps before I die I shall find something to say about this country here: it may be a monograph on the crayfish or an ode to the wood-thrush. Both are part of the same thing. But before I write at all I want to be sure I have something to say. A few years here will help me to know—there with you it would be too easy to be mistaken.

"I don't expect all to be right here, or easy. We have plumbed pretty well the dark side of country life. There will be times of loneliness and discouragement, and times when we shall be glad to come to you and the city for a time. And we shall always be glad to have you and other friends come to us here.

"Dear Steen, I know the love you hold for me. I know you cannot agree with me in this. And I write with no evangelical intention. I would not urge the course I choose on you or any other. I do not even claim complete assurance that it is right for me. I know that you and many others live in the city bravely and wisely and happily, and I honour you and them. But for myself, so nearly as I can see, I am choosing well. I shall love you always, and be grateful to you.

"Your friend,
"FRANK."

He ceased writing, and raising the shade, looked out the office window across the blue Lake to the grey line of sky. Then he gathered up the sheets, found an envelope, and carried the letter across the street to the post office.

He locked the office door, untied the old horse from his place in the shade, and jogged slowly down the main street of Green Bush toward the west. The sun was bright, and from under a hat brim crowded low over his eyes, he studied the roadside as he drove. At sunset he came within sight of the little lakes, their waters dyed gold and crimson by the colours of the sky. In the marsh where he had first seen Rose the blackbirds were whistling and cowbells jangled from the brush beyond.

At the gate he stopped, and climbed out painfully to let down the bars. Through the utter stillness a whip-poorwill called loudly. From the barnyard he could hear the chatter of little Rose, and then, as he listened keenly, the steady *purr-purr* of milk into a bucket almost filled. Presently, as he waited in the shadow, he saw his wife pass from the barnyard to the house, the shining bucket in one hand, the other clasping the fingers of the child. There was the slap of the screen-door, then lamplight shone redly from the vine-shaded kitchen window. He heard the rattle of stove-lids, and the fragrance of wood-smoke blew against his face. For a little while he rested his arms on the withers of the old horse to ease his weight from his hip, and laid his head on his hands, his eyes blinded with tears. Then, straightening with something like a smile, he let down the bars and led the horse to the barn.

THE END